Who's That Earl

Also by Susanna Craig

The Runaway Desires Series
To Kiss a Thief
To Tempt an Heiress
To Seduce a Stranger

The Rogues & Rebels Series
The Companion's Secret
The Duke's Suspicion
The Lady's Deception

Who's That Earl

A Love and Let Spy Romance

Susanna Craig

LYRICAL PRESS
Kensington Publishing Corp.
www.kensingtonbooks.com

LYRICAL PRESS BOOKS are published by

Kensington Publishing Corp.
119 West 40th Street
New York, NY 10018

All Kensington titles, imprints, and distributed lines are available at special quantity discounts for bulk purchases for sales promotion, premiums, fund-raising, educational, or institutional use.

Special book excerpts or customized printings can also be created to fit specific needs. For details, write or phone the office of the Kensington Sales Manager: Kensington Publishing Corp., 119 West 40th Street, New York, NY 10018. Attn. Sales Department. Phone: 1-800-221-2647.

Lyrical Press and Lyrical Press logo Reg. U.S. Pat. & TM Off.

First Electronic Edition: August 2020
ISBN-13: 978-1-5161-1057-5 (ebook)
ISBN-10: 1-5161-1057-9 (ebook)

First Print Edition: August 2020
ISBN-13: 978-1-5161-1058-2
ISBN-10: 1-5161-1058-7

Printed in the United States of America

To Brad, again. And always.

Acknowledgments

As I start this new series, I'm grateful to those who made it possible: my agent, Jill Marsal, who shepherded the idea through the submission process; my editor extraordinaire, Esi Sogah, who knows when to push and when to praise; the Kensington team, who turns the stories I give them into books; my family and friends, especially my husband and daughter, whose support takes many forms, including letting me listen to '80s music endlessly for inspiration; and finally, my readers, old and new.

Chapter 1

In spite of the eerie, not-quite quiet that settled over the island in the hours between dusk and dawn, Lieutenant Thomas Sutherland nearly missed the telltale rhythm of oars slicing through water.

Damn and blast. If he weren't careful, he'd find himself in enemy hands after all this time. Or at the mercy of his general, once he'd explained how he'd been distracted from his duties by the scent of flowers.

Seven years stationed in Dominica, eyes and ears trained on the most likely landing spot for the French fleet, had honed his focus. He'd even learned to ignore the whine and sting of the damned mosquitoes, though they seemed to have a particular affinity for his blood—or perhaps for the whisky that ran in equal measure through his veins.

But in all that time, he'd never figured out how to ignore the sweetly sensual aroma that hung heavy on the still, dark air. Night-blooming jasmine, whose perfume should conjure no memories for him. Particularly not memories of an English lass from Sussex.

With a scowl—three parts for Napoleon and one part for himself—he dragged his attention to the business at hand and scanned the sheltered cove for the source of the sound. Though the waning moon was no more substantial than the paring of a fingernail, it was enough to silver the thin, rippling line of water at the shore's edge. A thicker stripe of light ruffled and foamed where the surf broke farther out.

At last, his eyes caught the movement they sought. A skiff moved jerkily against the tide, riding low in the water beneath the weight of a passenger and an oarsman. Tracking their point of arrival, Thomas moved swiftly and noiselessly along the beach, clinging to the protection of the dense foliage as long as he could, pausing every now and then to scan the blackness behind the little boat. Somewhere out there lurked the ship from which the two men had been sent, their mission yet to be determined.

When nothing stood between him and the water but a stretch of gleaming white sand, he sank to his haunches behind an outcropping of rock and waited. The oarsman paused too, letting the incoming tide do a share of his work. Even at this distance, he looked too young for his task. The small craft scudded sideways through the shallows before the lad hopped out with a splash and dragged it onto the beach.

All this time, the passenger had sat without moving, without even turning his head to left or right. But the moment the skiff was securely lodged in the sand, he vaulted from it and stood, scanning first the beach, then the scrub, and finally the more distant trees. He made no effort to hide either himself or his actions, as if the risks of being seen were worth the reward of catching sight of whatever he'd come to find. He too was young, though older by far than the seaman who'd rowed him here. Perhaps twenty or twenty-two. And wearing a pristine British naval officer's uniform, which made Thomas not one whit less wary of the man or his intentions.

The arrivals spoke to one another, too low for him to make out their words. English? Or French? The distant rumble of the tide disguised the cadence of their speech. After a brief exchange, the seaman clambered back into the skiff. When he was hunkered low in the bow, invisible to all but the best-trained eye, the supposed officer turned and began to make his way up the beach toward the woods, a trajectory that took him no more than five yards from the place where Thomas crouched.

Without taking his eyes from the man, Thomas slipped his knife from the sheath inside the shaft of his boot and followed. They moved as one, any noise Thomas made masked by the other's fumbling progress through unfamiliar territory, the scuffle of steps slipping on loose sand, the careless crunch of seashells beneath his feet, the rustle of dried grasses against his legs. Bit by bit, Thomas closed the distance between them. Eventually, they reached a clearing where a small cabin stood, elevated on stilts to withstand the strong tropical storms. It formed the base for Thomas's lookout operations, though he also kept rooms in Roseau, where he went whenever it became necessary to gather other sorts of information or sometimes to send communiqués.

The stranger nosed about, first examining the structure, then peering into the dark woods that surrounded it. When he set one foot on the lowest rung of the ladder that led to the door, preparing to ascend, Thomas spoke.

"Where I come from, it's customary to wait for an invitation."

The unexpected sound of a human voice produced exactly the response he expected. The man turned suddenly, lost his footing, and tumbled to the ground before locating Thomas as he emerged from the shadows just a few feet away.

"Bloody hell," the man rasped, the air having been driven from his lungs by a combination of shock and the fall. "What are you doing?" His uncertain gaze shifted from Thomas's simple linen clothes to his primitive little cottage to the curved blade of his knife. "When they said you'd been here too long, Sutherland, they weren't wrong." He had the voice of a public-school prefect, almost too flawless an English accent to be believed.

Thomas took another step forward. "Aye? And what else did they tell you? The password, you'd best hope."

"P-password? I'm Captain Bancroft of the *Colchester*." Desperation now sharpened his drawling speech, and he scrambled backward as he spoke, scooting across the dirt like a frightened crab. "I come bearing a dispatch from General Zebadiah Scott."

A string of specifics primed to win a man's confidence. Thomas, however, held his in reserve. Had it always been in his nature to expect a lie, to suspect a trap? Perhaps he *had* been here too long.

After a brief pause, the other man spoke again. "General Scott says, 'Homeward, Magnus.'" Despite his vulnerable position, Bancroft—if that was indeed his name—enunciated the message like a man with no intention of repeating himself. Not even at knifepoint.

But repetition would serve little purpose. Thomas had heard him perfectly. He held himself rigid, determined not to betray the internal disturbance caused by two simple words. With them, any doubt about the genuineness of either Bancroft's identity or his mission had evaporated.

Apparently interpreting Thomas's stillness as confusion, Bancroft dared a slight clearing of his throat. "You have the necessary cipher, I assume."

A long, deliberate pause. "Nay."

Because for once, there was no code to be broken. *Magnus* was too obscure, and too personal, to require encryption. Though Thomas had not heard it for many years, the name was perfectly familiar.

How it should come to be addressed to him, here, was the real enigma. But no mere cipher could provide the necessary clarification. Only General Scott could do that, and he evidently preferred to explain in person rather than relay the whys and wherefores through an intermediary. Out of habit, Thomas cocked his head in a listening posture, though his thoughts were too jumbled for him to hear anything beyond the roar of his blood in his ears.

Fortunately, all of his senses had not deserted him. A sudden gust of perfume filled his nostrils. Night-blooming jasmine, again. And with it came the familiar memory. A woman's upturned face. Nut-brown hair, plump cheeks, blue eyes. He tried to shake her picture from his mind. Good God, what had—?

What *had* stirred the branches of that infernal shrub? There was no wind to speak of, and they'd come too far from the beach to blame the ocean breeze for driving the scent. Something, or someone, was on the move nearby.

With a swift, silent lunge, he closed the distance between him and Bancroft. Before the captain could react, Thomas had dragged him half-upright and pinned him to one of the stilts that supported the cabin, using both the man's body and the stout wooden post as a shield against the intruder. With one hand, he twisted Bancroft's arms behind his back, while with the other he held the knife to the man's neck.

"Christ," Bancroft whimpered, almost a prayer. The movement of the man's throat made the blade twitch. Reluctantly, Thomas shifted the position of his hand. He had no desire to spill blood—yet.

In another moment, the almost-forgotten seaman crashed into the little clearing. His eyes darted nervously from one pool of shadow to another. Though the boy could not have been more than twelve, he could not be safely ignored, for in one sinewy arm he held an oar over his head.

Thomas spoke low, before he could be picked out from the darkness. "Drop it, lad."

His voice drew the boy's eye to the perilous situation of his commanding officer. The same faint streak of moonlight that had silvered the waves now gleamed along the blade of Thomas's knife. The boy froze with the oar still upraised, swaying slightly beneath its weight and momentum. With a flick of his wrist, Thomas motioned for him to lay it on the ground.

"Do it, Perkins" Bancroft rasped. "I don't fancy having a mad Scotsman fillet me with a rusty cane knife."

Bewildered, the lad looked first to one and then the other before shaking his head and letting the oar drop. It landed with a dull thud, bounced off the hard ground, and struck Bancroft's shin.

The string of profanity that flew from Bancroft's lips marked him clearly as an Englishman—men almost always resorted to their native tongue when sick or in pain. Thomas was similarly convinced that no bones had been broken, else the man would have been neither so creative nor so coherent. "Cheer up, Captain." He thrust the knife once more into its sheath, then favored the man with a lazy smile. "The lad might've been carrying a pistol."

"I had hopes that the oar would be persuasion enough," Bancroft ground from between clenched teeth, still clutching at his injury.

Despite the warm, humid air, a chill settled over Thomas. The captain had ordered the seaman to follow him—and to come armed. As if they'd expected trouble. Or resistance.

"Persuasion?"

Bancroft winced as he struggled to keep his feet, leaning heavily on Perkins and gesturing for the oar, which he pressed into service as a makeshift crutch. Dust streaked his once-spotless uniform, one sleeve was torn, and sweat slid down his face in rivulets, making tracks in the smear of dirt across one cheek. Still, he had not lost his haughty demeanor. "General Scott made it clear that you have never shown any particular fondness for following orders."

Thomas shrugged gamely. Why else would he have been sent to this godforsaken spot to begin with?

"He asked me to make sure you understood that it's imperative you follow this one."

With the oar, Bancroft gestured toward the rough path their feet had carved between the spot where they stood and the beach, indicating that Thomas was to lead the way back to the boat.

Such a simple directive: *Homeward.*

But where, after all this time, was home?

* * * *

London in early January was still a bustling, hustling place. Though the great and wealthy overwintered on their country estates, the rest of the city went on about its business, oblivious to the gray skies and the cold, damp wind that cut right through a man's coat. Even a red one.

Thomas tugged uneasily at the collar of his uniform and fancied he caught a whiff of camphor. No surprise there. He'd had no use for the flash of scarlet and brass while working undercover, and no use for wool's sturdy warmth under a West Indian sun. In Whitehall, however, and for a meeting with General Scott, even he could muster a show of respect for authority.

Once across the almost-deserted parade grounds and inside the vast warren of offices and stables that made up the Horse Guards, he paused to shake the rain from his hat and tuck it under his arm. Directed down a northern corridor, he found himself counting his steps out of habit. It would not do for a man of his experience to get lost.

At last, he paused before an unmarked oak door. Before he could raise his knuckles to rap, it swung open, as if he had been expected. As if someone had been watching. But, of course, someone had been watching. Behind that sturdy panel—or rather, behind what he assumed would turn out to be a series of doors, each one more strenuously guarded than the last—sat the architect of Britain's military-intelligence operation.

"Lieutenant Sutherland." The officer who had opened the door wore a uniform that had never been sweat-stained, nor bloodied, nor stuffed in the bottom of a trunk, and he spoke as if there could be no question of the visitor's identity. "He's expecting you. Right this way."

Thomas had less than a moment to get his bearings. The small room contained a cabinet, a desk, and a chair for the one who worked at it, none for visitors. Before he could decide whether the two neat stacks of paper on the desktop contained information vital to the nation's security or were merely for show, the man had opened another door—just one, though it was the sort that was built into the wall in such a way as to make it easy to overlook—and ushered him through it. The latch clicked softly into place the moment he had crossed the threshold.

This office was larger than the anteroom, though not considerably so, and similarly furnished, though the desk was somewhat larger, and a pair of chairs sat before it in addition to the one behind it. Yet the dissimilarities were equally striking. In a word, the space was...*cozy*. A worn but gaily-patterned Turkey carpet covered most of the austere tile floor. Dark blue drapes had been looped haphazardly behind polished bronze hooks, inviting in what daylight could be coaxed through a single tall window. The desk, like the carpet, had seen its share of use, and its surface was positively littered with sloping and sliding piles of papers. Here and there, Thomas could see the corner of a map peeping out from the chaos, or the red-wax circle of some important seal. A cloud of smoke hung on the air, wreathing the white-haired figure who stood with his back to the door, looking out into the gray morning.

"Ah, come in. Come in." General Zebadiah Scott spoke around the stem of his pipe as he turned from the window and extended a hand of welcome. "I've been expecting you. Thought you would arrive sooner, but my sources tell me you were delayed in Portsmouth by some, ah, *personal* business."

At the twinkle in Scott's eye, Thomas busied himself with settling into the chair the general had indicated. All things considered, it was not shocking to discover that the man knew how he'd spent the days after his arrival. Hell, Scott could probably name every pub he'd visited, which was more than Thomas himself could do.

But Thomas's gaze had been driven to the floor by the unsettling sensation that Scott knew even more. Knew that for an hour, or even two, Thomas had been quietly weighing whether or not to return to London via a certain village in Sussex, just to prove to himself that the woman he'd met seven years ago had not been a figment of his imagination. Just to see if Miss Quayle was *Miss* Quayle still.

By morning, common sense had returned, along with a dry mouth and an aching head. Sternly, he had faced his reflection in the glass above the washstand and told himself that any such detour would be a foolish waste of time. Miss Quayle was no doubt Mrs. Somebody-or-other now, with children trailing from her apron strings. Better to remember her as sweet and seventeen and smelling of night-blooming jasmine.

He had not mentioned either his ill-considered plan or his far more sensible rejection of it to anyone. Had not so much as muttered her name beneath his breath. Yet, as Thomas discovered when he raised his head, Scott was still looking at him, with knowing eyes and a quirk about his mouth that could only be described as amusement. Some underling's dutiful report of Thomas's days of debauchery in Portsmouth would not have produced such a look.

"Ah, well. Welcome home, Mr. Sutherland." The general set his pipe on a crystal ashtray, so near a stack of papers that Thomas feared they might catch fire. With his wispy white hair, slight build, and wizened features, Scott strongly favored a mischievous elf. No one would suspect him for a creative genius, a military mastermind. Unless, perhaps, he owed some part of his uncanny abilities to sorcery?

"But I forget myself," he exclaimed, clapping his hands together and laughing. "I must say, 'my lord' now. Lord Magnus." He sketched a bow and was still chortling when he took up the chair behind the desk.

Thomas had spent almost every moment of seven weeks at sea—seven weeks with very little else to distract him, not even a storm or a sighting of a French ship—trying to make sense of the message Bancroft had delivered. He'd tested every possible meaning in his mind, including the one Scott had just given: that he, Thomas, now bore a title.

Time and again, he'd dismissed it as impossible.

Once more, he eased a finger beneath his collar. "I'm afraid, sir, I still don't understand..."

"How you came to inherit an earldom? Oh, in the usual way, as I understand it. The previous holder of the title died."

"Aye, sir. But how came *I* to be next in line for it? Or even in the queue, come to that? So far as I ken, I've nary a drop of noble blood in my veins."

That remark sent Scott rummaging through the stacks on his desk. From beneath a small avalanche of paper and even a book or two, he emerged with a letter bearing an official-looking seal. "But you do. Or, at least, your mother did. It seems Magnus is one of those peculiar Scottish titles that can pass through the female line." He extended the parchment, but Thomas made no move to take it, and Scott let it flutter from his fingertips to rejoin the pile.

His mother, his kind, delicate, clever mother, a countess...if she'd lived. In some ways, that might be the least surprising revelation of all. She'd been the source of all gentleness—and, evidently, gentility—in his childhood home.

Her death of some unnamed malady when he'd been fifteen had changed everything. Devastated, his father had packed up their belongings and dragged his son south, to England, where the older man had died just three years later.

Intending, in any event, to take the king's shilling, Thomas had used his small inheritance to purchase an officer's commission. How he had happened to catch the notice of then-Colonel Scott, he had never learned. No man ever knew quite how or why he'd been chosen for Scott's service, but the result was always the same: intensive training in the art of intelligence gathering, followed by a new life entirely, a life disconnected from whatever had gone before. Following a brief sojourn on the southern coast of England, briefer by far than a man might've wished, he had shipped out to the West Indies, where the French had been stirring up trouble. The Highlands might as well have been at the other end of the earth.

General Scott's voice broke into his reverie. "I daresay you remember Dunnock Castle?"

Thomas had spent summers in the shadow of its crumbling walls, on visits to his grandmother. Mama had insisted that the crowded streets of Glasgow were no place for a growing boy. Digging through those memories now yielded something akin to what one might find at the bottom of a long-locked trunk: the occasional treasure, but far more that was musty and ill-fitting.

Now, however, through a stroke of—no, he couldn't call it luck—it was his. "Dunnock Castle," he repeated in an absent murmur. "Mine."

"Yours," Scott concurred. "Although..." Once more the general began shuffling through papers. "There is the small matter of the lease."

"Lease?"

"As you know, the previous Earl of Magnus was rarely resident at Dunnock."

Thomas recalled his grandmother complaining that the laird was little more to the people of Balisaig than a name. Magnus was some gouty old man who spent his days in a warmer, drier clime. Thomas doubted that even his mother had suspected any connection between their families.

"So, in order to prevent the estate from falling into ruin—"

Further into ruin, Thomas was tempted to interject.

"—he leased it out. I had one of my aides gather the details for you. Ah, ha!" Having at long last laid hands on the papers he sought, he then began a quest for his spectacles, which he found resting on his forehead, where they had been perched since Thomas had entered the room. With a self-deprecating laugh, he knocked them into their proper place with the tap of one finger. "Let's see…" He scanned the first part of the lengthy document, then nodded. "Fetches a tidy sum in rents, I'll say that much for it."

Thomas's suspicions rose. "Who would pay a tidy sum to live in a ramshackle pile on the edge of nowhere?"

"Ah." Something that wasn't only amusement twitched at the corners of Scott's mouth. "That would be Robin Ratliff. The writer."

"Never heard of him."

"You must be the only one who hasn't, Sutherl—er, Magnus." The general laughed. "He pens gothic novels, of the sort that are popular in watering places and circulating libraries. Horrid stuff, my wife tells me. And she should know, based on the bills I've had from the bookshop."

Thomas mustered an answering smile. "About the lease…"

"Yes, right. The lease." He turned again to study the papers in his hands, flipping forward and back. "By and large, its terms are unsurprising. Of course, you may decide whether to renew it on the next quarter day, which should give you plenty of time to—oh." He paused, scanning the next line twice.

Thomas could not decide how to read the general's hesitation. "Time to what?"

"Well, I suppose it's only natural." His embarrassment was acute. "I've been assuming you had until Lady Day in March, you see. But the next *Scottish* quarter day is—"

"Candlemas," Thomas reluctantly supplied.

February second. Less than a month to get from London to Edinburgh, successfully claim the title at the Lyon Court, and then travel another hundred and fifty miles into the Highlands, to Balisaig. In the dead of winter.

Thomas's skepticism must have shown on his face, for Scott was quick to offer reassurance. "Not a pleasant journey, I know, but it can be done. And afterward, you'll be at your leisure to conduct an assessment of the property and its tenants' needs, make your determinations about the estate's management...before the, er, spring planting season," he added hopefully. Thomas rather suspected the man knew even less about farming than he did. "Why, maybe you'll even meet some likely lass and decide to settle down."

Settle down? Thomas nearly laughed aloud. General Scott commanded men of action, officers wedded only to their duties. Who would have pegged him for a matchmaker?

Not that Thomas had anything against marriage. He'd once come close— dangerously close, some might say—to making an offer he felt sure would have been accepted. The seven years since had been filled with reminders of the girl he'd left behind, but many more reminders of why a man in his position, a soldier and a spy, had no business thinking of settling down.

"And if I don't?"

"Don't...?" General Scott fixed him with a wary, questioning look, as if he felt certain he had misunderstood.

"Don't claim the title. Don't want anything to do with Dunnock Castle." What did he know of being a landowner? "I'll stick with what I ken."

The mischievous twinkle, the self-deprecating laugh—all gone so suddenly Thomas almost believed they had been a figment of his imagination. Scott's face was set in hard lines now, and he looked every inch a general. "I am well aware of the dangers our soldiers face, and the pressing need for information to keep them safe. The knowledge and experience possessed by the officers in my service is invaluable. But when one of my men is called to his domestic duty, I expect him to honor that call as swiftly as he would one of mine, Lieutenant."

Thomas had no doubt that the omission of his new title was deliberate.

"A man without honor has no place here," Scott continued. One hand waved across the surface of the desk, gesturing toward the maps and letters that documented the British Army's unceasing efforts to vanquish an enemy bent on terrorizing an ever-growing share of the globe. The territory comprised by that single word—*here*—was vast indeed.

There had been no mention yet of Thomas being forced to resign his commission in favor of a near-worthless earldom, and for that, he was grateful. But the general was telling him, in not so many words, that if he hoped for any assignment of interest or value in future, he would have to see to matters in Scotland without delay.

Not trusting himself to speak, Thomas held his hand out for the report, which Scott surrendered with a look of triumph. A quick shuffle through its pages told him that the investigation had been thorough indeed. Dates, figures, a detailed family tree. Familiar names—names of people he'd once called friends. People who were now his tenants. His responsibility.

These were not the responsibilities he wanted.

"Ratliff cannot be a man of sense," he said, blinking at the sum the writer paid for the privilege of shivering away at Dunnock.

Scott shrugged. "His books are full of stuff and nonsense, to be sure. But he's rich as Croesus—and more famous. Think what Ratliff's scrawl on that lease might fetch at auction," Scott murmured absently, tapping his lips with one fingertip.

Thomas hardly heard him. The general could insist he see to matters in Scotland. But he couldn't order him to stay. If the previous Lord Magnus had managed Dunnock from a distance, via solicitor, bailiff, and steward, then why couldn't he?

Even a cursory glance through the papers suggested that the old earl had not always chosen his surrogates wisely, however. Thomas could have his work cut out for him, finding the right man to see to things in Balisaig.

Scott shook himself, returning his attention to the matter at hand. "In any case, I'd advise you to start with Higginbotham."

"Higginbotham?"

"Ratliff's secretary—his public face, so to speak. Ratliff himself is said to be a bit of a recluse. Leaves all the business matters to Higginbotham."

All the business matters? Then Ratliff's secretary must already be involved in some aspects of the running of Dunnock. Perhaps this Higginbotham chap could be persuaded to expand his role. To leave one employer in favor of another.

And Thomas could carry on with his life.

"Manages a tight ship, by all accounts," continued General Scott.

A faint smile curved Thomas's lips. He could picture the fellow, ink-stained fingers, nose in a ledger. Ordinarily, he despised the managing sort. But under the circumstances...

"I know that look," Scott said warningly. "Promise me you won't antagonize Higginbotham, Magnus. You might find yourself in need of assistance when you reach Dunnock."

Thomas's smile grew. "*Antagonize* Higginbotham? I wouldn't dream of it, sir."

Chapter 2

Absently, Jane fingered the pearl handle of her penknife. Then, with one firm, deliberate movement, she drove its sharp tip through the papers and into the scarred oak desktop. Ordinarily, she wasn't the sort to be bothered by one troubling letter.

Today, however, the post had brought two.

They'd had the nerve to arrive together, in one packet, accompanied by a newsy note from Mr. Canfield, her London publisher, apologizing for the delay in sending them. He had been attending his elderly father in Bath, he'd explained, where that gentleman had been sent in hopes of improving his rheumatism.

With little in the way of expectation, she'd opened the first, a lengthy missive from a solicitor, announcing the demise of the Earl of Magnus, laird of Dunnock Castle. The heir had, at last, been located in some far-flung spot, remote enough that his immediate interference with matters at home was unlikely.

However, as Mr. Ratliff's legal counsel, he'd concluded, *I feel myself obliged to inform him that the renewal of the lease on Dunnock Castle cannot be unequivocally guaranteed.*

For more than five years, Dunnock Castle had been her home. She'd almost begun to think of it as *hers*—certainly the late earl had shown no signs of possessiveness where the ancient castle, and its lands and people, were concerned. But the new earl, no matter how far removed, might see things differently. She might, once again, find herself homeless.

With a heavy sigh, she'd tossed that letter onto the desktop and turned to the second, hoping for better news, only to be confronted by a detailed reckoning of the particular circle of hell to which authors of books like *The Necromancer's Bride* ought to be consigned.

She knew—had always known—that some people did not approve of novels. Particularly not the sort of lurid, gothic tales she penned under the name Robin Ratliff. She was no stranger to criticism.

But this was different. Not just a critique. A threat. Oh, a rather melodramatic one, to be sure—unless the writer's skills at dark magic actually rivaled her fictional creation's. Nevertheless, the words had sent an unwelcome sensation of alarm slithering down her spine.

Just for good measure, she tugged the knife free and stabbed the offending papers again.

From the puddle of canine devotion near the hearth came a weary groan. "I know, I know," she murmured consolingly. She did not intend to let idle threats and pointless worries keep her from her work.

Neither did she remove the blade from the wood.

Instead, she drew a half-filled page toward her, while reaching for a pen with the other hand. Leaning back into the chair, she brushed the feather across her lips as she scanned the words she'd written earlier:

Fog rippled through the undergrowth...Was that a spectral glow emanating from one of the vaults in the churchyard? No, the light came from farther off, somewhere in the woods...Allora's pale hand trembled as she laid it against the stone window ledge...

Jane's gaze drifted from the paper in her hand to the crackling fire. One of the dogs had begun to snore. This would never do. Tossing the pen aside, she pushed herself away from the desk and walked to the window to open it. The room was too warm, that was all.

She'd come all the way to Scotland for crumbling stone walls and wild landscapes. For whatever local legends she could unearth: will o' the wisps and witches, demon bear-ghosts and time-traveling stone circles. For *inspiration*.

Most of all, in Scotland she was free. And she was not going to let a pair of letters take her freedom from her.

Thrusting open the glass—which was as narrow and crisscrossed with lead as anyone of a romantic disposition could wish—she drew in a deep gulp of damp, wintry air. The gloom of twilight had newly settled in the vales and crags, and far below, parts of Dunnock Castle had already disappeared into darkness. In the distance, the loch was as black as a pool of spilled ink.

Her eyes traveled eagerly from one shadowy place to the next. Though the misty rain threatened to turn to sleet at any moment, her heroine, Allora, would not stay cozy and secure inside on a night like this. She would pick her way among the rugged rocks, though her slippers offered no protection from their mercilessly sharp edges. She would press on across the frost-bitten heath, despite being clad in nothing but her nightdress. She would make her way past the ancient kirk, slipping between the mossy gravestones, although she knew too well the rumors that—

"Gracious, ma'am! You'll catch your death."

Agnes Murdoch, the elderly housekeeper, stood just inside the threshold, drawn up to her full height of four feet, eleven inches.

Jane had had no notice of the woman's arrival, too lost in her own thoughts to have heard footsteps on the winding staircase of the south tower or even a tap on the door. The dogs' silence had long since been bought by Mrs. Murdoch's bits of cheese. One glance at the plush cushions by the fire confirmed that they had not stirred themselves to give warning, though one watchful eye gleamed from a mound of brown and white fur. Agnes might have something of interest in her pocket, after all.

Mrs. Murdoch looked from Jane to the desk and back again, evidently torn between her desire to snatch the window frame from her mistress's hand and slam it shut, and the more suitably servant-like behavior of snatching up the papers that had been scattered by the gust of wind.

Jane took pity on her and closed the window. The papers ceased their skittish dance across the polished desktop and onto the floor. She could only hope all the magic had not gone out of them.

"There's a gentleman below, asking for you, ma'am." Agnes announced at last.

"Who could be calling at this hour?"

One of Agnes's shoulders lifted. Abashed, she shook her head. "Dougan didna think t' ask his name."

Jane nodded her understanding. Dougan had the heart and mind of a child in a man's body. *Folks would consider it a great kindness if ye could see your way to keepin' him on*, Agnes had told her when she'd first arrived at Dunnock. *He likes to feel useful about the place.*

As it had turned out, feeling useful primarily involved Dougan marching back and forth across the parapet in his kilt, occasionally while playing the bagpipes, but Jane had readily agreed to retain him as gatekeeper. At the time, she'd expected no visitors.

Now, however...She glanced toward her desk and the letters. A shiver passed through her, and she stepped away from the window, though the glass was tightly closed.

Could the arrival be the new earl?

"Dougan didn't mention the man arriving in a crested coach drawn by six black horses, with outriders to match, did he?" The noblemen in her stories, nefarious rogues every one of them, always traveled in such a fashion.

"No, indeed." The prospect of entertaining such a grand personage visibly alarmed the elderly housekeeper. "Verra handsome he is, though."

In most respects, the housekeeper was as stern and proper as could be desired. Persuaded that Mrs. Higginbotham must be lonely in her isolation, however, she was also prone to take every opportunity to point out eligible men. Past efforts had ranged from the scrawny, red-faced cotter's son who had brought them fresh vegetables in the summer to the silver-haired sexton, who always had dirt beneath his nails. To Jane's relief—and Agnes's chagrin—the environs of Dunnock Castle included very few "braw lads."

Not that Jane was indifferent to the attractions of a fine masculine form. She was, after all, just four and twenty and blessed with excellent eyesight. But being appreciative of a man's looks did not mean being susceptible to his charms. She had taken pains to make herself perfectly independent, and she was more than content to leave such foolishness to elderly servants and the misguided heroines of fiction.

"That's as may be, I suppose," Jane retorted primly, grimly.

Agnes set her face in an expression to match Jane's. "Then you'll come down, ma'am."

It wasn't a question. Briefly, Jane considered ordering Agnes to send the man away instead. To tell him to call again in the morning. Or never. But curiosity burrowed beneath her skin, like one of the dogs nuzzling insistently under her hand to be petted.

"If I must."

Unwilling to appear disheveled before a stranger—before anyone, really—Jane paused to raise a hand to smooth her hair and then to shake the wrinkles from her skirt. Her efforts earned a sly glance from Agnes, who doubtless saw it as primping before meeting a handsome man. Finally, Jane gathered the wayward papers, depositing them in a neat stack beside the ones pinned to the desktop by her penknife.

With a nod to the housekeeper to precede her, she strode toward the door. Both dogs lifted their heads to watch her go, but neither showed any inclination to follow. No one would ever mistake them for watchdogs.

When she entered the room where the stranger had been left to wait, her first thought was that Agnes might also have mentioned he was tall. Six feet, at least, by Jane's estimate, and the cavernous Great Hall of Dunnock Castle had a way of making things look smaller than they really were.

Tall and broad. His arms were crossed in front of him, pulling his greatcoat taut across his shoulders as he studied a timeworn tapestry hanging above the hearth—the *empty* hearth. She did not make a habit of keeping fires burning to welcome guests. Despite the chilly reception, there was something easy, familiar, about his posture. She recognized his type. The sort of man who would sprawl if one offered him a chair. Which she had no intention of doing.

His back was turned to her, so she could assess little more than the cut of his coat—neither new nor fashionable—and its dampness. No coach and six for this gentleman, unless he'd left them in the village and walked.

As she approached, the scuff of her soft-soled shoes across the flagstone seemed not to alert him to her presence. Deep in thought, apparently. Or hard of hearing, like the sexton.

A half-dozen feet away, she stopped and spoke in a ringing voice. "You wished to see me, sir?"

His reaction—the slight lift of his shoulders, the slow turn of his head—hinted more at annoyance than surprise. "There must have been some misunderstanding." A Scotsman, by his accent, though his brogue was considerably softer than the ones she heard about Dunnock. "I asked to speak with Robin Ratliff's secretary."

"And so you are."

All of Dunnock Castle, the village of Balisaig, even Mr. Canfield, believed Jane to be the famous author's secretary—though personally she preferred the title of amanuensis.

Ratliff's genius, as she'd told the skeleton staff of Dunnock, demanded his total seclusion from the world. She managed to avoid questions largely by claiming he was traveling for research, or for pleasure, for months at a time. If anyone interrupted her while she was writing, Jane claimed to be merely copying out the author's notes.

She'd constructed an elaborate fiction, far more elaborate than the ones printed in cheap duodecimo volumes with Gothic typeface on the title page, the ones that found their way into housemaids' garrets and respectable drawing rooms alike. Ratliff's books had made her rich, but posing as Ratliff's assistant had given her something money and celebrity could not, something more valuable still. Believing her to be little more than a servant, people largely left her in peace.

Well, *most* people. Beneath her skirts, her toe began to tap as she glared at the stranger's back. She could see nothing more of his face than the firm edge of a jaw that hadn't been shaved that morning. His attention was still half-caught by the tapestry, which depicted some long-ago battle, the winning side led by the man who'd first been honored as the Earl of Magnus, so the story went.

"I was referring to Mr. Higginbotham," he said. How could a man sound both lazy and impatient at once?

"There is no *Mr.* Higginbotham." Out of habit, she dropped her gaze to the unrelieved black of her woolen dress and heaved a mournful sigh. "At least, not anymore."

It was a show of sorrow she had made many times, and always to the purpose. After the initial murmuring of pity, people looked past a respectable widow in her weeds, even a young one. Which was exactly how Jane wanted it.

In truth, there had *never* been a Mr. Higginbotham. Jane had invented him too: the perfect man, as kind, as gentle, as unlike a Robin Ratliff character, either hero or villain, as she could make him. Most important, he'd been generous enough to leave her with a widow's independence before she was even of age.

In addition to privacy, the assumed name of Mrs. Higginbotham also provided Jane with an extra measure of protection from anyone who wished her ill—or who would wish her ill, if they knew the truth. A society that frowned on female ambition. That threatening letter writer. Her family.

Not a soul from London to the Scottish Highlands recognized her as—

"*Miss Quayle?*"

At that, she jerked up her head. She had been so busy schooling her expression into something appropriately doleful, she had not realized the stranger had turned fully to face her. Now that he had doffed his hat, she could see his wavy dark brown hair and the thick brows that framed expressive hazel eyes.

A familiar face, and not only in the sense of easygoing. Known to her. Or at least, known to the woman she had once been.

Bewilderment, surprise, disbelief skated across Lieutenant Thomas Sutherland's sun-browned features as he took a tentative step toward her, one hand extended. She could almost fancy he had found something for which he'd long been searching and was afraid one false move might drive it away again.

Further evidence that her mind was prone to foolish fancies tonight.

"I have not been addressed by that name for many years," she said, ignoring the impulse to lay her fingers across his palm, as she had once done so long ago.

Her cool, distant tone seemed to recall him to his purpose. He straightened, dropped his hand to his side, and tucked his hat beneath his arm. "As I said, I have an urgent matter of business to discuss with Mr.—er, with Robin Ratliff's secretary."

"Amanuensis," she swiftly corrected.

"God bless you."

When she fixed him with an answering glare, she could see mischief sparkling in his eyes. "An amanuensis, Mr. Sutherland, is one who transcribes another's work, or copies a manuscript." The prim explanation only served to amuse him further. A dimple dented his left cheek as he fought and failed to check a smile. "A secretary's labors are considerably more demanding and diffuse," she continued, "and would, I'm sure, be far beyond my humble abilities." The less anyone expected of the fictitious Mrs. Higginbotham, the more time Jane could devote to the fiction of Robin Ratliff.

At that, Mr. Sutherland laughed aloud. Only after a long minute, and with some apparent trouble, did he manage to bring his humor under control. "Forgive me, Miss Quayle. But I've seen that gleam in your eye before. And it's not humility."

Miss Quayle, again. Her name, her dearest secret, all but shouted from the rafters, repeatedly. And in the Great Hall, where almost anyone, where—*oh dear God*—Agnes might overhear. This would never do. Impulsively, she reached out and laid a staying hand on his sleeve.

She knew instantly she'd made a dreadful mistake. She had no business building a bridge over the troubled stream of the past, forging a connection between two people whom the years had made strangers. And...*oh*, and worse. She was suddenly, almost painfully aware of the strength of his corded forearm.

What absolute nonsense! Feel the shape of muscles, through two layers of heavy wool? It was one thing to conjure up such a reaction for the heroine of one of her novels. Readers expected heightened emotions, exaggerated physical sensations. They wanted to experience everything her characters did.

It was quite another matter to discover that she, sensible Jane Quayle, wanted to dig her own fingertips into the cool, damp fabric of a man's greatcoat.

"I believe it would be best if we spoke somewhere else," she said, snatching back her hand.

He dipped his head in acquiescence, but the movement did not quite hide another mocking smile.

She led him from the hall, silently chiding herself for the rashness of her suggestion. At this hour, the only room in which she could be sure of finding both light and heat was the room she had just left: her private study.

As they ascended the circular stair of the south tower, she glanced surreptitiously over her shoulder. He was several steps below her, once more lost in thought. Where had he been all these years? What was the urgent business that had brought him to Dunnock Castle? And what could it have to do with her—in any of her guises?

He'd paused to remove his gloves, and she watched as he lightly trailed the long fingers of one hand over the curved stonework. Before she could stop it, her traitorous imagination had transferred his touch to her own skin, and a spark of awareness swept up her spine, like lightning arcing across a stormy sky. How very different these last seven years might have been, if only...

Narrowly, she caught herself before she stumbled against the next step. At the top, she paused before the door and drew a steadying breath. It was just a room. A room with a desk and a pair of glass-fronted bookcases, with comfortable leather chairs and an uncomfortable horsehair sofa. She hadn't bothered to redecorate when she'd taken up residence at Dunnock. She'd added only a few personal touches. So, despite calling the room her private study, the only truly private thing in it was the manuscript on which she was currently working.

Then again, perhaps *that* was his business. Perhaps he hoped to sneak a copy of the next Robin Ratliff novel.

A furtive smile twitched across her lips. Now her imagination really was running away with her. Surely Mr. Sutherland had his talents, like all God's creatures, but a *spy*?

He reached the top of the staircase just as she lifted the door latch. "Now," she said, swinging open the door and stepping inside, "about this urgent business—"

The dogs bounded forward at the sound of her voice, a blur of brown and white fur, long ears flapping in a breeze of their own making. The moment an unfamiliar man crossed the threshold behind her, however, they stopped in their tracks and began to bark. The low rumble of a growl traveled along the floor.

Bred to be a lady's lapdogs, the little spaniels tended to react strongly to men, a vestige of the days they'd spent being kicked and shouted at by the London dandy from whom Jane had—well, she liked to think of it as having rescued them, though *stolen* might be more technically correct. Reacting partly out of fear and partly to her flustered, frustrated state, they were now busy expressing their vocal distrust of Mr. Sutherland. Did they know more than she did?

She glanced back at him. One brow had risen in a sharp arch. He looked more amused than alarmed by this unexpected show of...well, call it *ferocity*.

With a snap of her fingers, she pointed at the floor. "Athena! Aphrodite!" To her surprise and relief, the dogs sat and were silent. But they did not take their eyes from the unwelcome visitor, and the fur on the back of Athena's neck ruffled when Mr. Sutherland stepped closer.

"Athena and Aphrodite." A wry smile curved his lips as he repeated their names. "Mr. Ratliff evidently has a flair for the dramatic. In the, er, classical sense."

She bent and plucked up a dog in each arm. Athena squirmed distractedly, while Aphrodite sniffed and snuffled, inspecting her mistress for any harm. *Flair for the dramatic*, indeed. "It's a comfort to have their protection in the wilds of the north."

"Protection, eh?" The second eyebrow joined the first somewhere in the middle of his forehead as he looked the dogs over. Athena, the larger of the two, still weighed less than a stone. "Were you counting on them licking intruders to death, Miss—Mrs. Higginbotham?"

Belatedly, she discovered it was no better to hear that name from his lips. "Do you doubt the efficacy of such an approach, Mr. Sutherland?"

Though she'd spoken in her most Mrs. Higginbotham-ish voice, the one she generally reserved for Agnes whenever the matchmaking fit was upon her, the effect on Mr. Sutherland was wildly different. His dark brows... well, *waggled* was the only word she could think of to describe their movement, and the smile that played around his lips now was positively wicked. "That depends entirely on who's doing the licking."

Innocent Jane Quayle ought not to grasp the bawdier implications of the exchange. Even the genteel widow Mrs. Higginbotham might claim ignorance. Robin Ratliff understood perfectly. Heat rushed into her face, which earned her another sharp yip of warning.

"Aphrodite, hush."

"I suspect they're snappish because we woke them from a sound sleep," Mr. Sutherland suggested then, smoothing his features into something like bland propriety, though she knew he had not overlooked the hot, knowing blush that had risen to her cheeks. "Probably chasing rabbits in their dreams, and our ill-timed arrival snatched victory from their jaws."

Athena squirmed more vigorously, and her round belly threatened to slip from Jane's grasp. If these dogs dreamed, it was of Agnes's cheese, and that was a prize that didn't often elude them. Aphrodite began to bark again in earnest.

"Perhaps I should go," he offered, though without enthusiasm, in a voice pitched loud enough to be heard over the racket, "and call again in the morning."

Yes. It had been a mistake to bring him up here. An invasion of her sanctuary. The dogs were trying to shield her. They sensed that the stranger had rattled her defenses. Far better to hold this meeting in the bright light of day.

Even by candlelight, however, now that some of her initial shock had worn off, she could see how tired and travel-weary he was. Icy raindrops still glittered on the shoulders of his greatcoat. His sun-warmed skin betrayed the pallor of fatigue, beneath a two or three days' growth of beard. He looked...well, *haggard* was the word that came to mind. No less handsome for it, to be sure. But definitely as if he'd been hurrying to get here. To discuss urgent business with...her?

The prospect of a sleepless night of wondering, and remembering, stretched before her. She shook her head. "I'll just take the dogs downstairs so we can talk in peace."

He glanced at them before settling his gaze on her. "If you're sure."

Of course she wasn't *sure*. Circumstances had forced her to make a number of quick decisions in recent years. A charitable soul might describe most of them as rash.

A nocturnal reunion with this man might be the worst of them, and that was saying something.

But curiosity was eating at her. What could have brought him back into her life? And if he'd managed to find her, who else might arrive on his heels? She nodded brusquely, aware that her grip on both the situation and the dogs was growing every minute more tenuous. "The sooner I give you an opportunity to explain the business that brought you here, Mr. Sutherland, the sooner you can be on your way."

Chapter 3

Left alone in the room, Thomas spent a full minute staring after her. *Disbelief* was far too mild a word to begin to capture his emotions. One woman had haunted his memory, his dreams, his imagination for years. Had he truly found her at Dunnock?

Or was this another episode like the one he'd experienced shortly after his arrival in the West Indies? According to the doctor, he'd been within hours of succumbing to some tropical fever. She'd appeared at his bedside and scolded him into recovery. When he'd come to himself enough to ask about her, the old nurse who'd been hired to care for him had favored him with a soft, pitying look. The kind of look ordinarily reserved for fools and madmen.

He sniffed the air for some hint of night-blooming jasmine but smelled only peat smoke. He hadn't hallucinated, though. Not this time.

The high-stickler Higginbotham, about whom he'd been warned, was none other than his Jane.

No sooner had the thought formed than he shook his head and snorted to rid himself of it. *His* Jane? Ridiculous. She'd been the acquaintance of a few weeks, seven years ago. No matter the hours they'd spent together, the confidences they'd shared. No matter the words he'd nearly spoken. No matter the memory of her sweet kiss and his whispered promise to call on her papa.

But when he'd tried to keep that promise, Mr. Quayle had declared he had no daughter and slammed the door in his face.

It hadn't taken years of specialized training as an intelligence officer to realize the man wasn't telling the truth. Mr. Quayle had been an exceptionally poor liar. But Thomas, believing he had more time and fearing that a challenge to the father might result in a punishment for the daughter, had bowed his head, apologized for the intrusion, and walked away, still clutching the nosegay he'd brought for her.

An hour later, a messenger had delivered new orders from General Scott. Come nightfall, Thomas had found himself staring up at the smoke-stained ceiling of a Portsmouth pub, wishing he'd probed Mr. Quayle's answer just a bit. Once under sail for Dominica, he'd tried and failed to shake the memory of her. Tried and failed to dismiss the spark between them.

At first sight tonight, she'd been so cool, so aloof, he'd almost begun to doubt his memory again. But when she'd laid her fingertips on his arm... well, he did not think she'd forgotten him, either.

Restless, he tossed his hat and gloves onto a low table and strode deeper into the room. Near the fireplace, his foot struck something hard. He looked down to discover he'd nearly tripped over a bone. A femur, by the looks of it, long since stripped of its flesh by the sharp teeth whose marks it bore. Beside it lay a coil of knotted, frayed rope. A smile twitched at the corner of his mouth. Were these not precisely the artifacts of pain and suffering that a reader of gothic novels might expect to find littering the floor of a crumbling castle?

Even if the devastation had been wrought by a pair of cosseted spaniels, and not some fearsome hellhound.

Closer to the hearth sat a pair of plump cushions, shielded from sparks by a brass fire screen. Their midnight-blue velvet was coated thickly with white fur, nearly obscuring the names embroidered in gold thread. The Greek goddesses of love and wisdom...Ratliff evidently had a sense of humor, as well as a flamboyant touch.

Rather than pushing the cushions aside to get closer, Thomas contented himself with stretching out his hands to the roaring fire. Once, the heat of the tropics had threatened to congeal his northern blood. He had not expected his return would prove an equally challenging adjustment.

Truth be told, he had not expected to return.

When his greatcoat began to steam, he shrugged himself free of it and looked about for a place to hang it that wouldn't be marred by its dampness. Behind the desk was a straight-backed wooden chair that might easily have passed for some sort of antique torture device, with its high, narrow back and straight arms. Nary a curve nor cushion in sight.

Nevertheless, someone had been sitting there. The desktop was covered with papers. Without intending to pry, he passed his gaze lightly over them. Fresh, black ink. A neat hand. Something about a girl, and a graveyard, and—*Ah.* This must be Robin Ratliff's work in progress. As Thomas draped his coat over the chair, he glanced once more about the room: the desk littered with papers, the overstuffed bookshelves, the dogs' beds. So this was the famous author's workshop? He'd expected something more lavish, given what General Scott had said, and what the lease to Dunnock had suggested, about the man's extraordinary wealth.

Taking in and evaluating every bit of available information had become something of a habit with Thomas. Nevertheless, if not for the penknife acting as a sort of macabre signpost, he would have overlooked the letter.

He had never considered himself an inordinately curious person, particularly about matters that did not concern him. But if nothing else, seven years of spying on behalf of the British Crown made it difficult for him to ignore a piece of paper that someone had found necessary to stab to death.

It might have been staged, of course. Some plot twist the writer had been testing out. But if so, he'd gone to a great deal of trouble to make the prop convincing. Unlike on the manuscript pages, the writing was difficult to read, obviously disguised—by using the opposite hand, if he had to guess. As best as he could make out, the letter writer intended to subject the author of some book called *The Necromancer's Bride* to the fate of its titular character, which evidently involved both occult offerings and more run-of-the-mill torment.

One word had been obliterated by the penknife—stabbed more than once, it would seem, for the paper was ragged, though the knife was sharp. The grisly details evidently extended onto a second sheet, which peeked from beneath the first. He flicked the corner of the top page with his fingertip but did not lift it to continue reading. He'd seen enough.

It was impossible to determine from a quick perusal whether the threat was sincere. On the other hand, elaborate plots sometimes masked far simpler dangers. He would not advise Ratliff to ignore it.

"Now, Mr. Sutherland, about this—"

He jerked his gaze to the doorway, where Jane stood framed, frozen in the act of brushing dog hair from her dress. Her blue eyes sliced coldly through him as her gaze shifted from him to the papers on the desktop and back again.

"What are you doing at my desk?" Though her voice was little more than a harsh whisper, it carried clearly across the room.

Her desk? Not Ratliff's? A sudden and irrational flash of anger burned away his previous amusement. Of course, the great man himself did not sit on a hard chair, hunched over a battered desk. He probably lounged on a pile of velvet cushions, like his dogs, while his—what was the word she'd used? Ah, yes, *amanuensis*—labored to catch every word that fell from his dissolute lips. Evidently, the man had no concern, no compassion at all for his employee. Why, the only concession to her comfort was the desk's proximity to the fire, but that spot had its disadvantages, too—namely a pair of noisy, ill-trained dogs, over which she clearly struggled to exert any control.

Surely, the late Mr. Higginbotham's family could have kept his widow from a life of drudgery, locked up in the south tower of Dunnock Castle?

With a conciliatory and not entirely convincing smile, he plucked up the shoulders of his greatcoat and let the garment drop once more over the chair's unforgiving rail. "I was just looking for a place to hang this."

"Oh." He caught a glimmer of chagrin in her eyes, but it did not fully displace her wariness. "I'm sorry about that. Visitors are a rarity at Dunnock. The servants are not accustomed—that is to say—" Finally, she crossed the threshold. "Mrs. Murdoch asked me to tell you she's prepared a room for you."

Quickly, he skirted the corner of the desk and stepped forward to meet her, hoping the movement masked his surprise at her words. Such an offer had been the last thing he expected, though it did not escape his notice that the housekeeper had been the one to make it, not Jane. "That's very kind of her."

"Apparently, the rain has turned to sleet," she explained when they stood no more than an arm's length apart. He nodded. The rain had been suspiciously cold and thick an hour ago as he'd walked from the crossroads, where the stage had dropped him. "If you tried to make it to the village now, you'd likely break your neck."

He could not quite persuade himself that it was concern he heard in her voice. The firelight lent her skin a warm glow that undercut the coolness of her demeanor, however. He let himself lean toward her ever so slightly. "How extraordinary to see you again, after all this time. And to find you *here…*"

He longed to reassure himself she was real, to touch her, to brush his thumb along her cheek, across her lips. She looked even better than he remembered. What once had been a mere pleasing plumpness about her figure had matured into the womanly curves of a painting by Rubens. Strong and sensual. Soft.

Though at the moment, that softness was well-hidden. Her expression, her demeanor, reminded him of an oyster's shell, snapped tightly shut to guard the vulnerable places within.

"Yes. A strange coincidence," she agreed, taking a single step backward.

Despite his desire to get closer, he understood her reserve. Seven years ago, they had been parted without so much as a chance to say goodbye. Their lives had marched onward, taking their separate courses, his marred by war and hers by widowhood. She had every right to be cautious. Still, he saw something more than chance in this encounter. "Oh, I wouldna call it a coincidence."

A wrinkle darted across her forehead. "Is it my imagination, Mr. Sutherland, or is your accent growing stronger?" The disapproving set of her jaw indicated she was unwilling to be charmed by it.

Some in Scott's service had been required to remove all trace of their origins from their speech. Thomas, on the other hand, had been known to play his up on occasion—though not for the purposes Jane seemed to suspect.

But this was different. Not a conscious affectation. Almost...natural. As if his return to Scottish soil had brought with it a return of the familiar cadences and colloquialisms of his youth.

He wasn't sure he liked it any more than Jane seemed to.

"Must be something in the air of the Highlands that brings it out," he said with a forced smile. "Dunnock is my home, after all"—or so General Scott had decreed with his curt order. "I rambled over the hills about Balisaig every summer when I was a lad," he clarified when she stiffened further. "My gran lived and died here."

Her gaze darted over him, lingering longest on his shoulders and chest. He liked the feel of her eyes on him. But she'd only been noting his lack of uniform, it seemed. "You're home on leave?"

He waited until she met his eyes again before saying with a half smile, "Not exactly."

He had spent every hour on the road between Edinburgh and here weighing his options, deciding what he would do when he reached Balisaig... when he reached *home*, as everyone was determined to have it. He'd claimed the title, but he wasn't ready to declare himself Magnus—not yet. Surely, he would get more honest answers about the state of things here if people didn't know they were speaking to the earl.

"Then why?" she demanded.

When he'd stepped from the coach, he'd intended to find lodgings in the village. The decision to come first to Dunnock had been a whim, born in part of his unreadiness to offer old friends some explanation for his return. Mostly, though, he'd been eager to take the measure of the man he hoped to hire to manage the estate.

"Perhaps I'd better discuss the matter with Ratliff himself, instead." A delay would give him time to decide what to say. The speech he'd rehearsed for the imagined Mr. Higginbotham wouldn't do at all.

"No." Her reply cracked the air between them like a whip. He drew himself up a little taller. "You can't," she added, in a tone slightly softer but no less determined.

Was the man ill? A hermit? "Tell him, 'tis a serious matter I've come to discuss."

"He's—he's in Edinburgh. Doing research."

Thomas tried to convince himself that the sudden pinch in his gut, the tension in his limbs, was irritation, annoyance. Perhaps even anger. He'd come all this way, when he might have met the man in Edinburgh and have done with this matter of the lease.

But if he'd come no farther than Edinburgh, then he wouldn't have found Jane.

He also wouldn't have seen the letter. If it had just arrived, as its position on the desk indicated, and Ratliff was away, then he could not yet know of it. Had there been others like it? Did the man know he might be in danger?

No, that sharp, twisting sensation inside him was an old companion, one he recognized too well: fear. Every soldier knew it, though he might call it by another name, to salve his pride. It was what kept him alert, out of danger. Any soldier who didn't feel it was probably dead.

Thomas was not, however, accustomed to feeling fear on behalf of another. Fear not for the faceless Ratliff, who was two days' journey off and would have to fend for himself. Fear for Jane, whose blue gaze was now regarding him with an uneasy mix of steadiness and uncertainty.

Based on that letter, a madman might have Robin Ratliff in his sights. But if the letter writer decided to make good on his threats and came to Dunnock, where the famous author was believed to reside, he would find Jane instead, all but alone. The scattering of servants—among them, a septuagenarian housekeeper and that fellow allowed to play at being gatekeeper—offered little security. To say nothing of those noisy fluffs of fur that passed for guard dogs.

Reflexively, Thomas curled his hand into a fist. He hadn't wanted the responsibilities of Dunnock's laird. But he couldn't let someone come to harm inside these walls. He glanced around the room. *His* walls.

Her gaze had shifted to the desktop. *"Oh. Of course."* She was speaking to herself more than to him, and in a tone of dawning realization. "And naturally, he chose someone familiar with the place. Someone whose time in the army gave him certain skills." Before Thomas could sort out her meaning, she jerked her attention back to him, and her penetrating eyes raked once more over his face, his clothes. He let her study him without interruption. In his experience, people liked to imagine themselves clever enough to read others. "I know why you've come," she declared.

"Aye, an' why's that?" Did she think he'd written that threatening letter? Was she about to accuse him of plotting to murder her employer?

"Mr. Ratliff's solicitor said the new earl had been found, but that he lived too far off to take matters in hand directly. You must be Lord Magnus's agent."

The laugh that burst from him was genuine, though it conveyed more shock than humor. Bad enough, in all conscience, to be the earl himself. But a landowner's agent? "Indeed I'm not. Such work would be far beyond my humble abilities, to borrow a pretty turn of phrase." His own unfitness for the task of managing Dunnock was why he'd come here with hopes of hiring Higginbotham, after all.

At least she hadn't been imagining him a would-be murderer—though it might have been more reassuring if she had. She needed to exercise caution with visitors. If that was her desk, then presumably she'd been the one to stab the letter with the penknife. Had that been her way of dismissing the danger it represented?

"If you're not here about Mr. Ratliff's lease on Dunnock…" Her brows dove into a worried V as she puzzled over the matter. *Of course. The blasted lease.* Had the solicitor indicated that Ratliff might be turned out by the new earl? Did she fear for her own position if that happened? "… Then what is it you want here, Mr. Sutherland?"

His mind spun. Since that day in General Scott's office, he'd had no difficulty coming up with a long list of reasons to leave Dunnock Castle as quickly as possible after his arrival. Now, however, if he hoped to protect Jane, he needed an excuse to stay.

"You said yourself that the situation here demands someone who knows Dunnock, someone with certain skills." He might not know the first thing about being an earl, but he was a damned good intelligence officer. His gaze landed once more on the letter. Here was the task to which he could apply his talents. "As I think you know, Robin Ratliff has received death threats. I'm here to investigate."

Chapter 4

Jane opened her mouth, but all that came out was a strangled, choking sort of noise, the sound of a gasp, a laugh, and a one-word shriek—*liar!*—colliding in her throat. Of all the preposterous explanations for him to offer, the one he'd hit upon was surely the most ridiculous.

"Are you suggesting Mr. Ratliff hired you?" She probed the claim, just to make sure she hadn't misheard.

"That surprises you?"

"*Shock* might be a more accurate description, Mr. Sutherland. *Utter disbelief* would not be an exaggeration. Why, I am tempted to call it *impossible*. The notion that Robin Ratliff has been writing letters and conducting business without the knowledge and assistance of his secretary—"

"Amanuensis," he corrected, with that playful smile she wanted to despise but couldn't. "Surely, you don't mean to suggest he involves his humble copyist in every decision he makes?"

"I—" She prepared to pounce on the falsehood. Two things held her back.

First was the simple fact that she was lying too. Lying to him—to everyone. Not that one person's lies excused another's, or that hers made him somehow trustworthy. But it felt hypocritical to fault him for fabricating an answer without knowing why. She, of all people, understood that one might have a perfectly good reason for doing it. She, of all people, knew how risky the truth could be.

And second, only two people knew about the threat to Robin Ratliff. She was one. The other was the letter writer. Which meant that Mr. Sutherland just might be...

No. No, of course he hadn't written the blasted thing. He'd seen it while nosing around her desk—as he'd obviously been doing when she came in, however much he denied it. It had been foolish of her to leave it lying about. But why assume there had been other threats? Why pretend to have been called here to investigate the matter?

And since his arrival obviously had nothing to do with a letter he'd only just seen, she still had no answer to the question of what *had* brought him here. She did not entirely trust his flat denial about working for the Earl of Magnus. He'd said he'd come on a matter of business, after all, and the solicitor's letter had alerted her to the most pressing business having to do with Dunnock Castle.

When Mr. Sutherland had discovered that the "Mr. Higginbotham" he'd traveled so far to see was in fact the woman he'd known years ago, his surprise had been genuine, of that she felt sure. Some part of even her wondered whether his lie was a fumbling, even endearing, excuse to stay and reacquaint himself with her.

If that was the case, should she be flattered or aggravated by his interest?

His sudden appearance had brought to mind the long-gone days of assemblies and pretty dresses, giggling behind her fan, a stroll in a moonlit garden with a handsome gentleman. She never allowed herself to feel lonely. But tonight she found herself recalling with a sort of fondness the time before she had discovered that the surest—and safest—route to her dream had to be traveled alone.

Aggravated. Definitely aggravated. The past belonged in the past, no matter how temptingly it beckoned.

But displaying her aggravation was unlikely to help her find out the truth. She might be better off to go along with his ruse, merely to keep an eye on him. Shaking off the sharp words she had been about to speak, she favored him with a smile instead. She would find a way to manage this situation, as she had managed so many others. "It seems Robin Ratliff still has the capacity to surprise me, Mr. Sutherland."

If the abrupt shift in her demeanor had caught him off guard, he quickly regained his balance. "The best storytellers are full of surprises, Mrs. Higginbotham. I, for one, find it dull—and a little suspicious—when things go entirely to plan. Of course, some surprises are pleasanter than others." He tipped his head as if to include her among the pleasant surprises.

"It's kind of you to say so, Mr. Sutherland. I should hate to be thought dull." She stepped toward her desk, almost brushing against him as she passed, and then jerked the penknife free of the wood. After returning that implement to its place on the engraved silver tray beside the ink bottle, she picked up the two letters, folded the one from the solicitor, and placed it in the desk's shallow center drawer, which she then locked with a tiny key she fished from deep within her bodice. "Or suspicious."

He watched her with a passable imitation of indifference to everything but the knife, and even that earned nothing more strenuous than a raised eyebrow.

"This, I suppose, is the sort of letter to which you are referring?" She held out the offending document but did not glance at it. Those hateful words did not need further opportunity to etch themselves onto her brain or to burrow beneath her skin.

He took it, keeping his eyes on her face for a moment longer than was comfortable before shifting his attention to the letter and reading it slowly through. She watched, reluctantly fascinated by the way the firelight highlighted his strong features. The fatigue she'd noted earlier had given way to a strange sort of animation. He was enjoying this—not the substance of the letter, nor the discomfort it had caused her, but the mystery, the challenge it represented.

When he finished, he turned the sheet over to examine the direction and the broken wax seal. "This was sent to London."

"Yes, it was delivered to his publisher, Persephone Press, and forwarded on to him here."

"Do you always open letters addressed to Mr. Ratliff?"

A beat of silence threatened to reveal more than she intended. "I have permission to do so when he is away, yes. So that nothing urgent or important is overlooked."

"Hmm. Almost like a secretary." He shifted his attention from the letter to her. "And is he often away?"

Whatever she'd imagined would happen if she ever saw Mr. Sutherland again, this brisk, businesslike questioning had not been it. He was obviously practiced at it. She felt unsettled, which was likely his goal. "Often, yes."

"And where does he go?"

"It depends." *On how far away I need him to be.*

An expression of wry humor etched itself into his face along familiar lines, and he shook his head. "I suppose I'm just unlucky to have missed him." She permitted herself a little laugh. "When do you expect him to return?"

"I—I couldn't say."

Mild surprise greeted her reply, and then he held up the letter again. "Is this it? No second page?"

"No."

The corner of his mouth twitched. She had not known that skepticism could call up a dimple, the same as a smile. "Mrs. Higginbotham, if I'm going to resolve this matter, I'll need your cooperation and honesty."

She tipped her head to the side to acknowledge his point and gave a sweet smile. "Of course. What possible good could come of being dishonest with one another?"

For a long moment, he simply looked at her, poised on the edge of speech but not speaking. She felt certain that the mischievous sparkle in his eyes, the slight play of amusement around his lips were matched by a similar expression on her own face. As if each of them knew that the other was not being entirely truthful but, instead of being dismayed or frustrated by the discovery, was intrigued by it.

What did it say about either of them that the prospect of a cat-and-mouse game was so appealing?

At last, he laughed softly, conceding the round to her. "May I keep this?" he asked, already folding the letter and preparing to slip it inside his coat.

"Of course." She wanted nothing to do with the thing. She ought to have tossed it into the fire to begin with. Though if she had, would Mr. Sutherland have found some other pretext for staying at Dunnock?

"Are there others in your possession?"

She widened her eyes in pretend shock at the prospect. "Why, no. If there are others, I assumed Mr. Ratliff would've given them to you."

Mr. Sutherland tucked the letter neatly into his breast pocket before favoring her with a lazy smile. "All he had, ma'am."

*All he had...*None, in other words. Oh, he was really too good at this, and such a realization ought not to make her pulse race. Or, if it was determined to race, then it ought to be an indicator of fear or distress. Certainly not excitement.

It was just that, well, years of virtual isolation in Scotland *could* be a trifle dull.

And Mr. Sutherland, for all the frustration she'd felt since the announcement of his arrival, was not dull. Even the first glimpse of him across a muddy street, seven years ago, had been enough to set a foolish young lady's pulse aflutter. The dashing uniform, the twinkle in his eye, the Scottish brogue...he'd exuded a certain roguish charm, though she'd tried to dismiss it as the effect of her sometimes-wayward imagination.

If anything, the years had improved him as a specimen of masculinity: broader shoulders, a more chiseled jaw. His hazel eyes still twinkled. Now, though, she saw something different in them. She had the distinct impression those eyes had seen things, somber things that made their moments of merriment more precious. There was a ruggedness about him now that drew her, much as she'd been drawn by the ruggedness of Scotland itself.

"Tell me, Mr. Sutherland." She gestured for him to sit down on the horsehair sofa. "What did you do in the army?"

He was looking down at the cushion where, to her dismay, a good deal of white fur had become interwoven with the upholstery. Athena often preferred the sofa to her place on the hearth. No one else ever sat there.

Still, it could easily be interpreted as failure on the part of the staff, or herself, to keep things orderly. It felt, somehow, like a sign of weakness. Softness.

A side of herself she chose no longer to show.

To Jane's surprise, he did not bother to try to brush it away, futile though the gesture doubtless would have been. She supposed it was consistent with his general devil-may-care attitude.

He did, however, grimace slightly as he sank down. The cushions were soft, too soft for anyone but a child or a small pet to feel comfortable, which was precisely why she'd offered that seat to him. It wouldn't do to make him too comfortable here. Nevertheless, a slight twinge of regret passed through her. She hadn't considered that a man of his size might go right on sinking to the floor.

In the end, the sofa held, though not without a creak of protest from its frame and a bit of awkward shifting about on the part of Mr. Sutherland, who no longer enjoyed the advantage of height. When he met her gaze again, his was still steadfastly amused and, yes, knowing. "Were you hoping to put your opponent out of sorts, Mrs. Higginbotham?" he murmured. "I shall remember that."

"Opponent? Why, whatever do you mean?" She straightened a bit in the overlarge leather chair she'd chosen, which had the unfortunate effect of lifting her feet from the floor in a most undignified fashion.

To hide a laugh, he passed a hand over his mouth and jaw, lingering just a moment to rub that bristle she found so fascinating, then stretched out his arm along the back of the sofa, looking far too much at his ease. Too late, she remembered her vow not to invite him to sit down at all.

"I've been in the West Indies, ma'am, doing most of what my commanding officers ordered," he answered her question at last.

Her lips quirked in reluctant amusement. "Only most?"

"It wouldn't do to raise their expectations." He winked. "Why, on six days out of seven, I did nothing at all."

That wink caused her stomach to perform a curious flip-flop, but she calmed it with an even breath and said, in that prim voice that almost always worked with Agnes, "What happened on the seventh day?"

"Oh, I did a bit of beachcombing."

She hadn't the faintest notion what he meant, except that it sounded idle and pointless but almost certainly wasn't. After all, everyone knew that the French and British had long been battling for supremacy in the Caribbean, which required any number of sailors and soldiers and ships.

She might not know what beachcombing was, but she was intimately familiar with the process of trying to persuade someone that she was what they believed her to be: merely a widow who wrote a neat hand, employed to turn a famous author's manuscripts into clean copies for the publisher. What, then, might Mr. Sutherland really be? It was fascinating to watch him spin and knit the wool before he pulled it over her eyes. Or tried to.

"No wonder you're so, er, brown." *Dreadfully* brown. More brown than a proper gentleman had any right to be. She certainly did *not* find herself wondering whether his sun-kissed skin felt as warm as it looked, or whether his chest and shoulders were as tanned as his face and hands. "I confess, when I said that your service had given you the skills necessary for this job, I was thinking of something quite different."

"Oh?" His eyebrows shot up. "Were there particular skills of mine you intend to put to the test?"

This time, she somehow managed not to blush. "Well, if you are here to investigate a death threat, Mr. Sutherland, doesn't that rather presuppose that there's a killer about? Given that we may all be in danger, one hopes you're a skilled marksman, or swordsman, or—" The customary steely note in her voice grew thin at its edges.

"Never fear, ma'am," he spoke across her. "I can handle my weapon."

She found his lazy, suggestive smile oddly reassuring, as if he believed the matter required no defensive tactics more substantial than witty repartee. She'd meant to sound skeptical, even dismissive of the prospect of danger. Somehow, however, the act of speaking the threat aloud made it far more real than the letter writer's poor penmanship had done. What if...what if someone really wanted Robin Ratliff—her—dead?

"But the goal," he continued, more seriously, "is never to need to outgun your opponent. If his weapon is drawn, the battle is already half lost."

She supposed that made a certain amount of sense.

"It's my job to anticipate his moves," he continued. "To be quicker. Cleverer."

"And all that—that *beachcombing* has made you quick and clever, has it?"

His arm dropped to his side, and he pushed himself up, onto the edge of the seat, closer to her. In the firelight, his eyes gleamed like whisky in the glass. "I'm still alive, lass. That's all you need to know."

She parted her lips to retort, but no words came.

It went against her nature to let someone else have the last word. Books were easier. The perfect line always came to her eventually, so that her characters were never at a loss. But right in this moment, she felt neither quick nor clever.

She felt afraid. Frightened of being forced to leave Dunnock, by fair means or foul.

Pushing to her feet, she said, "I'll ring Mrs. Murdoch to show you to your room." Mr. Sutherland had to be tired. Surely, tomorrow morning would be soon enough to begin figuring out what they really wanted from each other? She needed to be alone, to think. This ordinary January day had taken twists and turns even Robin Ratliff's readers would have decried as improbable.

But no sooner were the words out than she swayed unsteadily and found herself sitting down again. The room swam at the edges of her vision. Oh, this was patently ridiculous. She had never fainted before, and although she had once wondered whether it wouldn't be useful to experience the sensation, for research purposes, now was not the time.

Despite the horsehair sofa's effort to keep him prisoner, Mr. Sutherland had leaped up the moment she offered to rise, a more gentlemanly act than she had expected from him. Though that wasn't entirely fair, either. She had no reason not to think of him as a gentleman. But it wasn't improving her equilibrium to have him looming over her. A man who'd been traveling for days, wearing damp clothes, hadn't any right to smell so enticingly crisp and spicy.

Then he picked her up her limp hand from the arm of the chair and began to chafe her wrist. One broad, slightly callused thumb slipped beneath the fine lace edging her sleeve and passed over the delicate skin that guarded her pulse. "Mrs. Higginbotham? Are you all right?" She peered up at him, saw worry creasing the fine lines at the corners of his eyes, read concern in his wry, crooked smile. "Perhaps I ought to help you to your room instead." He bent lower, as if he might just lift her into his arms.

From somewhere, she mustered the wherewithal to pull herself free of his touch and to sit more upright. "I'm fine," she insisted, shaking the wool from her head. "Just stood up too quickly, that's all."

Obligingly, he took a step backward. "I'll ring for Mrs. Murdoch, then, shall I?" He crossed the room to the bell rope before she could protest.

"Wait." The last thing she needed was Agnes to fuss over her. She managed to get to her feet, one hand gripping the back of the chair to ensure she stayed there this time. The effort earned her a frown. "The dogs are with Agnes—Mrs. Murdoch. The bell will only set them off again. And the other servants will already be abed."

"Well, then, is it to be that wretched sofa for me tonight?" he asked with a wink.

Was it her imagination, or was his brogue getting stronger yet?

"Better that than the cushions on the hearth," she tossed back, drawing strength from his teasing as she flicked her gaze toward the dogs' beds, then back to him.

But he was looking past her, at the door that led to her chamber, almost as if he knew exactly what lay behind it. She supposed she shouldn't be surprised if his skill set included intimate knowledge of the floor plan of Dunnock Castle—or, more likely, an uncanny ability to scout out ladies' bedrooms.

When his gaze focused once more on her, the current that passed between them was undiminished by the breadth of the room. As strong and as unmistakable as it had been when it shot across the Tenchley assembly seven years ago. Her pulse kicked up a notch. The heat of his gaze was doing strange things to her insides, and she dug her fingers more firmly into the supple leather of the chair.

It wasn't difficult to picture him as a strapping Highlander in a kilt, with his claymore drawn and upraised...standing watch at the foot of her bed...or closer still... "I suppose a guard might come in handy if the fiend who wrote that letter decides to show his face," she whispered.

He appeared to weigh her words—both spoken and unspoken, if she weren't mistaken. "Aye, lass. That it might." His voice was low, warmer even than his eyes, though at this distance, his expression was unreadable. "So, time to rouse the dogs." He jerked the tasseled cord of the bell pull, then gave a surprisingly crisp bow, a reminder that he was still a soldier, for all that nonsense about beachcombing. "I'll meet Mrs. Murdoch below. Good night, Mrs. Higginbotham." With those words, he turned and left, as confident of his destination as if he owned the place.

Relief—for that was what she chose to call it—coursed through her. She'd been spared the consequences of her own foolishness. Really, to have almost *fainted*! After all, she wasn't a frail Robin Ratliff heroine in need of protection. And Mr. Sutherland wasn't her hero.

Probably not the villain of the piece, either, though he'd been dishonest about why he'd invaded Dunnock, her sanctuary. If she wanted her peace and privacy back, she was going to have to establish firm boundaries. Keep her guard up, not lower it, as shock had led her to do tonight.

That's all you need to know, he'd said.

"Oh, no, it isn't."

She spoke aloud in the empty room, a retort unworthy of Robin Ratliff's notoriously wicked wit. But it would have to do.

With a sigh, she sank back into the chair. Her arms and legs were as weak as if she'd been battling quicksand, fighting even as she was being sucked, inexorably, back into the morass of her past.

Tomorrow, she meant to find out whether Mr. Sutherland had come to throw her a lifeline or push her under.

Chapter 5

In the fine medieval tradition, the circular staircase of the south tower had been designed and built to delay, if not prevent, an invasion. The tight spiral wound upward on the left, preventing a right-handed warrior from ascending with his sword raised. The steps were so narrow they could only be climbed single file. And it was impossible for the person at the bottom to see what defenses might await him at the top.

So when Thomas met Mrs. Murdoch a dozen or so steps from the bottom of the staircase, the elderly housekeeper had little warning of his descent, and Athena and Aphrodite, who had been trotting at her heels, went wild. The staircase funneled the cacophony of their shrill barking and Mrs. Murdoch's exclamations upward, nearly deafening him. They stood for a moment at an impasse, the housekeeper too startled to move and Thomas unable to go past her.

If the stairwell had been wider than the breadth of his shoulders, or the step on which he stood were deeper than half the sole of his boot, he would've turned around and gone back up. It had taken all his strength of will to say good night to Jane and walk out of that room. Tonight, a new image of her had been seared onto his memory: pale, trembling, almost overcome—and he'd very nearly gathered her into his arms and promised to keep her safe forever. But she didn't trust him, any more than her dogs did.

And with reason.

Seven years ago, he'd left Sussex without even an opportunity to explain. No wonder she'd given him a cool greeting. To reappear in her life, as abruptly as he'd left it? And then not even able to be honest with her about what he'd been doing in the intervening years, or why he'd come here tonight?

It had been harder to lie to her than he'd expected. Difficult, but necessary. He didn't know what threats or problems the castle held. He didn't even know her, certainly not the woman she'd become. To tell her, or anyone, the truth—that he'd spent the better part of the last decade serving as a spy and had now inherited an earldom he didn't want—was to close a chapter of his life forever.

And he'd come dangerously close to doing it anyway.

"Whisht, lassies, whisht," Agnes was pleading, struggling to lay her hands on the dogs without losing her balance. When he eventually thought to press himself flat against the curved outer wall, the dogs skated past, clinging to the turn, their brown and white bodies low and wary. "Och, sir, I'm dead sorry," the housekeeper declared when the echoes of their barking had subsided. "'Twas the bell that set 'em off tae start, but they've always been dead skittish around men."

"Mrs. Higginbotham will be glad to see them, I think." More comforted by their presence than by his, at least. "She said you'd been kind enough to prepare a room for me, Mrs. Murdoch."

"Aye, that's so, Mr.—"

"Sutherland."

Her wrinkled face creased in a broad grin. "Ah, I thought I heard a wee bit of the Scots in your voice."

"A wee bit," he agreed a trifle reluctantly, recalling Jane's accusation. He held out a hand to help the housekeeper make the dangerous turn so that she could descend the stairs. "But I've been away for more than ten years."

"Ah, well." She dismissed the last decade with a wave of her other hand, a hand he would have preferred she kept flat to the stone wall for the sake of balance. "You're home now."

Was he? How could a place be so familiar, and yet so strange?

Then again, he might say much the same about Jane.

Once at the bottom of the staircase, Mrs. Murdoch began to bustle down the corridor he'd walked along earlier with Jane. "How long has Mrs. Higginbotham been at Dunnock?"

She didn't pause as she answered. "As long as Mr. Ratliff has."

Was she being deliberately evasive? His stride was easily twice hers, and he quickly reached the housekeeper's side. "And how long is that?"

"Oh, a few years now."

Nearly six. He knew as much from the papers General Scott had given him to study. But, of course, that time line did not account for the year or so between their meeting in Sussex and her arrival in Scotland. The period in which she'd been married and widowed, taken employment, and agreed to travel to what Englishmen who didn't know better thought of as the end of the world.

When Mrs. Murdoch ushered him across the Great Hall, he began to wonder whether she hadn't decided to show him out the door instead of to his room. "Dougan put your things in the gatehouse," she explained. "Bit of privacy for you there."

A bit of privacy for Jane, as well. Once the castle door was shut, he would be as far removed from her as he could and still be within Dunnock's walls. Perhaps he'd underestimated the servants' protective instinct.

Almost immediately, he regretted leaving his greatcoat and gloves behind. The damp, icy air made him think with unexpected longing of sweat and sand and the whine of mosquitoes. Once more, he silently cursed General Scott for insisting on his coming to Dunnock. If his chilly reception from Jane tonight was anything to go by, even their unexpected reunion might not be enough to salvage this journey.

Mrs. Murdoch turned her face into the wind, favoring him with red cheeks and sparkling eyes. "There's nowt like th' fresh Scots air to remind a man he's a Highlander," she insisted.

The echo of his own ridiculous explanation for his brogue forced another wry smile to his lips.

The gatehouse consisted of a suite of rooms built into the castle's outer bailey, where in days long gone by, the guards would have lived and slept and kept watch through the narrow slits high in the walls. Vaguely, he wondered whether he would be expected to share the dark, humble quarters with Dougan. But when Mrs. Murdoch shouldered open the door—"sticks a bit, always has"—he saw that the rooms behind it had been transformed from their original purpose as guardsmen's quarters. The apartment was spacious and modern, comfortably furnished. They passed through an office to the sitting room, and beyond that he could see a bedchamber.

"Lord Magnus's steward, Mr. Barrie, did live here for many a year," Mrs. Murdoch explained. "He—the earl, that is—shut up the rest o' the castle and let most of the staff go. Didn't fancy worryin' himself about it, it seems. Then, after Mr. Barrie took sick an' died, Mr. Ratliff came."

Thomas smoothed his features into an expression of mild interest. "But Mr. Ratliff isn't—" He bit off whatever he'd been about to say. Who knew what Mr. Ratliff might be? "Who manages the land?" he asked instead.

She shrugged. "Someone in Glasgow? Or maybe it's London." *Edinburgh*, he very nearly corrected her. But any of those cities clearly lay beyond the borders of the housekeeper's imagination. "Mrs. Higginbotham gets letters from him from time to time."

More letters—and likely unpleasant ones too, concerning matters about which she could do very little. She must have come to dread the arrival of the post.

"I thought p'rhaps *you*'d come to...well, er...see about things." Mrs. Murdoch folded her hands in front of her and gave him a significant look.

Do I look like a steward?

He didn't dare ask, afraid the answer might be yes. Then again, with his sun-browned skin and scuffed boots, perhaps he no longer looked enough like a gentleman even for that.

"I've come to investigate a threatening letter sent to Mr. Ratliff," he said instead. Hardly a lie now. He certainly meant to uncover who'd written the damned thing, though he was far more concerned with the possible danger to Jane. No need, in any case, to claim more of a role for himself. While he was conducting his investigation into the letter, he could look into the state of affairs at Dunnock as well. Surely, that would satisfy General Scott's demand.

The housekeeper's eyes grew wide at the mention of a threat.

"Tell me, what sort of tenant has Mr. Ratliff been?" he asked.

Surprise at his question flickered across her features, and she drew her folded hands closer to her body, in the manner of one guarding something—a secret? Or was she simply a loyal servant, disinclined to speak of her master's affairs? "I couldn't say, Mr. Sutherland."

"Why not?"

"Why, I've never met the man."

"Never—?"

She gave a crooked nod of confirmation. "Keeps to himself, he does. Spends most of his time abroad." Clearly, she found such behavior strange.

Research, Jane had said. Who would have imagined that such fanciful books required extensive research? "Yes, Mrs. Higginbotham mentioned that he's in Edinburgh now."

"Och, is he?" She sounded unsurprised, and supremely uninterested. "Well, he's gone more than he's here, and that's a fact."

Curious behavior, to be sure. But then, General Scott had hinted that he ought to expect as much. Who but a great eccentric would pay a prime sum to live at Dunnock?

Or *not* to live there, as the case might be.

"Thank you, Mrs. Murdoch. You've been most helpful." With a wave of his arm, he ushered her back into the office. The housekeeper readily accepted his dismissal, and after making a surprisingly spry curtsy, she wrested open the stubborn door and stepped back into the courtyard.

Another blast of wintry wind and a flurry of snowflakes whirled their way into the room in her wake.

As soon as the door was shut, he set about getting his bearings, a habit of long standing that made it less likely for a soldier to be taken by surprise in unfamiliar surroundings. The office was small and square, with a bare stone floor and whitewashed walls. The plain, serviceable furnishings were sufficient for bookkeeping and meeting with tenants: a table, a pair of wooden chairs, and a desk.

How long since anyone had done the estate's business there?

He shook off the question and moved to bolt the door. He'd met Mr. Watson, the earl's—*his*—land agent in Edinburgh and been unimpressed. But he had no real reason to believe that Dunnock's affairs could not be competently managed from afar, if he could find the proper person.

He could no longer solve his dilemma by hiring "Mr. Higginbotham" to take care of Dunnock, however. How long might it take to find a steward worthy of the name? What sorts of decisions would he be expected to make in the meantime?

Damn and blast.

As if hoping the questions would not follow him, he hurried into the sitting room, where the fire blazing in the hearth made the space comparatively warm and bright. The walls had been paneled sometime in the last century, and most of the furniture seemed to date from an earlier generation as well, though it was more elegant than that of the office, with a wool rug on the floor and a few inexpensive prints decorating the walls. The sofa looked at least as inviting as the one he'd been sitting on an hour before. The well-stocked tea tray resting on a table by the fireplace made the room welcoming. The fire had been lit too recently to drive away the dampness and mustiness of disuse. Otherwise, everything looked to be in perfect readiness for guests.

But, of course, Ratliff was never here to entertain...

Picking up the candle from the tea table in one hand and a slice of plum cake in the other—he'd not eaten since leaving Perth hours ago—Thomas made his way into the bedchamber. Like the sitting room, its walls were paneled and its furnishings old-fashioned but comfortable. Someone, presumably Mrs. Murdoch, had turned down the bed to air the linens, and Dougan had deposited his trunk and satchel against one wall. Though farthest from the door, this room was the coldest, and he did not linger. Unpacking could wait until morning.

Back in the sitting room, he addressed himself to the remaining contents of the tray, which included a reasonably hearty supper and a half-full decanter of whisky, he was pleasantly surprised to discover. He liked Mrs. Murdoch better with every passing moment.

Full and warm, he leaned back in the chair and loosened his cravat. Beneath the crackle and hiss of the fire, the silence of the room was oppressive. No dull roar of the ocean or squawking birds overhead. Nary a reminder of the life that had been his for so long.

He ran a finger beneath his collar and gave another tug; the clothes and manners of a gentleman chafed at him now. They'd been his, once. But they'd not suited the role he'd been ordered to play in the West Indies, so he'd put them off in favor of tattered linen and unkempt hair, no one's idea of a British agent on the lookout for French landing parties. In Dominica, *he* had been the eccentric, the mad Scot who wandered the beaches and was known to drink too much.

Now, he would have to figure out the proper part to play here. His eyes traveled the room, and when his gaze lighted on the decanter, he leaned forward to splash a measure of the amber liquid into a tumbler.

The whisky burned a little as it made its way down his throat. Not enough, but a start. He raised the decanter in mock salute to no one in particular and tipped it over the glass again. The loch was surely frozen over now, and it didn't have much in the way of a beach to wander, in any case, but he knew of no reason why he couldn't go right on being the mad Scot who drank too much.

After watching the firelight through the contents of the tumbler for a long moment, he returned the glass to the tray untouched and reached into his pocket to withdraw the anonymous letter. By itself, it wasn't much of a clue to go on, the paper unremarkable, the hand obviously disguised. Had there really been no others like it? And if there'd been only the one letter, had he made too much of the threat? Jane's reaction to his claim that he'd come to investigate the matter had been more than skeptical, as if it were not just unlikely Ratliff had hired him, but impossible. As if she'd known he was lying.

Absently, he rubbed his thumb over the torn place her penknife had made. She hadn't been frightened by the letter. She'd been angry. Angered on Ratliff's behalf? Perhaps. But there was something else, some detail that was eluding his grasp. He was half-tempted to find a copy of *The Necromancer's Bride* just to see what all the fuss was about.

After picking up the paper and returning the document to his breast pocket, he pushed to his feet. A good night's sleep would clear his head. Tomorrow, he would find out who handled the post in the village and see what information could be gleaned there.

Which of his old haunts, his old friends, would he find still standing? Some would surely recognize him in Balisaig. Not as Magnus, of course. As that troublesome Lowlands boy who'd once come with the summer sun to drive his gran to distraction. He rubbed the back of his knuckles over his unshaven jaw. Perhaps he ought to have thought of a disguise. He might've let his beard grow during the journey. Or at least a mustache...

Instead of making his way to the bedchamber, he strode to the door of the gatehouse and threw back the bolt, needing one last look. Years on an island, weeks at sea...he found it disorienting, a little disconcerting, to be locked in a windowless room. He dragged the door open, wondering as it juddered over the grove in the floor how Mrs. Murdoch had managed to get the better of the rusty hinges and the door's weight.

The wind moaned as it rushed past him; the stout oak panel had muffled it almost as well as the stone walls. The courtyard was empty, and no light gleamed anywhere. Dunnock loomed over him, a darker shadow against a blue-black, starless sky.

The castle doors, which Mrs. Murdoch had shut behind her, were the only opening in the castle's inner bailey, designed by the builders as a second line of defense against any intruder who managed to breach the outer wall and get past the guards in the gatehouse. Though he wasn't intimately familiar with the layout of the castle, he knew that the living quarters lay on the opposite side, where high walls and the loch below provided a final measure of security. By putting him here, Mrs. Murdoch had managed the impossible: show a stranger hospitality, but keep him far away from anything valuable.

But the only treasure inside Dunnock that interested him was Jane.

What might have happened if he had accepted her offer of a night spent on that awful couch or the cushions on the hearth? He'd slept in worse conditions, and the discomfort would have been a small price to pay for a chance to stay close to her. But, of course, she'd only been teasing—at least, she'd only intended to tease. She didn't trust the spark of attraction between them, either, and that was doubtless a sign of her good sense.

Now, however, as he stood staring into the darkness, he found himself wondering whether he would wake to discover that seeing her tonight had only been another fever dream.

And if that were the case, perhaps all the rest of it was simply a nightmare.

A particularly sharp blade of air sliced through him, and he shivered against its rawness. Shaking his head at his own foolishness, he pulled the door shut again and bolted it. For now, at least, she was safe up there in her tower. And since Ratliff had left his dogs behind, Athena and Aphrodite were with her, ready to sound the alarm if needed.

Only when he had readied himself for bed and slipped between the cold sheets did Mrs. Murdoch's comment about the dogs wiggle its way back to the front of his mind.

They've always been dead skittish around men.

He supposed she'd meant to say that the man's dogs disliked *other* men. It was all a bit odd, though. Not unlike Ratliff himself. The reclusiveness, the lengthy absences—it all added up to a strange, shadowy figure, a man only Jane seemed to know well.

Thomas had been wrong when he'd said she hadn't changed. The girl he'd known had been open, trusting—too trusting, perhaps. The woman was guarded, wary, reserved. What had happened to make her so?

He stared up at the ceiling, waiting for the bed to warm enough for him to fall sleep. He hadn't told Jane the truth about who he was or why he'd come.

But he was beginning to suspect he wasn't the only one with a secret.

Chapter 6

Jane lay on her back staring up into the canopy, Athena and Aphrodite snuggled against her ribs on either side. The bed had been her one true indulgence, with its silky linens, an extravagant number of pillows, and curtains of wine-colored brocaded velvet cascading down in swags from a gilded tester. Every woman deserved such a bed, all to herself—well, shared with her dogs, of course. It was a haven to which she could retreat when the words wouldn't come or lofty critics turned up their noses.

Tonight, however, though the bed was as comfortable as ever and the hour was late, sleep eluded her. Restlessness prickled beneath her skin, like an awkwardly situated itch that demanded to be scratched at the most inopportune moment. She felt every bit as unsettled as she had earlier in the evening, maybe more so, despite telling herself repeatedly that nothing had really changed.

She was perfectly safe—the writer of that letter had sent it to London, not here, obviously not knowing where she lived.

She still held the lease on Dunnock and had received no official word it would not be renewed.

Work on *The Brigand's Captive* was coming along nicely.

The only real difference between last night and tonight was the arrival of Mr. Sutherland, which hardly signified, because—

She heaved a sigh. Athena protested the movement of her human pillow by laying a paw on Jane's upper arm to hold her in place.

Jane had been telling herself for an hour or more that it was perfectly pointless to let herself get worked up about Mr. Sutherland. No matter that he had appeared out of nowhere on the same day as those dreadful letters. No matter that he had offered an explanation that held less water than a tin pail with a guinea-sized hole. No matter that he obviously intended to stay and poke around in matters that didn't concern him...or did they?

No matter that she'd once fancied herself in love with him.

She stifled another sigh. No matter how hard she tried, she couldn't talk herself out of her unease. While he might not be dangerous, he was definitely trouble.

Years ago, she had made the decision to close the door on one life and open another. The moments, the people, the places—all shut up and tucked away in the darkest corner of the deepest drawer in her memory. Now, however, in what might have been a scene from one of her own books, the box in which she'd buried her past had started to rattle ominously. What lay inside was still alive and demanding to be let out.

And it was all Thomas Sutherland's fault.

She'd spent no—well, very little—time in the last seven years thinking about him. What a shock to discover that the attraction she'd felt to him at seventeen hadn't faded. She supposed it wasn't exactly surprising for a young woman to be drawn to a tall, handsome gentleman, to enjoy his laughing eyes and ready smile, to wonder what it would be like to run her fingers through his dark, wavy hair.

But it had always been more than that.

Now, as then, he exuded confidence. Confidence without arrogance, which in her experience was a rarity, especially among men. Something about the way he carried himself, his willingness to laugh at himself—she'd never known anything quite like it, either before or since. She...well, to be honest, she envied it.

She was proud of her success, confident in her creative abilities. Nevertheless, a certain degree of anxiety lingered. It wouldn't be going too far to call it fear, though precisely *what* she feared was difficult to pin down. Maintaining the world she'd made for herself required control and reserve and, yes, secrecy. Unlike some, she couldn't afford to be easygoing.

But when Mr. Sutherland's ample personal charms were combined with the way he'd looked at her years ago—the way he'd looked at her tonight—it wasn't hard to understand why she was lying awake thinking of him, even if she shouldn't.

The first time she'd seen Mr. Sutherland had been in Ford's general store. Her brother Jonathan had stopped for something, most likely a stick of barley sugar, on his way to the rectory, where the curate tutored him three times a week in Greek. Though Jonathan might not have been past the age of skipping lessons to go fishing, he had surely been past the age of believing no one would be the wiser if he did. Long past the age of needing his elder sister to walk with him to the rectory, in any case. But Jane had clung fast to the custom, which offered her three golden opportunities each week to get out of the house.

When the bell above the shop door had tinkled, announcing the arrival of another customer, she had turned out of habit, a movement that afforded her a more thorough look at the man she'd first noticed standing across the street. By his dress, she could guess he must be part of the small band of officers that had recently arrived in Tenchley. Village gossip said they'd been stationed temporarily on the coast while awaiting further orders.

Will Ford had called out a greeting from behind the counter, and the newcomer, Mr. Sutherland, had answered in a pleasant Scottish burr that had tickled strangely in her ear. He'd been speaking to Will, of course.

But he had been looking at her.

She could not remember ever seeing approval in anyone else's gaze. When examining her only daughter's appearance, Mama had been prone to purse her lips and shake her head. Papa had often frowned. Even Julia Holloway, her dearest friend, had been known to cluck with pity and call her plain.

Nothing in Jane's experience had ever encouraged her to be any kinder to herself than others were. When she peered into her glass, she saw just what everyone else did—or so she assumed: an unfashionably plump girl with heavy brown hair that refused to hold a curl. Her blue eyes, though a pretty-enough shade, were insufficiently striking to constitute a "redeeming feature."

But if Mr. Sutherland's expression had been anything to go by—the sparkle in his own eyes, the beginnings of a smile—he saw something others didn't.

Mortified by his notice, suspecting a trick, she'd promptly spun about and busied herself with a display of rather gaudy ribbons. Young men in red coats expected a great deal of attention and generally got it. She refused to answer his expectation.

If she had ever considered that their first meeting would not also be their last, she might have behaved less rudely.

Three days later, she'd found herself at tea at the Holloways, where she was allowed to visit unaccompanied, partly because their house was in sight of Papa's, but mostly because Sir Richard was the mayor of Tenchley and almost as protective of Jane as of his own daughter.

For that reason, she had certainly not expected to find three of the officers among the company. Sir Richard had made the introductions.

"Miss Quayle, may I present Lieutenant Sutherland?"

An awkward curtsy, made more so by her inability to drag her eyes from the twinkle of recognition in his.

An answering, easy bow. *"A pleasure to* meet *you, Miss Quayle."*

Afternoon had stretched into evening, tea into supper and cards. He'd hardly left her side. Eventually, she had made up her mind that if he was determined to be gallant, she could make an effort to be amusing. He'd listened attentively while she'd told tales about the village and its residents, not really intending them to be comic, though he'd laughed, and so had she. He'd said she had a gift for storytelling. More than once she'd caught Julia's eye across the room, sparkling with encouragement.

When Sir Richard had walked her home, and her father had frowned at the lateness of the hour, she'd once more expected that to be the end of it. But two days later, as she'd walked with Jonathan to the rectory and then seated herself on an iron bench outside to wait, Mr. Sutherland had appeared out of nowhere to join her.

Every other day, for several weeks, they'd passed the hours of Jonathan's lessons together. Beneath the mellow September sun, they'd strolled arm in arm over the rough ground of the churchyard—an ideal location to woo a budding gothic novelist, though she had not dared to speak to Mr. Sutherland of her writing, and she had tried not to think of his attentions as wooing. He'd told her of Scotland and of army life, and she'd been unexpectedly fascinated by both—fascinated by him and his inexplicable fascination with her. And at the end of those idyllic weeks, fascination having deepened almost imperceptibly into something more, she'd happily promised him a pair of dances at the village assembly.

As late as the afternoon of the assembly, she'd been afraid it would prove to be a promise she wouldn't be able to keep. It had threatened rain all day. Mama had been recovering from a head cold and refused to venture out. Papa had been delayed on business in a neighboring town and was not expected until after nightfall.

Sir Richard Holloway had once more saved the day. His special pleading on Julia's behalf had earned Mama's grudging permission that Jane might attend with them. She'd fussed over her appearance as much as she could without drawing her mother's or brother's unwanted speculation. She'd prayed for the rain to hold off and been astonished when her prayer was answered. She'd entered the assembly on Sir Richard's left arm—Julia had been on his right—and scanned the room with eager eyes.

When she'd seen no telltale flash of scarlet, her foolish, girlish heart had threatened to break.

Mr. Sutherland and the other officers had arrived very late. He'd found her in the wallflowers' corner, just as the company had been about to disperse to dine. Though the dancing was already over, she'd put her hand in his, expecting to be led into the crush of the supper room, stiff with disappointment. Instead, he'd taken her outside, into what passed for a garden, though an early frost had left it sere.

They'd walked for some time in silence before he'd worked up the—no, not *courage*; she had not believed even then that he lacked courage—the resolve, then, to tell her that the delay had been caused by some of the other officers receiving their new orders late that day. His own would surely arrive soon.

Even expecting it, the news had momentarily robbed her of breath. Their time together, though mostly stolen, had given color to her colorless days. No sooner had his words been spoken than the familiar grayness had begun to press on the corners of her vision.

Then he'd looked down at her, the mischievous sparkle in his eyes turned to toe-curling warmth.

"Miss Quayle, may I steal a kiss?"

She'd heard rumors about soldiers using their uncertain, dangerous futures to lure favors from young ladies, favors that couldn't be taken back. Even officers were not always gentlemen.

"It's a sin to steal, Mr. Sutherland," she'd told him, the mixture of longing and grief in her voice sounding more prim than anything. *"And I wouldn't want another's sins on my conscience."* Then her breath had caught in her throat, and she had to moisten her lips before she could continue. *"I'll grant you one instead."*

She'd waited, eyes closed, lips pursed, heart frozen in her chest, while his fingers came up beneath her chin and his mouth descended softly over hers. A hint of gentle pressure, a flicker of heat, and her first kiss—their goodbye kiss, she'd called it—was behind her.

He was, she felt certain, a man of the world. Of experience. Yet when he drew back and straightened his spine, she saw a touch of bewilderment in his face. And then he'd said, his voice a trifle unsteady, *"May I call on you at home tomorrow?"*

At home. Difficult not to infer that he meant to speak to Papa. Might tonight be not the end after all, but a beginning? Behind him, stars had twinkled in the sky. The clouds had moved off. Her heart, which had seemed to stop beating an age ago, had stuttered back to life. After a moment's hesitation, she'd nodded her consent.

Had he done it? She'd never known, because by dawn the next morning, she had—

Ruthlessly, she slammed shut the lid on her memories before anything else could escape.

Subsequent events ought to have driven Thomas from her mind. Instead, she could recall those golden weeks with him in perfect clarity, when she'd still been naïve, prone to believing in love at first sight, as told in tales of romance. But since the night of the assembly, she'd been forced to confront reality. Now she knew exactly how such fictions were made. She understood the source of their power, and she used it for her own ends.

Carefully, so as not to disturb the dogs, she burrowed deeper beneath the covers and closed her eyes. It had taken a great deal of effort to push the memory of those days, the memory of him, down into the locked box with the rest of her past, where it belonged. Thomas Sutherland might have elbowed his way into Dunnock Castle. But she didn't have to give him space in her head. Nor in her heart.

And certainly not in her bed.

* * * *

Despite the nuns' warnings, Allora was determined to discover the source of the glowing light. The convent walls, once her only security, had become a prison to her, and that light, a beacon of freedom. If only she could find a way to—

"Nose to the grindstone already this morning, Mrs. Higginbotham?"

Jane managed not to jump at the sound of Thomas's voice. Years of practice, including almost daily interruptions by Agnes, had trained her not to scurry to hide what she was working on. Such a reaction inevitably piqued curiosity.

The dogs, however, had never shown much aptitude for feigning calm. Athena, who had been sleeping quietly on the sofa, leaped up and stood with her paws on its rolled arm, barking furiously at the intruder. Aphrodite, disconcerted to find herself alone in the front of the hearth, flattened her body, laid back her ears, and began to growl.

Their reactions still seemed to amuse Thomas, more than alarm him. But at least he did not stray any farther into the room this time. With exaggerated care, Jane blotted her page, cleaned her pen, and corked the ink bottle, ignoring both the dogs' behavior and the unexpected guest.

"I've always been an early riser, Mr. Sutherland," she explained, finally. "I generally begin at dawn, work until mid-morning, then take the dogs out for some exercise."

At the mention of going out, Athena and Aphrodite momentarily forgot their distrust of Mr. Sutherland and bounded to her at the desk, tails wagging. "Sit," she ordered sternly. This time, only Athena listened.

When Jane glanced toward the doorway, Thomas was fighting a laugh. *Drat him.* It was only half-past nine, and now she was going to have to take the dogs down for a romp in the courtyard if she wanted any peace. "May I ask what you're doing here?"

He was leaning with one shoulder against the door frame, arms crossed over his chest. If he'd shaved this morning, then his razor needed a good stropping. And that loosely knotted cravat and tousled hair? *Disheveled*, her brain declared. *Disarming*, retorted some part of her that didn't ordinarily do much thinking.

"I'm going down to Balisaig." Whether or not he'd enjoyed a more restful night than she had, his eyes were bright and full of their customary mischief, more appealing than they had any right to be. "I came to fetch my coat and hat."

The village? What did he hope to discover there? "On the chair by the door," she said, with a dismissive wave of her hand. "Now, if you'll excuse me, I must get back to—"

Aphrodite jumped up, put her paws in Jane's lap, and gave a sharp bark of reprimand, as if to say, "You promised."

This time Thomas laughed outright.

She fixed him with a hard stare. This disruption to her routine was all his fault.

He straightened his posture but was otherwise uncowed by her stern expression. "Seems a pity that Ratliff makes you work while he plays."

"*Research* is not play."

"He's left a whole sheaf of pages for you to copy, I suppose?" His gaze settled on the desktop.

Instinctively, she began to gather her papers, breaking one of her own cardinal rules. "You needn't concern yourself with my—"

"Come with me."

"—work," she finished as he spoke across her. "What?" She'd assumed he would be eager for an opportunity to pry into things without her looking over his shoulder.

"Come with me. We can even take the dogs." Recognizing that they were under discussion, Athena stood up, and Aphrodite stopped pawing at Jane's knee long enough to look over her shoulder. "Perhaps if we wear them out," he suggested with a shrug and a grin, "they won't have as much energy for distrusting me."

Did he hope the long walk might have a similar effect on her?

Filled with morning light, the first sunshine in a week, the diamond-paned window gleamed like the gemstone after which it had been patterned. Last night's flurry of snow, dusted along its edges, had already begun to melt. The dazzlingly bright world beyond was as unlike the scene she'd been writing as could be imagined. With her index finger, she scooted another page onto the stack she'd made.

She had a book to write, and people who depended on her to be responsible. She was no longer a silly girl, to be taken in by the offer of a stroll on the arm of a handsome gentleman.

Unbidden came a far more recent memory: the feel of his corded forearm beneath her hand last night.

Her fingers curled into the unbending wooden arm of the chair instead. "I should be working."

His head tipped to the side as he studied her. "That's no' a 'nay,' lass."

For a moment, she refused to say more, refused to be charmed by that hint of a brogue, which he put on and left off at will. But he showed no sign of taking that broad hint and leaving her in peace.

She pushed herself to her feet. Aphrodite and Athena began to dance around her ankles. "All right, Mr. Sutherland. I'll fetch my pelisse and meet you in the courtyard in a quarter of an hour." All smiles, he bowed, retrieved his things, and turned toward the stairs.

Half an hour's cold walk into the village, the time spent there, and then the journey back again, longer because uphill. Dogs yapping incessantly all the while.

Ample time for the aggravation of his company to break her of this foolish fascination with him.

Chapter 7

Several inches of snow blanketed the inner courtyard, broken only by the path of the housemaid's footsteps leading to the gatehouse when she'd brought his breakfast and his own longer stride walking toward the castle. While waiting for Jane, Thomas stamped his feet to keep them warm and admired the play of sunlight through the sparkling clouds he raised. The winters of his childhood had never looked like this, for snow had fallen more rarely and melted more quickly in Glasgow. Perhaps it had been ungentlemanly of him to expect Jane to trudge through it. But as soon as he'd seen it, he'd wanted—needed—to share its magical brilliance with her.

And he could not quite face the prospect of visiting Balisaig alone.

True to her word, she came through the castle gate with a few minutes to spare, preceded by the dogs, who charged into the snow, snuffling and plowing with their noses buried and then snapping it up in their jaws. She laughed at the sight, the same merry sound he'd heard her make more than once so long ago, and he wondered with an unexpected stab—part jealousy, part pride—whether her husband had often managed to make her laugh like that.

Her heavy wool pelisse was black, in a style that might best be described as serviceable. But she'd paired it with a hood trimmed with silvery-gray fur that gleamed in the morning light and made her eyes more blue, and he did not think he would ever tire of looking at her, better than every dream his tired mind had conjured when he'd been a world away.

The dogs spotted him first and began their customary protest. She squinted a little as she focused her gaze on him, not quite a frown, and snapped her fingers at the dogs, a more than usually ineffective gesture because muted by her gloves. He could not help but laugh at her show of sternness. Why, he could almost taste the tartness on her tongue!

He found himself suddenly grateful for the chill in the air. Oh, but the thought of tasting her was a dangerous one indeed. Perhaps he'd been unwise to invite her to accompany him. Or selfish, at least.

"Whisht, lassies," he crooned, his voice pitched low beneath their shrill yapping, and held out his hands, palms up, for their inspection. They paused momentarily in their furor. One—Athena? Yes, Aphrodite had the more spotted coat—cautiously sniffed the air in his direction; both gave him a wide berth as they scooted past and out the castle gate. He'd count it progress.

If only he could soothe Jane's ruffled fur as easily.

He held out an arm for her, but she thrust her hands into her muff. "I don't think they like you, Mr. Sutherland."

"Mrs. Murdoch told me they haven't much liking for men at all," he replied lightly, falling into step beside her as they passed beneath the portcullis and into the breathtaking world of snow-dusted trees and snow-capped crags. He had known the beauty of the Highlands only in summer and had just completed a grueling journey over rutted, mud-slick roads, so the transformation was as extraordinary as it was unexpected. "But I shan't give up hope just yet."

"I—I had them of a...gentleman who treated them ill," she explained, her slight hesitation over the word *gentleman* suggesting she did not find the man's behavior worthy of the designation.

But he latched onto quite another part of the sentence. "*You* had them? I understood them to be Mr. Ratliff's dogs."

"No." He could not see her face around the hood's fur trim, but he could hear the tight-lipped grimace in her voice. As if she had said too much before and did not intend to make the same mistake again.

There was definitely something strange about the situation, something he couldn't quite put his finger on, something she didn't want to reveal. "If they don't get on any better with him, I'm surprised he tolerates it."

"You seem to have formed an unfavorable opinion of Mr. Ratliff. Wrongly, I might add."

"For your sake, I'm delighted to hear it." He did not want to think ill of Jane's employer. But he wasn't exactly eager to imagine that Ratliff got on with the dogs either, particularly not if it was because he enjoyed a too-intimate relationship with their mistress. And when he recalled those extravagant embroidered cushions by the hearth, and realized they might have been a gift from him, as much to please her as to please her dogs, well...

"How long have you worked for him?" he asked when he could trust his voice not to betray his suspicions.

"More than six years."

It wasn't complicated arithmetic, by any means. Still, he ran the numbers through twice, coming to the same realization each time: Within a twelvemonth after he'd left England, she'd been both wed and widowed. Then, evidently denied the support of either her family or her late husband's, she'd been driven to support herself by taking employment with a man who might or might not be a perfect scoundrel, the man who'd brought her here and all but abandoned her.

They walked in silence for nearly a quarter of a mile, and still he could give no name to the sharp-edged emotion cutting through him. He'd been holding onto the memory of her, of her kiss, proof of sweetness in a stale, sour world. The promise of connection for a man who had sometimes feared he'd lost hold of everything that mattered, including himself.

On the night of the dance, he'd wondered at the foolishness of the local lads, letting her languish among the wallflowers. But it had needed only one of them to come to his senses. Of course, she'd married, just as Thomas had told himself she would.

Once, though, he'd brashly thought to be the one to win her hand. If he'd demanded an explanation of her father, defied Scott's order, delayed his departure by even a day, would something, anything have been different? For either of them?

Yes. You'd have lost your commission and probably been lashed to within an inch of your life, good sense reminded him. *And she would have had nothing more to do with you.*

The self-deprecating sound that burst from him had little enough of humor about it, but he tried to pass it off as a laugh at the dogs' antics. They'd charged ahead, snuffing at every rock and tuft of grass transformed into a fantastical creature by the snowfall. Heaven help him if they managed to scare up a hare. They'd be gone in a flash, and he'd have to track them until he found them, or he'd be out of Jane's good graces forever—if he weren't already.

"See, I told you the walk would do them good."

"I never doubted the benefit of the exercise, Mr. Sutherland." Her words hung on the air in an icy cloud. "Only the timing."

"And the company?" he prompted devilishly.

She paused and looked up into his face. "Honestly, I do not know." Her cheeks and the tip of her nose were rosy with cold. "You must have had some reason for wishing me to walk with you."

"Of course."

Her eyes flashed, as if she'd caught him in some mischief.

"I ken you're remembering what happened the last time I had you out for a stroll?"

"Certainly not." The pink in her cheeks deepened.

"Nay?" In the intervening years, he ought to have been too focused on his survival to have spent much time swooning over a girl he'd known for only a few weeks. But he'd held onto those moments like a nun clutched her rosary, lingering over each detail, seeking...something. Solace in the past. An escape from the present. A promise of hope for the future. "I think of it often."

Her breath caught on a startled gasp that parted her lips most invitingly. That sharp intake of breath, combined with another blush, revealed that those stolen moments had meant something to her too. Even if she'd been telling herself they shouldn't have.

Slowly, he dipped his head, searching her eyes. "I was beginning to fear you'd forgotten."

Their first kiss had been swift and secretive, hidden from the prying eyes of the village by the darkness of an autumn night. Now, they stood in the open beneath the wintry sun. The bright, cold air surrounded them like a second embrace and drove them closer together, seeking one another's heat.

He put his arms around her, one hand against the middle of her back, the other cupping the back of her head. Beneath her hood, he could feel the heavy twists of her hair against his palm. She withdrew one kid-gloved hand from her muff and laid it flat against his chest, over his heart, neither drawing him closer nor pushing him away.

Just before his lips met hers, a low growl rumbled in the stillness. Together, they glanced downward, to the source of the sound. Athena had the fabric of Jane's skirts between her teeth and had sat down to give herself more leverage as she tried ineffectually to drag her mistress away from him. Aphrodite danced around them, unsure how best to assist in dividing them.

Jane laughed nervously. "See, I told you they were excellent protection."

When he lifted his head, he scanned their surroundings out of habit. He saw nothing, partly because all around them was a glaring sea of whiteness. And partly because his mind was still full of Jane, the scent of her, the feel of her, the remembered taste of her...

"Protection from whom?"

Cold air swept between them, as she eased herself from the circle of his arms. Satisfied, the dogs once more charged ahead. "From ourselves, perhaps?" she suggested with another weak laugh. She tugged at her pelisse to straighten it, then tucked her hands back into her muff. "I have *not* forgotten that night, Mr. Sutherland. But I do not believe it would be wise for us to resume our acquaintance right where we left off. For one thing, I feel certain kisses would distract you from your investigation into that letter."

"Oh?" He was beside her in two strides. "Do you have a great deal of experience in such matters?"

She glanced at him through narrowed eyes. "Do you?"

"Do I have experience in doing my duty, in spite of distraction?" He made no effort to hide the frustration he felt. "May I remind you, ma'am, that I am a soldier?"

Her chin jerked up a fraction of an inch. "You may rest assured I had not forgotten that, either."

They walked the remaining quarter of a mile in silence. At last, the wee village of Balisaig spread out below them, a point of visual interest in an otherwise-unbroken landscape of white. A few shops and houses dotted either side of a surprisingly wide central road that followed the line of the valley, connecting it with the world beyond the Highlands. In the distance rose the spire of the kirk, and farther beyond black smoke billowed from the blacksmith's forge.

Very little had changed from his memory of the place, and he could not quite decide whether that was a good sign or a bad one.

He dragged his feet through the final snowy steps, stopping at the village edge.

"Just what *are* you hoping to discover in Balisaig?" she asked, seeming to read something in his hesitation.

Surely a more complicated question than she had intended. Earlier, he had wondered why she had not returned to her late husband's family, or to her own. But hard on the heels of that question had come the memory of her father denying her very existence...

No, it was not always possible—and almost never easy—to go home.

"I suppose Robin Ratliff chose such a remote spot in hopes of finding peace and quiet," he said, an oblique sort of answer to her question.

"Creative types generally prefer freedom from distraction, yes."

"Freedom from distraction is a luxury most will never know," he tossed back. "With so little else to divert the people here, there must be a great deal of curiosity about him. People wanting to know what happened to such and so a character, or when his next book might be making an appearance, that sort of thing."

She withdrew a hand from her muff to wave the question away, like a bit of annoying fluff. "Hardly enough to drive away Mr. Ratliff's muse."

"Perhaps not. But something managed to drive *him* away, it seems."

The hems of her skirts churned up a swirl of snow as she turned sharply toward him. A shadow flickered across her gaze and was gone. Easy to miss, if one were not accustomed to being vigilant, to watching for shadows on a darkening sea.

"If it's village gossip you're hoping to hear, then I suggest you start at the Thistle and Crown." She paused in front of the stone pub, with its faded shingle swinging above the street. He wondered whether she had spent long enough in the Highlands to know that the crown in question had naught to do with any of the Georges. "That's also where all the mail for Balisaig, including Dunnock Castle, is delivered."

Laying his hand on the latch of the door, he motioned for her to precede him inside.

"Oh, no," she demurred. "The post came yesterday, remember. I've another errand to run today. Then I must return to my work."

He paused. "I hope you do not mean to suggest that you will go back to Dunnock alone?"

A shriek drew their attention to the village square, where a ragtag group of boys and girls were engaged in a fierce snowball fight. Their laughter and boasts rang in the cold air. Athena and Aphrodite had inserted themselves into the fray, he saw, and were nipping at heels and tugging at sleeves and mufflers indiscriminately, happy to prolong the game by interfering with victory on either side, which the children appeared to encourage.

"I'll have the dogs with me," she said.

Dissatisfied, he shook his head. "If Mr. Ratliff had believed the dogs were sufficient protection for you, Mrs. Higginbotham, he wouldn't have hired me. Meet me here in half an hour's time," he said as he pushed open the door and prepared to step through it. "We will all walk home together."

Chapter 8

As soon as the door had shut behind him, Jane let out a breath—part exasperation, part relief. It carried with it the words she knew better than to say. Though she felt certain his protectiveness was overdone, a squabble on the streets of Balisaig would serve neither of them well.

Whether part of that deep exhalation was a sigh of disappointment—of longing—she refused to examine.

She strode across the street and into the apothecary's shop. In the winter, when travel was difficult and the peddler's cart did not visit, the apothecary stocked a miscellany of goods in addition to his medicines. Though she did not intend to buy anything today, she let her fingers trail through a selection of brightly colored ribbons in passing. The fluttering silk called to mind that morning in Will Ford's shop, and she jerked her hand away again.

"More paper already, Mrs. Higginbotham?" called Mr. Abernathy from behind a counter, where he was grinding something to a fine powder with a mortar and pestle. He was a short, stocky man of forty or so, with a ready smile and a reassuring manner.

"Oh, no, thank you," she said, looking around for Mrs. Abernathy but seeing no sign of her. "I'm just warming myself after the walk down."

"If you were lookin' for my wife, she's just stepped down to the manse with something for Mr. Donaldson," he explained, rightly guessing the true purpose of her visit.

Mr. Bartholomew Donaldson had been in Balisaig for less than a month. Objecting strenuously to the notion that even the clergyman was expected to enter the Thistle and Crown to collect his own post, he had begged Mrs. Abernathy the favor of gathering his for him. Rather than express annoyance at his sanctimony, the apothecary's wife seemed to relish the opportunity to help—or at least the opportunity to be among the first to discover the young clergyman's business.

"Oh, of course. Have you heard we've a visitor at Dunnock?" she asked a moment later, trying to assess whether gossip about Thomas had already begun to spread. It would be perfectly useless to try to hide his arrival.

"Oh, aye?" Predictably, his voice held no shock at the news. "Well, if you need anythin', or he does..." He smiled, but Jane could see the glint of curiosity in his eyes before he restored his spectacles to their proper place and returned to his work.

She was examining a pair of surprisingly pretty clocked stockings, comparing them in her mind's eye to the black woolen ones she usually wore, when a gust of cold air swept across the floor, announcing the opening of the door and the arrival of another customer. Quickly, she laid the stockings back into their flat, narrow box and pushed it away from the edge of the counter, so that it was not readily apparent what had caught her eye.

But the woman who had entered the shop was not a customer. "Thinkin' of some new stockings, Mrs. Higginbotham?" Very little escaped the notice of Mrs. Abernathy. She peered over Jane's shoulder, then pulled the package closer, the very devil offering the apple to Eve. "Och, they're lovely, aren't they? I'd be that pleased to see you treat yourself."

A little flush of embarrassment swept up Jane's throat, as if she'd been caught doing something far more scandalous than looking at a new pair of stockings. Jane certainly did not *need* them. No one ever saw her stockings—well, except for Esme, when she did the laundry—and that was unlikely to change. She slid the package away from her again.

Mrs. Abernathy shook her head, and red-blond ringlets bounced beneath her the brim of her fashionable bonnet. "Ye canna wear the widow's weeds forever, my dear."

Jane shook her head. If Mrs. Abernathy only knew...

Untying the ribbons of her bonnet as she went, the apothecary's wife slipped behind the counter and favored her husband with an airy kiss of greeting. "Och, the air is fine and fresh this morning. You were smart to come down again, Mrs. Higginbotham."

It was her way of asking why Jane had made the trip into Balisaig two days in a row. After all, the air was always fine and fresh in the Highlands.

Fresh enough even to strengthen a Scotsman's brogue.

Jane screwed her eyes shut, weighing whether to ask for a headache paper. After this morning's aggravations, she felt certain she'd need one soon enough. When she opened her eyes again, she found both Mr. and Mrs. Abernathy watching her. Jane's gaze wandered guiltily back to the stockings. Clearly, she ought to have concocted some plausible excuse for visiting. Her stock of paper was more than adequate, but perhaps she could justify a bottle of ink...

"I suspect it's got summat to do with the stranger," Mr. Abernathy ventured, in a voice that he might have intended for his wife's ears only, but which carried easily through the shop. "Invite her in for a cup o' tea, won't ye?"

She fixed Jane with an assessing look. "Will ye come up, Mrs. Higginbotham?"

"I really shouldn't. The dogs—"

Mrs. Abernathy waved away that feeble excuse. "Mary MacIntyre is pullin' them about in her da's handcart, last I saw. One o' the dear things was wearin' a baby's bonnet."

"That would be Aphrodite," Jane said. Both dogs readily tolerated the girl's exuberant affection, but Athena's tolerance had limits.

So, with a nod, Jane followed Mrs. Abernathy up the narrow staircase at the back of the shop to the suite of rooms above, which had been perfectly adequate living quarters for Mr. Abernathy, the bachelor. But last winter, on a visit to Glasgow, the apothecary had met and married Mrs. Abernathy, and she had proceeded to cram the apartment with fine furniture and feminine touches. If the couple were ever blessed with children, they would have to be stacked like cordwood along one side of the sitting room, between Mrs. Abernathy's tambour and her harp.

It was nonetheless a pleasant spot, which Jane had discovered she enjoyed visiting occasionally. Though she cherished her independence, sometimes the cavernous, empty rooms of Dunnock were too much to bear.

While Mrs. Abernathy laid aside her bonnet and drew off her gloves, Jane began to follow suit, then paused, wondering at the state of her hair beneath her hood, remembering the touch of Thomas's hand against those heavy coils. Uneasily, she reached beneath to check that the pins were still in place.

"There's a glass above the table at the top of the stairs," Mrs. Abernathy reminded her with a speculative look.

"And have you think me vain?" Jane brushed off the suggestion with a laugh and flipped the fur-trimmed hood away from her face. Three or four hairpins clattered onto the floor, and a lock of hair slipped down over her shoulder. Silently, Mrs. Abernathy bent and picked up the pins, then held them out to Jane, who scrambled to tuck the sign of her almost-indiscretion out of sight.

Not, of course, that anyone in Balisaig had any reason to suspect that Jane's cheeks were flushed and her hair was mussed because Thomas Sutherland had very nearly kissed her.

Perhaps she ought to have let him. As a purgative, of course. To be rid of unwanted memories and to prove herself master of the situation.

But she couldn't deny she was curious. That kiss so long ago had been brief, chaste—the kiss of a young man, though eager, determined to act the gentleman. Still it had fueled her imagination and left her wanting more. Time had changed both of them. It was impossible not to wonder what his kiss would be like now.

Her fingers trembled as she tucked the last pin into place, arranging her hair into a more than usually severe knot. She winced as she grazed her scalp with its sharp points.

Better not to tempt fate. One kiss might lead to another...and another...

Afterward, she sat down hard in her customary chair before the window, at the little piecrust table the Abernathys used for breakfast and tea. Her clumsy movements rattled the china. Mrs. Abernathy, who surely must be observing Jane's odd behavior with interest, merely seated herself opposite and rang the bell for the maid.

"Coffee, please," she said when the maid entered, then tipped her head and studied her guest with a quirk of concern across her brow. "On second thought, it looks to me as if Mrs. Higginbotham could use a cup of tea."

A short time later, when the tea steamed from two delicate cups and the maid had retreated to her work in the other rooms, washing the breakfast dishes or airing the beds, Mrs. Abernathy held out the sugar bowl and declared, seemingly out of nowhere, "Company is well enough, but houseguests can be such a bother."

Jane dragged her attention back to the present moment. "Yes," she agreed, dropping two lumps of sugar into her cup. "Particularly uninvited ones."

"Particularly *handsome* ones." Mrs. Abernathy smiled around the edge of her cup as she sipped her tea. "Or so I've heard."

Jane gave the contents of her cup an unnecessarily vigorous stir. "Have you? Well, handsome is as handsome does, they say. In any case, I cannot think Mr. Sutherland will stay long. He has business with Mr. Ratliff but did not find him at home. My employer has gone to Edinburgh, and I do not expect him to return anytime soon."

"Ah, well. He's given Balisaig somethin' to see, at any rate." Mrs. Abernathy returned her cup to its saucer. "January always welcomes a distraction, I find. This winter has been particularly dreary."

More talk of distractions. Thomas had been right, of course. No one was ever entirely free of them, though in coming to the Highlands, Jane had made every effort to minimize them. But what if Mrs. Abernathy was also right? Maybe Jane did crave a distraction. Maybe that was why she'd almost let herself kiss Thomas. It had nothing to do with *him*, per se, or with their past, or with what they might be to one another if either of them could trust enough to tell the truth.

Fortunately, she had a great deal of experience in working through distractions. And this one wouldn't last long. He would learn little of interest at the pub. He would grow bored waiting for Robin Ratliff to return. Things would surely return to their normal course soon enough.

A normal course that did not include suggestive banter or ill-advised touches or almost-kisses on the path into Balisaig.

"Speaking of distractions…" Mrs. Abernathy's voice recalled her attention to the table, as she refilled Jane's cup from a teapot painted with pink cabbage roses. "Let's talk of something else. It seems our Mr. Donaldson ordered a new book of sermons. They arrived on the late coach yesterday."

"I hope they're more inspiring than whatever model he's been using."

Mrs. Abernathy pretended to be shocked at Jane's wickedness. But Jane could tell by the twinkle in the other woman's eye that she had had similar thoughts—and also that the book of sermons was not the most interesting information she had to share.

"He had a letter too."

"Oh?"

"From Edinburgh. Some friend—a fellow clergyman, I presume—has heard that a gentleman arrived from abroad earlier this month to claim the title of Lord Magnus. Mr. Donaldson speculated, and I'm inclined to agree, that if he's traveled as far as that, it will not be long before he pays Balisaig and Dunnock Castle a visit."

Jane shaped her lips into another *oh*, but in the end she could not muster even that monosyllable.

The solicitor's letter had made the new earl's interference sound like a remote possibility. How could he have been so wrong? Shouldn't he have known at least as much as Mr. Donaldson's friend?

Then again, she realized belatedly, the solicitor's letter might not have been up to date in its information. It could have been posted quite some time ago, then left to sit on Mr. Canfield's desk for weeks while that man was enjoying the society of Bath. Even now, another might be on its way, announcing Lord Magnus's imminent arrival. Why, she probably had last night's snowfall to thank for the fact that the earl wasn't even now on her—or rather, *his*—doorstep.

She lifted her gaze from the table to the window, scanning the sky for the slate-colored clouds that would be welcome harbingers of more snow. But the sky was clear, a brilliant cerulean blue, and already the snow that had gathered in the corners of the window ledge had begun to melt.

The truth was, it would be good for the people of Balisaig and the surrounding farms to have the attention of their landlord after all this time. It was only she who had cause to dread his arrival.

"Are you all right, Mrs. Higginbotham?" Mrs. Abernathy seemed to understand that his arrival would not necessarily be a cause of celebration for everyone.

Jane started at her friend's touch on the back of her hand. "Of course. Just surprised."

"Mr. Ratliff is in Edinburgh, you said? Then he must know, I suppose. I wonder at him not sending you word."

"I—" Jane had to pause for a fortifying gulp of tea before the words would come. "When he's involved with his work, he often loses track of more mundane matters."

One delicate golden-brown eyebrow arched in disbelief. *"Mundane matters?* But if the earl comes and decides to stay, you'll all be turned out of Dunnock."

Oh, God.

Behind her, the mantel clock gave a tinkling chime, reminding her of the passage of time. If she didn't collect the dogs and leave Balisaig soon, she'd be forced to walk once more with Thomas. And she needed to be alone, to think, to prepare. Her lease on Dunnock expired within a matter of days, and she was not fool enough to imagine that the new earl's timing was a coincidence.

To think, she had almost let that other letter rattle her. This was the real threat. She was going to have to start over.

Again.

"I have to go." She rose abruptly and would have sat down again just as quickly, but she refused to give in to another episode of this uncharacteristic wobbliness in her knees. She had never been missish, even when she was a miss.

The sudden movement nearly upset the tea table. But Mrs. Abernathy, evidently prepared for such a possibility, laid one hand on its fluted edge to steady it, then rose and gripped Jane's hands in hers. "Oh, my dear Mrs. Higginbotham. Dinna fash yourself. Mr. Ratliff surely has matters well in hand."

A burble of hysterical laughter rose in Jane's chest, but she managed to check it. "Oh, yes. He's very clever."

Together, they gathered Jane's things, and Mrs. Abernathy preceded her down the stairs. When they passed Mr. Abernathy's work table, he glanced up to wish her a good morning. Though he, unlike his wife, was not noted for his perceptiveness, Jane could see worry flicker into his eyes as he peered over the tops of his spectacles.

"Good morning to you, Mr. Abernathy," she said in her calmest, most reassuring voice. It would be all through the village by midday if she gave in to tears.

They were prickling behind her eyes, though, and stinging in her throat, and the pressure grew worse when Mrs. Abernathy picked up the package of stockings and wordlessly pressed them into Jane's hands.

"I haven't got my reticule," Jane protested. "I cannot pay for them."

"A gift," Mrs. Abernathy said. Everything about her demeanor declared the stockings an effort to atone for her having been the bearer of upsetting news.

Jane nodded and tucked the thin package into her muff. If she was going to have to refashion her life, she could do so in a pair of new stockings, at least. "Thank you, my friend. Truly."

On the street, she was nearly run down by a laughing Mary MacIntyre, who was looking over her shoulder at the contents of the handcart she was pulling, rather than where she was going. Inside sat the two dogs side by side, fur wet and paws muddy, tongues lolling in exhausted enjoyment. The baby bonnet had disappeared. Jane hoped it had not been ingested.

"I'm afraid I have to be heading home now, Mary," she said, laying a hand on the girl's head to slow her progress. "So I'll be taking Athena and Aphrodite."

"Aww, not yet, Mrs. Higginbotham." Mary looked up, her pleading brown eyes framed by a tangle of red-brown hair. "I'll bring them home later, I promise."

For just a moment, Jane considered relenting. The dogs were worn out, and she could not face the thought of having to carry them up the hill. Then Aphrodite, ready to be free, stood on her hind legs, nearly upsetting the delicate balance of the little two-wheeled cart. Jane lifted her out and smiled consolingly at Mary. "I think it's for the best if they come with me."

Besides, the longer she delayed, the more likely she would have unwelcome companionship. Her eyes darted to the pub, whose door thankfully—though curiously—remained closed. It ought not to have taken so long to ask about the mail. Perhaps Thomas had found old friends inside. He had said, after all, that Balisaig was his home.

A sudden chill swept through her that had nothing to do with the ankle-deep snow.

Home.

He'd said that *Dunnock* was his home, hadn't he?

Other snippets of conversation came rushing back to her, fitting together more neatly than she wanted to admit. Thomas's obvious lie about what had brought him to Balisaig. Mrs. Abernathy's revelation that the title had been claimed by someone who'd come from abroad. Mr. Donaldson's speculation that it was only a matter of time until the earl showed up in the village.

Jane did not realize her gaze had narrowed until she felt a cold, wet nose nudge at her exposed wrist. When she glanced down, she had to relax her hard-eyed squint to focus on Aphrodite, dangling from Mary's thin arms. "Are ye all right, ma'am?" the girl asked, worriedly.

"Perhaps Mr. Donaldson isn't always wrong."

Her answer did nothing to allay Mary's visible concern. "How's that?"

But Jane only gathered the dogs and began to walk away, one thought pounding through her head like a feverish pulse.

Lord Magnus is already here.

Chapter 9

Just inside the doorway to the Thistle and Crown, Thomas paused for a few moments to let his eyes adjust. The glare of sun against snow made the pub comparatively dim, though its stone walls were whitewashed and the large window facing the street was clean.

He was still blinking away spots when a voice said, "I dinna believe it."

Eventually, Thomas was able to pick out a man standing behind the bar, his hip propped on a tall stool, his fair hair overlong. He must have been the one who had spoken, as the pub was otherwise empty.

"If it's no' Tommy Sutherland, back from the dead."

Recognition—of that teasing voice, that ready grin—began to dawn, and Thomas responded in kind. "From England, don't you mean?"

"Hell. England." The man shrugged good-naturedly. "What's the difference?"

Thomas strode toward the bar, hand outstretched. "Eleazor Ross, is it really you?"

"An' who else would it be, I'd like to know?" The other man, unsatisfied with the offer of a mere handshake, bounced to his feet, laid aside whatever he had been looking at and crossed the well-scrubbed wooden floor to give his old friend a back-slapping hug. His kilt swung with the energy of his step. "But I'll thank ye to remember it's still just Ross."

The matter of names had been the subject of jokes among them when they'd been lads. Even then, Ross had been determined to leave behind the scourge of Eleazor, insisting on being addressed only by his surname. Now, he had grown into the sort of powerfully built man whom very few people would be brave, or foolish, enough to tease about the matter.

When they broke apart, Thomas said, "What of your family—are they well?"

"Och, well enough. Da's worn out with the work, but sometimes he comes down in the evening," Ross explained, jerking his chin upward to indicate the family apartments above. "My sisters are all married and gone, but for Davina." The youngest sibling, whom Mrs. Ross had died bringing into the world, had been a towheaded girl when Thomas had last visited Balisaig. "An' what of you?" Ross tilted his head to inspect him. "Ye didna get so brown in England, I ken."

"I joined the army. They sent me abroad."

"O' course they did. None better than a Scotsman when there's a job to be done." Ross nodded knowingly as he returned to his stool. "What brings you home now?"

Home. There it was again, that insistence that he belonged to Balisaig, rather than the less-pleasant reality that it, in fact, belonged to him.

Thomas opened his mouth to explain the lost years. His father's refusal to allow him to return in the winter following his mother's death, when word had come that his grandmother was ill. The bitter knowledge that Gran had had no member of her family to walk with her on that last journey to the kirk. The unexpected commission. The maddening heat of Dominica. General Scott's final, unsettling order.

But the words *I'm Magnus*—perhaps the only true answer to Ross's question—wouldn't come. At least, not yet. When they were finally, inevitably, uttered, they seemed certain to drive a wedge between Thomas and the friends of his youth.

He glanced around the empty pub. Though the mugs had been washed and the tables wiped, the scattered chairs still spoke of last night's conviviality. A larger group had clustered by the fire to discuss something of interest or importance. In the corner, two figures had tucked themselves away from the crowd to huddle over a battered chess set. The misshapen stub of a tallow candle, employed to replace a missing pawn, still decorated the board.

He knew it would be more fitting to describe the kirk as the soul of the village, but it was here folks gathered, day after day, night after night. Here they shared the news, their sadness and their celebrations. Here where they fought and argued, yes, and here where they knitted themselves together again.

This community had welcomed him once. Would it do so again?

In the end he said only, "Got a job to do up at the castle," and reached for the book Ross had been reading when he arrived, hoping for some distraction.

What he found was indeed distracting, though not at all what he'd sought. The compact duodecimo volume, cheaply bound, contained the first part of a novel. Specifically, *The Necromancer's Bride* by Robin Ratliff. The very last name he'd wanted to see.

"Ah, that would be Elspeth's," Ross said, snatching the book from his grasp. He laid it behind the bar, out of reach, but not before tucking something between two pages to mark his place. "You remember Elspeth Shaw? She's the barmaid here now. Her sister Esme's at Dunnock."

Thomas nodded, remembering the maid who'd brought his breakfast. He would have had only the vaguest recollection of the Shaws if not for the thick file General Scott had handed him, which had been supplemented by the estate records he'd collected from Mr. Watson. When the long journey, first from London and then from Edinburgh, had grown too tedious for him to bear, Thomas had finally given in and read through those papers, which had revealed at once too much and too little. He knew, for instance, that Mr. Shaw was Dunnock's most prosperous tenant farmer. But he did not know what it might signify about the state of their affairs that the man's daughters had put themselves into service.

"She certainly has interesting taste in reading."

"That Ratliff chap spins a good tale," Ross defended her—and, evidently, himself.

"So I've heard. Tell me," he said, leaning against the bar, "is there anyone else still here I'd remember? What about Theo?" Theo Campbell had been the third in their mischievous trio, all those years ago.

"He's the blacksmith, now. Comes in for his pint and his pie, most nights, when he's not payin' court to this lassie or that." Ross paused to pull two foaming mugs of ale and set one in front of Thomas. "Where are ye sleepin'?"

"Dunnock's gatehouse."

Ross made an expression, somewhere between surprised and impressed. "So, you'll have seen Mrs. Higginbotham, then."

"Mrs. Higginbotham? Aye. I've seen her. Spoken with her."

Nearly kissed her.

He could not quite decide what unsettled him most about that phrase, the *kissed* or the *nearly*. He'd been desperate to discover whether her lips tasted as sweet as he remembered. But was she right? Was it unwise to try to pick up where they'd left off?

He'd held onto their first kiss for so long, it had become a perfect, delicate crystallization of the past. A second kiss might melt that precious memory like a snowflake.

Or would those memories, those feelings, those kisses form a powerful, dangerous avalanche that would sweep them both off their feet?

Thomas shook his head to drive off such thoughts, blinking again like a snow-blind man. "Why?" he demanded, when he once more focused on his friend's amused expression. "Haven't *you* seen her?"

"Oh, aye. Comes in regular to fetch the post, she does. Stops in for a chat with Mrs. Abernathy across the way more often than not. Usually makes it down to the kirk on Sundays. She's got a capital pair of spaniel pups."

Even her dogs were well liked in Balisaig, it seemed. "Don't the people hereabouts find her rather...reserved?"

Ross lifted one shoulder. "Well, folks make allowances for a Sassenach, ye ken?"

"Sassenach," he echoed. *Outlander.* The word held a world of meaning. Accurate, certainly, in Jane's case. But might it not also apply to...?

Ross chuckled at something in Thomas's expression. "P'raps we ought to do the same for you."

Thomas forced himself to laugh with him. Yet he *was* afraid. It was impossible not to wonder, again, whether their friendship could survive the revelation that Thomas was now an earl.

He drank deeply from his mug before he could answer with his customary easiness. "Nay, Ross. Balisaig's known me too long for that."

The other man gave a self-satisfied nod, evidently willing to wave away the years that might have come between them. "Aye, that we have. So, what's this job of yourn?"

"Well, now..." Thomas wiped the foam from his lip with the back of his hand and lowered his voice, despite the empty pub. Old habits died hard, and people were usually more ready to help an investigation if they believed they'd been taken into another's confidence. "What do you know of Dunnock's tenant?"

Ross's answer was familiar. "Nowt but that he writes books," he said, tapping the cover of the volume he'd put under the bar. "Never seen 'im."

Thomas tried to read the other man's expression. Interest? Distrust? Surely the people of Balisaig wondered about the mysterious Mr. Ratliff? Unless their own distress made idle curiosity a luxury they could not afford.

"He doesn't visit the village, then? Never darkens the door of the kirk?"

"Some folks claim he's ill," Ross explained. "Though I canna say I ever heard tell of the apothecary being called. Esme told Elspeth he spends more 'n half 'is time abroad."

Thomas made a noise he hoped would pass for surprise.

"I dinna see that it matters much," said Ross, after taking another deep drink. "It's not like we've ever clapped eyes on Lord Magnus, either. Folks get on, whether or no' there's some great man at Dunnock."

With sudden energy, Thomas thumped down his own mug and strode toward the window. Most of its panes were filled with rondels of glass, through which little could be seen but colors and the hints of shapes. Nevertheless, he attempted once more to take stock of the street and its handful of passersby. "Do they? Get on, I mean."

When Ross made no answer, Thomas turned to find himself an object of scrutiny, far more intense than any the man had spared for either Ratliff or Jane. "Aye," he said at last. "Just like we always have. Maybe ye've forgotten."

Had he forgotten? Or had memory exaggerated the struggles and sacrifices of this rural village? Had he given too much weight to his gran's complaints about the earl's indifference?

A fortnight past, he might have latched onto Ross's words with eagerness, seeing them as his ticket to return to General Scott, report that all was well, and request his new assignment.

Two things now gave him pause.

First, tucked among the stacks of papers, leases, and accounts, he'd found pamphlets of advice about land management. As he'd learned as he rode along, landlords throughout the Highlands were clearing more land for grazing. Displaced tenants had been reduced from farmers to crofters. All was done in the name of improvement, but Thomas could easily see that the change did little to improve the tenants' lives.

Mr. Watson's endorsement of the plan would have been enough to fuel Thomas's doubts about the idea, if not for the concern that Dunnock must remain profitable or all would suffer. He thought of the Shaws. Ross was right—the people here were tough, survivors through many a struggle. Modern agricultural practices could not be ignored, however. If they did not keep up with the times, the people of Balisaig were doomed to be left behind. Change, in other words, was inevitable. But it would go more smoothly with a steady hand to guide it.

And that steady hand ought by rights to belong to the Earl of Magnus. To him.

Damn and blast.

His second point of hesitation was Jane. It had been far easier to imagine leaving Dunnock behind when it had not also involved leaving her. And the notion that he might be leaving her in danger only made matters worse.

How long, though, could he stay at Dunnock without revealing the real reason he'd come?

In three days, Ratliff's lease expired. Thomas could renew it, of course. He'd brought the necessary paperwork from Edinburgh. A few strokes of the pen and he would be assured of a profitable tenant for at least another year. He could return to London, resume his military duties, and manage Dunnock from afar, as his predecessor had done.

But if, as he was beginning to fear, circumstances demanded that he stay in Balisaig and take up his responsibilities here, then naturally he'd take up residence at Dunnock, sending the writer—and his lovely amanuensis—packing.

His gaze drifted back to the window. He needed to think like a laird. Or an intelligence officer. Not a lover. Because he hadn't set out on this journey to woo a lass and settle down with her, despite General Scott's broad hint. And in any case, the lass he'd found was not terribly interested in being wooed.

At least, not if the current set of her shoulders was any indication.

For despite the mottled glass, he had little doubt that hers was the figure striding across the street toward the pub, her skirts swaying with barely contained energy, the dogs dancing at her heels.

The sight surprised him. He'd fully expected to discover that she'd set out for Dunnock without him, merely to prove she could. But she hadn't, and perhaps that was a positive development?

He bent low enough to peer through one of the occasional clear panes of glass from which the window had been fashioned.

The stern set of Jane's jaw and her flashing eyes came into sharp focus. Definitely not a good sign.

God, he wished he could believe he was not the object of that fierce look and even fiercer posture. But he could figure the odds quick enough, given her obvious destination. And he was about to find out precisely what had driven her in his direction when the door to the pub would swing open in a half-dozen strides. Five...four...

"How many letters does Robin Ratliff get in a week? Or a month?" he asked, turning swiftly toward Ross.

Ross looked bewildered at the question. "I couldn't say. Everything that comes for Dunnock is addressed to Mrs. Higginbotham. She told Elspeth that Mr. Ratliff's publisher sometimes forwards things from London for him, under cover to her."

Just as the threat had been. Thomas nodded. Even if only a clerk in London and the handful of people in Balisaig knew where to find the famous author, it would not be difficult for the one who'd written the letter to discover it. Years as a secret agent had taught Thomas that someone determined to do harm would find a way to get the necessary information.

If the letter writer succeeded in tracking Robin Ratliff to Balisaig, he'd be frustrated to discover that the author was away. Jane herself could easily become the target of his violence.

"If you notice any changes, anything unusual in the post for Dunnock, tell me," he demanded, just as the door swung inward, temporarily blocking him from the view of the person who'd opened it.

He expected to hear the dogs charging in, barking. He expected Jane to announce herself with an exclamation. Even an oath.

But she did no such thing.

"Good morning, Mr. Ross." Her voice was all sugary sweetness, a demeanor that lost some credibility when she snapped, "No, Aphrodite. Sit. Stay with your sister."

"They're most welcome, Mrs. Higginbotham," insisted Ross. "An' you yourself, of course."

"I couldn't possibly. The snow's begun to melt, and they're wet from the ends of their noses to the tips of their tails. I won't stay a moment." She stepped just beyond the arc of the door's path and began to close it behind her. "I was only looking for Mr. Sutherland."

With a merry twinkle, Ross's eyes directed her to where Thomas stood. She turned abruptly and, despite the honeyed voice she'd used with Ross, looked him up and down disapprovingly. As if he'd been deliberately hiding from her. As if he were the one who'd left muddy paw prints on her skirts.

Her attention snapped back to Ross. "Has Elspeth finished the book I loaned her?"

"I canna say for certain, ma'am, but I don' believe so," Ross said, when he'd recovered from his surprise at the abrupt change of subject. His hand moved beneath the bar, and Thomas suspected he'd pushed the book well out of Jane's sight. "We'd a full house last night, what with the weather turnin' poorly."

"Of course. No rush at all. Please tell her I'll bring down the third volume whenever she's ready for it."

Ross dipped his head. "Indeed I will, ma'am."

She half-turned and glanced over her shoulder at Thomas. "Are you ready to return to Dunnock, sir?" The treacle in her voice almost made him miss this morning's tartness.

But the square set of her shoulders promised that he'd be treated to the other side of her tongue again as soon as they were alone.

"Aye, Mrs. Higginbotham," he said, offering a wink and a nod to Ross, who was fighting down laughter. Jane spun on one foot, providing Thomas with an unexpected opportunity to admire the curve of her hips beneath her swaying skirts as she preceded him to the doorway. "Lead the way."

Chapter 10

Despite the breadth of Balisaig's only thoroughfare, the distance between Mr. Abernathy's apothecary shop and the Thistle and Crown was short. Too short for Jane to be able to reach any decisions about Thomas before she found herself once more walking up the rough path toward Dunnock beside him.

The more she considered the facts, the more certain she grew. She hadn't the faintest idea how it might have come about—oh, these Scottish laws were strange!—but Thomas Sutherland, lieutenant in His Majesty's army, must now be Lord Magnus.

What to do with this knowledge? Accuse him? Admonish him? Of all the fibs and fractured truths she'd told and been told in her life, she could recall none like this. An earl, pretending to be a commoner!

"Did you learn anything of value in the pub, Mr. Sutherland?"

He hesitated before replying. "I made a start."

The glance he'd exchanged with Mr. Ross popped into her mind, the sort of amused, knowing look only old friends could share. He'd spent his boyhood summers in Balisaig, he'd told her. Now, he was sneaking about, spying on his own tenants. For what possible purpose?

Until she found out, she intended to maintain a proper distance between them. She thrust her hands deeper into her muff to discourage Thomas from offering her his arm.

"From the pace you're setting, I ken you're unhappy with me about something, lass," he said after a moment.

She had to slow her steps and draw breath to reply. "I don't know what you—"

"Tell me," he said, ignoring her instinctive denial, "are you angry that I tried to kiss you? Or that I didn't finish the job?"

She turned to look up at him and found him watching her with that familiar quirk about his lips and twinkle in his eyes. The burning sensation in her chest now blazed up into her cheeks.

"Contrary to your ridiculous speculations, Mr. Sutherland, I haven't spent the last seven years—or even the last hour—thinking of your kiss."

Yet another lie. Was that all they had for one another? But she could see no other path forward, at least not one that wasn't treacherous in the extreme.

He tipped his head to the side, and that dratted dimple reappeared as he regarded her with playful skepticism. "Oh, aye?"

The heat in her cheeks made the cold air sting her face as she resumed her purposeful stride toward the castle. He easily matched her pace.

"I suppose it would be useless to deny that there's always been a certain, uh...*spark* between us," she confessed after a moment, wishing she didn't sound so breathless.

The crunch and squeak of snow was loud beneath their feet. "But you wish you could deny it." It wasn't a question, exactly, though the words were tinged with something she was tempted to call disbelief.

Did she? She didn't know anything to a certainty, not anymore.

Well, perhaps *one* thing.

"You didn't come to Dunnock because of that letter."

Surprise flickered into his eyes. Surprise, and even a little shock. As if he'd half-expected her to see through his story, but had not expected her to call his bluff.

But how long could they both go on holding all their cards close to the vest?

"So why did you say you had?"

The quickness of his response proclaimed its honesty. "Because when I saw it lying there, I was alarmed. I can only excuse myself with saying that my protective instinct took over." A sheepish smile curved his lips.

"It's only words on a piece of paper."

"A simple letter can be the harbinger of far more serious things," he insisted, even as she lifted one brow in an incredulous arch. "I suppose it's in a soldier's nature to assume the worst and do what I can to keep others from harm."

Unbidden, the image of him as a Highland warrior rose once more in her mind. "And a Scotsman's."

He tipped his head in acknowledgment. "Still, I should have realized straightaway that you didn't need my protection."

"How could you possibly have realized any such thing?" She hoped she was past succumbing to flattery. "You haven't any idea who sent that letter. And you don't know what I'm capable of, either."

"Well, there *was* a knife protruding from your desk." The mischievous twinkle had returned to his eyes.

"I thought maybe it was the ferocious watchdogs that gave you pause."

His laughter was loud in the stillness, echoing off a nearby outcropping of rock and the more distant walls of the castle. Uncertain whether to join in or succumb to embarrassment, she turned and walked quickly on.

She had not gone many steps before he chuckled softly. "Now, that reminds me of how you turned your back to me the first time I ever saw you. In that little shop in Tenchley."

Embarrassment fluttered in her belly as she glanced back at him over her shoulder. "You fancied it a challenge, I suppose?"

He looked at her intently, brows lifted. "Wasn't it?"

"I—"

When no more words came to her rescue, she began to march forward again. He did not immediately follow. After a few steps, she looked back again and found him watching her, his eyes traveling lazily over her figure. "Let's just say, I liked what I saw."

"That's ridiculous. Why, all you could see was my—" *Oh.*

"Aye," he readily agreed. "And I wanted to see more."

As she spun fully to face him, so that her backside was no longer on display, her foot slipped on an icy patch hidden beneath the soft snow. Swiftly, he closed the distance between them, catching her by the elbow to steady her. She gasped, taken aback not by his strength, but by his gentleness. His arm tautened, absorbing her momentum and keeping them both upright, yet the pressure of his fingertips was not so great as to leave a bruise. When he seemed certain she would not fall, he let her go, though truth be told, she still did not feel entirely steady on her feet.

She did not know whether to blame his touch or the sudden loss of it.

"You're beautiful, ye ken?" His voice had deepened, giving the words an unusual intensity. For once, he sounded serious.

"No, I don't *ken*," she retorted, more snappish than the dogs, who were walking tranquilly along beside them, noses low to the ground and feathery tails waving almost languidly, fatigue having won out over their usual skittishness. "When I look in the glass, I only see what's there: a rather plain face, hair an ordinary shade of brown, and an…ample figure."

"Then your glass needs a good polish, lass." He shook his head. "Your hair is the deep glossy brown of roasted chestnuts, and your eyes…" His hand rose as if he longed to cup her check, to tilt her face to the feeble winter sun. Then he seemed to think better of touching her altogether and dropped his arm to his side. "Your eyes put me in mind of the summer sky on a rare perfect day—the sort we think back on when 'tis rainy or cold, the light we dream of in the dark of night."

She had never expected poetry from Thomas Sutherland. Hearing it fall from his lips in the softest Scottish brogue made the normally steady rhythm of her heart wobble a bit.

"And as for the rest?" His eyes raked over her curves and a low, appreciative rumble rose in his throat. That look, that sound quickened her breath and made her all too aware of the rise and fall of her breasts. "Ordinary? Ample?" he repeated derisively. "I hope your Mr. Higginbotham wooed you with better words than those."

Your Mr. Higginbotham.

In an instant the butterflies in her chest transformed into great, leathery-winged bats. She'd been so consumed by his secrets, she'd almost forgotten her own.

Her consternation must have shown on her face, for he dropped his gaze to the ground between them even as he stepped closer still. "Did you love him very much? I think you must have, to have married so soon after we—so soon after I left."

After *he* left? Then he didn't know…

"I—"

"I suppose he swept you off your feet?" Was it her imagination or did his voice waver? Certainly, he'd lost his usual mocking tone. "Or perhaps—perhaps you knew him long before I came into Sussex, and I was…presumptuous in my attentions."

"No." The protest rose instantly, unthinkingly, to her lips, though it might reveal more than she intended.

But he did not seem to hear it. "No wonder you gave me such a cool reception last night. You mourn him still, I see." His lifted his head, and as he took in her black pelisse, his eyes held none of that teasing lasciviousness.

Enough. She straightened her spine, and her chin jutted forward. "Mr. Higginbotham did indeed use all the right words to woo me. A poet could not have done better. He was unfailingly courteous and kind. Most attentive during our courtship. And generous to a fault after we were wed."

With every phrase, Thomas's eyes grew darker, more pained, and despite her stiff posture, her resolve began to sag. She longed to lay a hand on his arm, to soften the blows her words were inflicting. Her own story was proof positive that one might have honest reasons for keeping a secret.

For example, might not a newly arrived landowner look for a chance to investigate the state of things quietly before making any decisions? Such a man might want to take stock of his inheritance without anyone fawning over him or complaining to him. He might hope to gauge how the friends of his youth would react to his unexpected inheritance.

Yes, there were times when a lie might make it easier to get at the truth.

"He sounds the perfect gentleman, an ideal husband," Thomas said, his voice free of its playful brogue, wrung of all emotion.

Did she even remember the truth? Did she remember how to trust?

"Of course he was," she replied, surprised at her own firmness. "After all, I invented him."

As soon as the words passed her lips, she sucked in her breath, wishing she could recall them. But the secret, once spilled, slipped away like quicksilver, impossible to put back into the vial. He was still looking at her, though she had no name for the wide-eyed expression he now sported.

Tugging her hands free of her muff, she lifted her skirts in great handfuls, turned, and darted toward the castle gate.

Chapter 11

Bewildered, Athena and Aphrodite stood beside Thomas and stared after her fleeing form. Then, with an anxious glance upward, as if only just discovering they'd been abandoned with their enemy, they dashed after their mistress, leaving him alone to weigh the meaning of her words.

There is no Mr. Higginbotham, she had insisted on the night of his arrival. *I invented him.*

He'd suspected her of hiding something, yes. But not that. She'd made up both her husband and his death? She wore widow's weeds for a man who'd never existed? Thomas could not easily sort his emotions in that moment.

"Jane, wait."

Perhaps more related to the slick terrain than to his command, her steps slowed, but did not stop.

On the ground a few feet before him lay the bottom of a thin, narrow box, its lid having been knocked free and then trampled by the dogs. Jane must have dropped it as she ran. From it spilled something blue, a puddle of springtime against the snow. He bent and retrieved both the box and its contents: a pair of ladies' silk stockings, with a latticework of delicate embroidery running along their length. A gift? An indulgence?

He stuffed them into the deep pocket of his greatcoat and hurried after her, reaching her side just before she slipped through the inner bailey of the castle. Though the dogs raced ahead, she stopped, head and shoulders bowed.

When it became clear that she did not intend to speak first, or perhaps at all, he said simply, "I don't...understand."

Her reply was muffled. "I made him up."

"But why would you do such a thing?" Certainly he had no right or reason to be angry at her for keeping secrets. In fact, some small, terrible part of him dared to rejoice at the realization that he would not have to compete with another man's memory. In spite of himself, however, his voice rose, shock and surprise coloring his question.

Her head snapped up, her hood slipping back over her hair with the violence of the movement. "Why would a young woman, living alone, want the protections, the freedoms, our society affords widows?" Her eyes lit with the spark of some otherworldly fire. "Can you not imagine?"

"I—"

In truth, he had never before given the matter much thought. He had always regarded widows as objects of pity. He had never considered that a woman might be tempted to don those weeds as a means of resisting the restraints society put on her. At seventeen, he had been free to follow a path of his choosing. His fortune, such as it was, had been his to command. His person, too—whatever the British Army might assert to the contrary. At seventeen, Jane too had wanted to strike out on her own, it seemed. But she had been driven to play the part of widowed "Mrs. Higginbotham" just to have some scant measure of control over her life. Would he have had the strength to do what she had done, for just a taste of independence?

"I'm sorry it was necessary," he said, his voice low. "But I confess, I'm glad to know you're not really a grieving widow." Fishing deep in his pocket, he withdrew the pair of bright-colored stockings and held them out to her.

She took them, though with something like reluctance, or wariness at least, as if they belonged to someone else. Methodically, she wrapped them around one hand with the other to form a neat bundle. Why did she have them? Was she considering leaving off her false mourning? Did his arrival have anything to do with it?

"No, I have not lost a husband," she said, watching herself wind the stockings into a ball before stuffing them into her muff. "It does not therefore follow that I have not grieved."

Before his parted lips could decide which question to form, she explained.

"I lost my family. I have not seen them since the night of that assembly. While you and I were dancing and talking and—" More heat flamed into her cheeks, but she dashed it away with sharp shake of her head. "My mother found something of mine, something she misunderstood. Something of which she strenuously disapproved. She showed it to my father. By the time Sir Richard and Julia walked me home, my fate had already been decided. Papa ordered me to leave the house. I was granted a few moments to gather my things and kiss my sleeping brother goodbye. Under cover of helping me pack, our housekeeper gave me what I fear must have been her life's savings. By dawn I was on the stage bound for London. Alone."

"Jane." Her name burst from his lips, half sigh, half groan. He knew not what else to say. The circumstances that had driven her here were worse, much worse, than he could have imagined. The part of him that generally acted first and reflected later, the part that had longed for the glorious adventure of a soldier's life, itched to leave right that moment for Tenchley and set her father straight. But the part of him that had been trained to perform the careful, sometimes tedious, always dangerous work of an intelligence officer knew that rashness would solve nothing.

And squeezed between those two shares of his soul was an uncomfortably sharp splinter that wondered just what her mother had found.

"For seven years," he said, "I have puzzled over why your father told me he had no daughter."

The color leached from her face, and the rough sound in her throat made him think she was about to be sick. He held out a hand to her, and to his surprise, she took it, gripping the breadth of his palm with small but surprisingly strong fingers. After a moment, she had steadied herself enough to meet his gaze. He saw pain written there, the dull sort that spoke of some chronic, incurable wound. "You kept your promise?" she whispered, still clutching his hand. "You called on him? On me?"

"I did."

If he believed in destiny, he would've been tempted to say he was keeping that promise still. Despite the years and oceans that had come between them, here he was.

Here they were.

"How did you end up in Balisaig?" he asked. Had she thought of him, the stories of his misspent youth with which he'd regaled her? Try as he might, he could not recall whether he'd ever named the village.

She drew back, the slightest movement, but he understood then that, however much she had needed to tell someone—tell him—what had happened, she was not yet ready to share the entire story.

After another pause, however, she continued, though not exactly with an answer to his question. "The journey to London was an education." A shudder of memory passed through her. "After my second attempt to secure lodgings, I realized that it would be necessary to lie. A young, unmarried woman could have no hope of finding a respectable place, but perhaps a widow...? Mrs. Higginbotham was our housekeeper, and since it was her money, I began giving her name. Eventually, I found employment and was able to return her generous gift, with interest. When the opportunity to travel farther afield came, to put more distance between myself and Tenchley, I took it."

A great deal had been glossed over in that telling, he knew. For one thing, she'd not mentioned Ratliff. But for now, the outlines of the story were more than enough. "Have you continued to correspond with Mrs. Higginbotham?" he asked. "Or your friend?"

Her eyes, which had been focused somewhere on the past, grew wide. "Heavens no. I'm sure my father saw to it that my name was unspeakable in Tenchley. Julia's reputation would have been ruined if a secret correspondence with me had been discovered. I would never have put her at such a risk. Nor could I do anything that might jeopardize dear Mrs. Higginbotham's position."

"Then you know nothing of how your family fares?"

She paused, as if bracing herself. "Mama died of a sudden illness, four years ago. My father grows ever more bitter. I know what little I do because—because I reached out to my brother, once I was sure he was at Oxford. He understood, I think, that I was not entirely to blame for what happened."

Entirely? Nothing she could have done would ever excuse her father's willingness to send his own child to the wolves. He and his own father had not always seen eye to eye, but even in death his father had not abandoned him as utterly as Mr. Quayle had deserted Jane.

Again a pair of opposing instincts warred in his chest—on one side, a fierce desire to stay and protect her from future harm; on the other, a warrior's need to seek out the one who'd harmed her already and make him face justice.

She shivered, and the movement transferred itself to him through their still-clasped hands. "You're cold," he said, squeezing her fingers and then releasing them, fighting the impulse to wrap his arms around her instead. "I suppose it would be ungentlemanly of me to offer to warm you."

"Mr. Sutherland." She shook her head and heaved a sigh, but as he'd hoped, his playful suggestion had driven some of the sorrow from her expression. It was replaced with reluctant amusement. "You really do spend a great deal too much time thinking about the effect of your kisses."

With her teasing reply, the weight that had settled in his chest lifted just a bit. "Nay, lass," he replied with a wink. "'Tis *your* kiss that preys on my mind."

Two bright spots of color came into her cheeks. "You really mustn't say such things." Her voice dropped to almost a whisper. "Two strangers ought not to be spending so much time talking about kisses."

"Strangers?" he echoed, trying to keep a fresh note of pain from his voice.

"What do we really know of one another? If this morning has proven anything, it's that we've piled up a great many secrets between us—my reasons for claiming to be Mrs. Higginbotham, your real reasons for returning to Balisaig."

Truths rose to the tip of his tongue. Just as quickly, he swallowed them. This was neither the time nor place to reveal anything to her. To say nothing of revealing everything.

She had already revealed that she feared Lord Magnus's power to have her once more turned out of her home. Choosing this moment to announce he was the earl would surely cause more problems than it solved.

When he made no reply, a flicker of something—disappointment?—crossed her eyes. Her hood wobbled with another shiver. "I should go in. I have a great deal of work to make up now." The ordinary primness had returned to her voice. With the slightest dip of a curtsy, she turned, slipped through the doorway, and was gone.

Though tempted to follow, he didn't. She'd already given him more than he had any right to expect, and it was his turn to consider in what way he might best repay the debt.

He walked along the outer bailey, thinking first of returning to his quarters to mull over everything he'd learned. Restlessness sent his feet in the opposite direction. Morning had not yet given way to midday, and he could not bear to shut himself away in a windowless room while the sun shone, feeble though its warmth might be.

Reluctant to prod her secrets further, he decided to prod the castle's instead. Poking his head into every open archway and unlocked door, he scouted the castle's guardrooms (unmanned) and storerooms (mostly empty), coming, at last, to the stable, which housed a pair of donkeys and a tabby cat, which shot out of sight as soon as he entered. Dougan, who had been whistling tunelessly while he curried the rough-coated beasts, looked over one shoulder. The donkeys continued to eat and paid Thomas no mind.

"Good morning, Dougan," he said, tipping his hat. The man's once-red beard and hair had begun to turn white, and even in the dim light of the stable, Thomas could see that his kilt had been carefully patched in places.

"Aye?" He sounded nervous. Mrs. Murdoch had warned Thomas that Dougan was shy of strangers but had a good heart.

"Don't let me interrupt your work. I'm just familiarizing myself with the lay of things. I suppose there isn't much use for horses?" The donkeys could be employed for pulling a cart or even turning over the kitchen garden. Most of the soil of the Highlands was put to better use grazing cattle and sheep than raising grain. Dougan shook his head in silent agreement and went back to plying the comb. Thomas was on the point of going out again—he hadn't been looking for company, after all—when an empty stall in the shadows caught his eye.

Or rather, *not* empty. What filled it wasn't horses or feed, however, but something oddly shaped, hidden beneath several dusty tarps. Probably nothing more exciting than a broken-down wagon or stacked crates. He took three meandering steps in its direction, as if the matter were really of very little interest to him.

"Dougan," he said, lifting the corner of a tarp the merest fraction of an inch with the tip of one finger, "would you happen t' ken what's—?"

Dougan dropped his currycomb, which hit the straw-strewn stable floor with a dull thud. "Och, nay, lad," he exclaimed, eyes starting from his head. Thomas couldn't immediately decide whether the man was denying knowledge of what was hidden in the stall or warning him away from further exploration.

Either way, Thomas's curiosity was ignited. He gripped a fistful of the coarse, dusty fabric.

Dougan took a step closer. "Mrs. Higginbotham wouldna like that."

Mrs. Higginbotham? He thought of all Jane had already told him. What else was she hiding?

"I promise you, I'll bear the brunt of her wrath," Thomas vowed, giving a sharp tug. No time like the present to begin his role as laird of the castle.

The first tarp slid onto the stable floor in a mud-colored puddle of holland cloth, revealing the dashboard and tongue of a carriage. A curricle, to be precise. The shadows were too thick to determine much more.

He reached for one of the two remaining tarps, and Dougan began to wring his hands. When the second tarp fell away, the third gave up its feeble attempts to shield the curricle from prying eyes and dropped in a heap. A cloud of dust and chaff billowed upward, and the tabby cat, which had worked up the courage to poke her whiskers from her hiding place in the crevice between two stalls, darted to safety again.

Thomas could not prevent a low whistle of astonishment. "Well, what have we here?"

The racing curricle, its wheels and body a glossy red trimmed out with black, would have been the envy of every buck from Balisaig to Brighton. Even in the feeble light filtering into the corner of the stable, it gleamed. Somehow, he could not imagine such a flashy equipage had belonged to the late Lord Magnus. Which left only one obvious suspect: a profligate novelist with, as Thomas had already noted, a flair for the dramatic. Oh, yes. This curricle had Robin Ratliff written all over it.

But why hadn't Ratliff driven it to Edinburgh? The uncertain weather, perhaps. Or a not ill-founded fear of attracting the wrong sort of attention. Highwaymen would expect its driver to be worth a pretty penny, to say nothing of the value of the curricle itself.

Then again, Thomas could see no sign that the man kept horses for it. And not just any horses would do. A matched pair, black of course, well-bred and highly fed, the care of which would probably be more than poor old Dougan could handle.

As if he could read the direction of Thomas's thoughts, the old gatekeeper bent and plucked up a corner of one of the tarps, fingering it uncertainly. "Mrs. Higginbotham isn't going to like this at all," he moaned.

"Well, now. And who's going to tell her?" Thomas slapped the man's shoulder and offered his widest grin.

"Och, she'll ken. Even if you're careful, she'll take one look at the way the tarps lie and see they've been moved. An' heaven help ye if ye've scratched the paint." Dougan shook his head mournfully, as if Thomas might as well accept his fate and present himself to the executioner accordingly.

Thomas was only half-listening. Though not much of one for road races, he was finding it difficult not to wonder how well the curricle handled and how fast it could go. Whether anyone in the vicinity had a pair of horses they might let him borrow, just for an afternoon.

"Come, lad," Dougan insisted, shaking off Thomas's hand. He gathered up a tarp in his arms, and with a reluctant sigh, Thomas helped him spread it over the curricle, once more hiding it from view.

After they had replaced the third tarp, Dougan stepped back and passed a critical eye over their work. Again he shook his head despairingly. "She'll ken. Just ye wait an' see."

"And what then? I did no more than look. Surely, Mr. Ratliff can't object to that."

"Eh?"

"Mr. Ratliff, the writer. The one who rents Dunnock. The one who owns this curricle."

Dougan's look conveyed quite clearly that though he knew folks called him "soft in t' head," he regarded Thomas's head as softer still. "It's Mrs. Higginbotham's rig. Ha'n't ye heard a word I've said?"

"No, Dougan," Thomas corrected with a laugh. "She does a good many things on Mr. Ratliff's behalf, and I wouldn't be surprised to learn that he ordered her to check on his curricle from time to time—though why he doesn't just drive the thing himself, I canna guess. But she's his employee. And a lady. She wouldn't…"

His protests were growing feebler as the shake of Dougan's head grew more pronounced. "Mrs. Higginbotham drove that there curricle through the castle gates an' told me tae see that none other ever touched it," he said. "Right smart, she looked."

Thomas could well imagine. Too well. The color in her cheeks, the blazing look of triumph.

He was tempted to continue to insist on the impossibility of it all. But the morning had provided him with other evidence that Ratliff was an uncommonly generous and trusting employer. In fact, Thomas had never heard the like.

Mrs. Higginbotham's name on the post.

Mrs. Higginbotham's skittish spaniels underfoot.

And now Mrs. Higginbotham's red racing curricle…

Of course, the name was a fiction. Jane had just confessed to inventing Mr. Higginbotham out of whole cloth.

Absently, Thomas smoothed a wrinkle from the tarp, tracing the sharp cutaway of the curricle's side. No one at Dunnock Castle or in the village of Balisaig had ever seen Robin Ratliff, either. Everything about the man was as shrouded in mystery as this carriage.

Was it…was it possible she'd also invented—?

He clipped the thought short, before it could fully form.

It had always been in his nature to act first and think later. General Scott had done his best to train away those impulses. An intelligence officer gathered and weighed evidence. He did not leap to conclusions. No matter how tempting.

With a nod to Dougan, Thomas turned and left the stable.

Chapter 12

The convent walls had been built to safeguard its occupants from intruders. Getting out was easier. Allora managed the task with nothing worse than scraped knuckles and a perfectly mendable rent in her second-best muslin. Once over the wrought-iron gate, she directed her footsteps toward the forest. Fog lay like a damp, ghostly blanket over the valley. Though it had doubtless aided her escape, it also hid the mysterious glowing light from her view. Determined to discover its source, however, she forged ahead, her heart stuttering at every rustle of leaves and crackle in the undergrowth.

In ten years, she had never been allowed to venture beyond the convent's walls. Her knowledge of the surrounding landscape consisted of the views she had taken from various vantage points, when she was supposed to be improving her sketching. Now, on the ground, everything looked different. Was she even headed in the right direction?

Just when despair had almost driven her to turn back, her shoulder struck something and forced a muffled gasp of pain from her lungs. Her sight rendered almost useless by the dark and the fog, she groped with numb fingers to identify what she'd stumbled against. The wall stretched as far and as high as she could reach without taking another step. Not a fence, then, but some sort of structure. A farmer's cottage? A hermit's hut?

Cautiously, she crept along the wall until she reached its end. Voices rose to her ear. Men's voices, two or three, at least. They spoke to one another in a language she did not understand, their voices as rough-hewn as the boards from which the cabin had been built. Had she stumbled on a den of the brigands with which the forest was rumored to be rife? A strange thrill went through her. She had so little experience with the ways of men.

Hardly daring to breathe, she peered around the corner. Light spilled from a partially opened door to fall at her feet. Perhaps the men inside had seen the strange light. Perhaps one of them could be persuaded to guide her to it. At least, she—

"Well, well." The voice spoke low in her ear, so close she could feel the man's hot breath strike her cheek. Like the crack of a whip, his hand clapped over her mouth, pinning her against his hard body. "What's a lovely lass like you doing out on a night like this?"

"Mrs. Higginbotham?"

Her heart beating almost as fast as her heroine's, Jane jumped and gripped her pen tighter, narrowly managing to keep from throwing it across the desk and ruining an evening's work with spattered ink. When she had drawn and released two calming breaths, she looked toward the doorway, where Elspeth Shaw, barmaid at the Thistle and Crown, stood, still wearing her apron over a woolen work dress, her cheeks ruddy with cold, and her reddish-blond hair in a flyaway braid.

"Och, now. Did I give ye a fright?" The amused twist to the young woman's lips undercut the apology in her voice. "Mrs. Murdoch told me tae come up."

After another deep breath for good measure, Jane glanced toward the window, where nightfall stained the sky. Were late-hour visitors to become a regular occurrence? "What brings you here on a night like this, Elspeth?" Jane asked, and nearly rolled her eyes at her unintentional echo of the brigand's question. She'd been thinking only of the weather on the pages of her book. But it must be clear tonight in Balisaig. Elspeth wouldn't have made the climb to Dunnock after dark if a fresh blanket of snow had fallen.

Jane had had most of a lifetime to make her peace with interruptions. Freedom from distraction, as Thomas had so succinctly put it, was a luxury most would never know. Prior to coming to Dunnock, she'd certainly never had a separate room in which to write.

Still, tonight's interruption struck her as particularly ill-timed. She'd struggled half the afternoon to settle to her work, while her mind had insisted on reliving her foolish admission, reflecting on her suspicions about Thomas, and regretting yet another lost opportunity for a kiss. By dusk, her frustrations had been ratcheted up to a fever pitch.

She always strove for artistic detachment, but tonight, her heroine's besetting sin—curiosity—combined with her ill-advised attraction to a most unsuitable, even dangerous, man felt a little too familiar. Perhaps the anonymous letter writer was right, albeit inadvertently. Perhaps her books were a dangerous influence on the hearts and minds of susceptible young women.

Swallowing her annoyance—with herself as much as the interruption, Jane laid aside her pen. Elspeth Shaw was something of a friend, and certainly a devotee. She had done nothing to deserve this rudeness.

As she rose from her desk, Jane spied a small book tucked in the young woman's hand and recalled her promise to provide the next volume of *The Necromancer's Bride* whenever Elspeth was ready to read it. Though she had a great deal of evidence that her stories were popular with readers, she would always thrill to the idea of someone being willing to trudge up the side of a mountain on a winter's night just to find out what happened next.

Before she could say anything, though, Elspeth's eyes widened. "What's that you're wearing, Mrs. Higginbotham?" she asked around a choked laugh.

Jane glanced down at the loose-fitting gown of brocaded silk. "A banyan," she answered curtly. It had always struck her as unfair that a gentleman might wear something so relaxed and comfortable about the house and still be thought of as respectably dressed, while a lady serving tea in a dressing gown would start a scandal. So before she'd left London, she'd had a banyan made to Robin Ratliff's measurements. It was her favorite costume for writing.

"I suppose you've finished the second volume of *The Necromancer's Bride*," Jane continued, gliding toward the bookshelf and ignoring Elspeth's snickering.

"*I* finished it two days ago," the young woman insisted, thrusting out her chin. "But Ross wouldn't let me return it to you. He's a slow reader, he is," she added, and winked.

In spite of herself, the twitch of a smile rose to Jane's lips. "Is he?" Was this the reason for Elspeth's oddly timed visit? Had Mr. Ross been reading the book surreptitiously and sent the barmaid after the next installment the moment he'd finished the last? Then again, the ending of the second volume of that particular story had been timed to leave the reader wanting more...

Another little bolt of pride shot through her and turned the curve at the corners of her mouth even higher. What would any of them say if they ever discovered she was the one responsible for piquing their curiosity so wickedly well?

Experience had given her one answer to that question. Would she ever dare to trust anyone—trust Thomas—enough to find out if there were other answers? She'd already told him more than she'd intended to. Was she brave enough to spill the most important secret she kept? This time, would he follow with secrets of his own?

"'Course," Elspeth continued, breaking into her thoughts, "he'd have me tell you I'm here on account of the letter."

"Letter?" Something new and decidedly colder slithered along Jane's spine. She held out another neatly bound duodecimo volume, and the young woman exchanged it for the one she cradled in the crook of her arm.

"One for Dunnock got mixed up with someone else's post."

"Oh? Whose post?"

"Mr. Donaldson's."

She wished it had been almost anyone else in the village. "And he returned it to the Thistle and Crown?" she asked, knowing the clergyman's fear that someone might suspect him of frequenting the pub.

"Nay. Mrs. MacIntosh brought it back this afternoon." Elspeth nodded toward the book Jane now held. "I tucked it inside to keep it dry."

Instinctively, Jane's fingers tightened against the leather-covered boards, trapping the letter more securely between the book's pages. The younger woman frowned, evidently disappointed that Jane wasn't showing more enthusiasm about the missive—or at least, curiosity.

Jane merely bowed her head. "Thank you, Elspeth."

At that clear sign of dismissal, the young woman shrugged and hugged the new book to her, no doubt satisfied she'd done her duty and obviously pleased to have what she'd really come for. Mr. Ross wasn't likely to get more work out of her tonight.

When she was gone, Jane returned to her desk. Her slippered footsteps were loud in the unusually quiet room. No snoring dogs—they'd gone on their nightly visit to Agnes in search of treats. Even the fire had died down too low to snap and hiss.

After she sat down, she laid the book carefully on the center of her desk, covering up Allora's exploits, and stared at the reddish-brown cover for a long moment. The sweat of several pairs of hands had darkened the leather; the embossing was bisected by a circular stain, as from the bottom of a damp glass that had been set down upon it, probably at the pub, and one corner of the bottom board was tattered. All those signs of use warmed her heart, a reminder that the volume had made the rounds of Balisaig, just as other copies had been passed around other villages. *The Necromancer's Bride* had raised hairs and disrupted sleep and won hearts throughout Britain. She needed to remember that, whenever doubt...threatened...

Stiffly, she extended one fingertip and lifted the cover.

The letter looked up at her, the blob of wax with which it had been sealed staring from the folded rectangle of parchment like a bloodshot eye. Snatching up her penknife from the tray, she slit the seal with a surprisingly steady hand, and then used the tip of the blade to unfold the pages, as if she feared the paper itself might have been soaked in something dangerous to the touch.

Whatever she had been expecting—a letter from the solicitor, informing her that the request to renew the lease on Dunnock had been denied, or another ill-written screed about the deleterious effects of gothic novels on young people's, particularly young ladies', brains—she was not prepared for what she found.

The short note had been composed of words clipped from newspapers and pasted to the page. The varied fonts marched across the paper in ragged, jagged lines that might have been comical if they hadn't spelled out her—that is to say, Robin Ratliff's—doom.

Closing her eyes, she withdrew her finger and let the cover of the book drop shut. Had this letter come from the same person as the last? She found herself almost hoping so, although the method of composition made it impossible to know for certain. Otherwise, she would have to face the fact that because she had dared to tell a few fanciful stories, not one, but *two* people wanted her dead.

Briefly, she considered casting it into the fire, book and all. To do otherwise would be to agree that the letter writer deserved her attention.

But he—or she—had it already. Turning the letter to ash would change nothing, would do nothing to quiet the fear hammering in her head and in her chest. Then again, what would?

"Thomas."

The whisper came from deep within her. If she'd been sentimental, or a fool, she might have said her soul.

The sound of his name broke the spell of the silent room, and her eyes popped open. With a resolute grimace, she once more laid open the book and picked up the letter to study it. She suffered from no delusion that her books were for every reader. Criticism did not bother her. But this? Who would take the time to track down and cut out every word in this artful, awful threat? She turned the letter over to see whether the direction had been done in the same peculiar fashion. Who on earth had—?

The letter fluttered down onto the desk before she even realized it had slipped from her fingers. The same childish hand as the previous letter leaped from the center of the otherwise blank page. The very same... though with one important change. This letter hadn't been addressed to Mrs. Higginbotham or forwarded from Mr. Canfield. She closed her eyes again, but the words were seared into her eyelids, as if written in flame.

Mr. Robin Ratliff

Dunnock Castle
Balisaig, Inverness, Scotland

Slowly, she opened her burning eyes and focused her gaze on the far side of the room. Sometime between the last letter and this, the writer had discovered where Ratliff—*she*—lived.

Her hands shook—she hadn't the strength anymore to stop them—as she tore a scrap of paper off the bottom of the page on which Allora had fallen into the arms of her unlikely hero. She scrawled a few words across it and prayed they would be legible.

Could Thomas protect her from a madman? She didn't know.

And if she didn't believe in his promise of safety, what was it that she sought from him?

Mustering her courage, she rose and rang the bell.

* * * *

In the end, Thomas had decided not to confront Jane with his suspicions. Instead, he'd walked twice around the outer bailey before returning to his rooms in the gatehouse, no less restless than he'd been when he started. Esme had come while he'd been out, straightened the sitting room and aired the bed. While he appreciated the maid's efforts, the present orderliness was ill-suited to his mood. Like his mentor, he found it difficult to think when things were too neat.

Though the sun was shining, its brightness amplified by the snow, in the gatehouse all was dark. He lit a lamp and began to poke into the corners he'd been too tired to explore last night. He found old estate records that ought to have been sent on to Mr. Watson and never had been, a few coats, and a tricorn hat twenty years out of fashion, packed in camphor in the clothespress. And in a corner cupboard, the complete works of Robin Ratliff.

Tracing a finger along the row of spines, he considered what, if anything, the books might reveal either to confirm or deny his theory of their authorship. Though General Scott had made clear Ratliff's work was widely read and wildly popular, it felt like an invasion of Jane's privacy to be thinking of reading them himself, now that he'd begun to suspect her of writing them. He'd already learned some of her secrets today; would he discover more between the covers of her novels? Then again, if he meant to find out anything about the writer of that horrible letter, perhaps it would be useful to know what had stirred his ire.

He lit candles from the lantern until the room glowed, then settled on the sofa, one leg stretched along the seat, the other foot on the floor, and opened the first volume of *The Necromancer's Bride*.

Some hours later, he was nearing the end of the second volume, fully absorbed by the story of poor, orphaned Ophelia, found in the forest and raised by peasants, though obviously not of their stock. He'd toed off his boots to sit with both feet on the sofa, knees propped up to hold the book, as he had not done since he'd been a lad—if then. Even the laden dinner tray Esme had brought him earned only a scant share of his attention, what little he could spare from hair-raising accounts of the myriad cruelties Ophelia had been forced to endure and the frequent eruptions of strange sounds coming from Lord Ruthveyn's castle, in whose shadow they all struggled to survive. The rich, sensual voice on the page, far different from the sometimes prim and always proper one with which Jane spoke, almost made him second-guess his belief that she was really Ratliff.

From time to time, he paused to try to understand what had angered the letter writer, as if there might be some logic to his position. Certainly, if one presumed that it was dangerous to form an attachment to fictional characters, to the point of distraction from one's other duties, then the book did indeed pose a serious risk to its readers.

Then, of course, there was the looming castle and its mysterious lord who did little to fulfill his duties to the people of his estate. For the inspiration there, he hadn't to look any further than Dunnock and the failings of the late Lord Magnus.

Perhaps also the current one.

Mostly, though, in those moments of reflection, he found himself remarking on how much the heroine's experience mirrored Jane's—both young women with gifts that put them entirely out of step with everyone who surrounded them.

In chapter twelve of the second volume, Ophelia's foster family agreed to a proposition so shocking, Thomas found himself sitting bolt upright, both feet once more on the floor. Lord Ruthveyn, known to meddle in dark magic—hadn't his intended bride died at her own hand the night before their wedding?—offered a large sum of money in exchange for the hand of the lovely, innocent young woman, and without even a show of reluctance, the destitute couple renounced their parentage and sold her to him.

More and more, Thomas was forced to conclude that his surmise had been the correct one: Jane had been moved by her own family's cruelties to pen this tale. Like her heroine, she had been betrayed by those she had trusted and forced to make her own way in a hard world.

Pages fluttered beneath Thomas's fingers as he sped through them. Ophelia's proud ascent to the castle, unwilling to shed a tear. The apparently empty castle, with no sign of the necromancer. The shrieks and groans from the dungeons that broke her slumber. He owed Ross an apology for his silent mockery this morning in the pub. Expecting any moment to come across the fateful scene when Ruthveyn and Ophelia met, Thomas too would have resented an interruption.

Given freedom to wander the castle, for she saw no one to stop her, Ophelia discovered no instruments of torture, no frightful laboratory. She found herself most often in the vast library, staring up in amazement at the great walls of books. One evening, as she walked along the shelf, trailing a fingertip across a row of dusty spines, a voice spoke.

"Why do you never open any of them?"

She located the figure in the shadows, standing beside the chair in which he must previously have been sitting, watching her. By his words, she knew it had not been the first time he had done so.

It could only be Lord Ruthveyn, though he was younger than she had imagined and not half so frightening to look upon. His features were sharp and his skin sallow, with a curtain of dark hair framing his face, but he was not altogether unhandsome.

She curtsied. "Because I never learned to read, my lord."

Over the next few chapters, Ruthveyn dedicated himself to teaching her, in increasingly intimate scenes between the unlikely pair that kept Thomas's eyes skating over the pages. Eventually, Ophelia had learned enough to be able to read to Lord Ruthveyn every evening before she retired, while he quaffed what he called a forgetting potion—strong liquor the young woman was too naïve to recognize as such. Just when Thomas felt certain that the rumors of sorcery would be disproven in the scant pages of the volume that remained, Ruthveyn entered the library with a brimful goblet for Ophelia.

"Cupidio," he explained, ordering her to drink it.

Lord Ruthveyn had been too thorough a teacher for her not to understand the implications of the brew's name. But she required no love potion to fulfill at last the wedding vows she'd made. Her fascination with him, however unwise, was strong enough already. Nevertheless, she drained the glass as she'd been told, licking the last honeyed drops from her lips.

"Well?" He stood with arms crossed, his expression stern yet hopeful.

With undisguised eagerness, she dropped to her knees before him, though in truth, nothing had changed. The tremor of desire that stirred deep within her belly had naught to do with what she'd drunk. "Teach me to please you, my lord."

End of Vol. II

In his haste to reach for the third volume, Thomas upset what remained of the pot of tea, grown fortunately cold, as most of it landed in his lap, the rest of it dripping onto the sofa and carpet, narrowing missing the books he'd left lying about.

He was still sopping up the mess when someone knocked.

Muttering curses under his breath, he stomped through the office in his stockinged feet and dragged open the heavy outer door. All was in darkness; the hour must be very late. When cold air hit his wet clothes, the curses ceased to be muttered. "Damn and blast. What now?"

Elderly Mrs. Murdoch looked up at him reprovingly from beneath a hooded mantle. "Well, I never," she snapped, shoving a folded piece of paper at him. "Mrs. Higginbotham sent me tae give you this."

She was gone before his words of apology could reach her ears. He stood in the doorway looking after her, letting the cold air seep through his wet clothes as a punishment for his ill-mannered behavior. Once she had disappeared inside the castle, he retreated into his rooms. Before the fire, he unfolded the note, a ragged scrap on which an unsteady hand had scrawled

Robin Ratliff is in the castle and wishes to speak with you tonight.

An unexpected message, to be sure—and oddly cryptic. The few words, the rushed delivery, hinted at a state of distress. The hand that had held the pen had shaken too much for him to feel certain it had been Jane's. Perhaps his surmise had been wrong. If she were Ratliff, why would she choose this moment to reveal the connection?

Unless something had happened to prompt her to tell him the truth?

After a final swipe at his tea-stained clothes—thankfully, his waistcoat and coat had long since been shed and tossed aside—he shoved his feet into his boots and his arms into his battered greatcoat. Those issuing midnight invitations must excuse his dishabille.

Inside the castle, he crossed the deserted Great Hall and ascended the south stair as quickly as its narrow, curved steps allowed. The study door stood open, giving him a clear view of the room, of Jane, before he could be seen. She was pacing before the fire, staring down at the floor, evidently deep in thought. With her hair hanging over her shoulder in a long, thick braid, she looked as young as she had when they had first met.

Cautiously, he ventured across the threshold, but the dogs were nowhere in sight. She paused her restless steps and looked up, startled. He bowed. "I had a note I'd find Robin Ratliff in the castle. Where is he?"

For a long moment, she only looked at him. Then she spread her arms. "Here."

She'd obviously intended to surprise him with a dramatic revelation, and despite his suspicions about the author of *The Necromancer's Bride*, she'd succeeded.

She was clad in what appeared to be a man's dressing gown; its rich purple silk caught the light as she moved. No question, though, that it belonged to her, for it had been tailored to her shorter frame. It was just the sort of costume a dissolute gothic novelist might wear—and it drove all thought of Mrs. Higginbotham's dismal black dress from his mind.

He took another step toward her, but she turned one of her hands palm outward to stop him. It seemed she wasn't done with revelations yet. "I thought you would want to know that another letter came this evening," she said, gesturing toward the desk with the flick of her other wrist, though her gaze never left his face. "Lord Magnus."

Chapter 13

Jane had hoped to feel a sense of relief at telling someone her deepest, darkest secret. A sense of triumph at having guessed another's. Instead she felt vulnerable. Agitated.

Or maybe those feelings were the fault of the letter.

She watched Thomas stride toward the desk. Neither his expression nor his posture betrayed any reaction to her use of his title. Perhaps she'd been wrong after all? He picked up the letter and studied it for so long, she felt certain he had forgotten about her. Then he returned the paper to its place and, without looking up, asked, "How long have you known who I am?"

So, she'd guessed right. She drew a breath, wishing he would look at her. "Last night, I thought for certain you must have been sent by the new earl, despite your denial. But while I was in the village this morning, I heard news that he had recently been seen in Edinburgh and would likely make his way to Dunnock to take stock of things. When I thought of how far you'd come, your family connections to the Balisaig, I began to realize it was far more likely you *were* Lord Magnus. All the pieces fit."

"Do they?" He raised his face to hers. The customary lightness of his expression had been replaced by a degree of bitterness, a shadow of self-doubt she would not have thought him capable of feeling. "If you were suspicious of me from the first, I suppose I ought not to be surprised that you wouldn't kiss me."

For years, she had hidden, denied, lied. But where had it got her?

"I wish now that I had."

He came around in front of the desk, leaning his hips against it as he crossed his arms over his chest. "Do you?"

She nodded, glanced toward the letter on the desktop, and licked suddenly dry lips. "I could use a distraction."

Some of the familiar, mischievous warmth flickered in his answering gaze, though he said nothing.

"You weren't entirely shocked when I said I'm Robin Ratliff, were you?"

He lifted one shoulder in reluctant acknowledgment. "Your note tonight and the snow were the last pieces in the puzzle. It was easy enough to see that no carriage had come in or out today, which meant the mysterious Ratliff had to have been in the castle all along. What you'd told me this morning, about Higginbotham and about your family, made me wonder whether there wasn't more to tell. After we parted, I took a stroll around the outer bailey and came upon old Dougan caring for his donkeys. Despite his stern warnings, I poked around a bit in an empty stall and found—"

"The curricle," she finished, pursing her lips and shaking her head. She might have known she'd be betrayed eventually by one of the little extravagances she'd allowed herself.

"The *red racing* curricle," he agreed. And winked. "Perfectly suited to what I thought I knew of Dunnock's tenant. But Dougan insisted it was yours. When I added it together with the rest, I began to suspect how things lay. But I spent the afternoon reading *The Necromancer's Bride*, just to be sure."

She glanced toward that awful letter, then back at him, and pushed her chin forward, defiant. "And?"

With a wry laugh, he unfolded his arms and parted the sides of his greatcoat.

For a moment, all her attention was taken by the discovery he was wearing nothing more than a thin cambric shirt, which had come mostly untucked from a pair of worn but well-fitted buckskin breeches. Even his cravat was missing, and the wedge of tanned skin revealed by the deep V in his shirt was shadowed with dark, curling hair.

"Spilled half a pot of tea on myself hurrying to get my hands on volume three, didn't I?"

The damp fabric clung provocatively to the taut muscles of his abdomen, and lower. "Oh, my." Thanks to Elspeth's visit, she'd had a recent reminder of the dramatic break between the second and third volumes of *The Necromancer's Bride*. Heat rushed into her cheeks. "I suppose you want to know what happens next?"

His expression was...well, she couldn't quite put a name to it. Sly, perhaps. Intrigued. And more than a little impressed. "That much, lass, I think I can guess."

She looked him up and down again, let her gaze linger over every detail. He was entirely too handsome. And too confident. "With all due respect, Lord Magnus, I doubt it."

He had the grace to laugh again, though once more a shadow flickered across his eyes. He did not seem to relish hearing his title bandied about, as other men did. "If I'm wrong, then Robin Ratliff must have had some verra disappointed readers."

He was teasing her, of course. Nevertheless, the words cut uncomfortably close. "A few, over the years."

It was his turn to inspect her, though his gaze stayed focused on her face. "Your parents among them, I ken. You said your mother found something of yours, something that distressed her. Something you'd written, I take it?"

Jane nodded. "Left to her own devices, she would, I think, have found it in her heart to forgive me. But Papa—" The memory burst from the place where she'd hidden it away, as swift and dangerous as a bullet from a gun. *The crackle of paper as Papa shook the dreadful proof of her sins in her face. The little globule of spittle that formed in the corner of his mouth as he spewed his wrath. Tears streaming down Mama's cheeks all the while. The billow of smoke as her precious manuscript hit the drawing room fire.* "My father disapproved—disapproves, I daresay—of anything that smacks of fancy. Novels most of all."

The flash in Thomas's eyes caught her off guard. Had anyone ever been angry on her behalf? His chest rose and fell on a breath drawn sharply in through his nostrils and then slowly exhaled, though she could not see that it calmed him at all. "So he—"

"Burned it." She spoke across him before slipping out from beneath his glower to sit on the awful sofa. "In his defense, it *was* a rather shocking bit of prose. Fortunately, I kept another copy hidden under a loose floorboard in my room. When I reached London, the first publisher I spoke with told me it ought to have stayed on the ash heap. Such a scene could not possibly be included in any book that was meant to be purchased by circulating libraries."

"And you passed that advice on to Robin Ratliff, did you?" He pushed himself away from the desk and came to join her, settling into the leather chair as if it had been made for him.

It was her turn to laugh, a trifle wryly. "I did. But Robin Ratliff opted not to take it. Fortunately, Persephone Press paid well for the book, all the same."

With a nod, he leaned forward, resting his elbows on his knees. "Are there others who have been...troubled by your work? Not just ordinary critics. How many letters...?"

She glanced toward the desk. "Like that one? None. I've never—" Further words caught in her throat as he rose and retrieved the parchment, then returned to the chair and held it in front of him. She wanted it to swat it from his grip before its poison seeped into his fingertips. "I suppose," she managed, "over the years, there have been a score of good folks who've written to me or to Mr. Canfield to complain that my novels were frivolous trash or that their daughters were useless while under a particular book's spell. I'd never read one that truly troubled me until yesterday. And until tonight, I've never felt...afraid."

"One can't help but be alarmed at the sight of something like this," he said matter-of-factly. He turned the paper this way and that, so that the firelight caught the raised edges of the many jagged lines of type, ripped from their proper places and glued together to create something new and altogether terrible. "The one who wrote this wanted to frighten you as much with the form of the letter as with the words themselves. The apparent madness required to create such a thing, the attempt to remain utterly anonymous...it chills the blood. Quite deliberately."

It was, she supposed, some comfort to know her reaction had been neither unexpected nor overdramatic. "But that's not all," she insisted. "Turn it over. Look at the direction. Robin Ratliff has never received a single piece of post at Dunnock Castle. But this p-person knows th-that he—I mean, *I*—"

With his free hand, Thomas caught hers in a firm, reassuring grip. His fingers were warm—or rather, hers were as cold as ice, though she hadn't realized it until that moment. "He knows less that he thinks he does. For one thing, he believes himself to be addressing a man, not Jane Quayle."

"And if he comes bursting through that door," she demanded, glancing over her shoulder, "will it matter?"

He squeezed her fingers until she returned her gaze to him. "It might."

Of course, she'd wanted him to say *yes*, to insist that she was perfectly safe. And yet, there was a comfort in his honesty, something that made her willing to trust him despite the secrets he'd kept.

"You said 'attempt'—that this sort of a letter was an *attempt* to remain anonymous. Does that mean the attempt might fail?"

As he studied the document once more, he lifted one shoulder, twisted his neck as if to stretch it. But he never let go of her hand. "You must understand that others are far better at this than I. It requires an eye for detail." He underlined a string of words with his thumbnail. "See the shape of the letters, the little break in the top of the *o*? That will have come from a specific press. The idea is to determine which papers and magazines were used, in order to narrow down the suspect's location. If the newsprint matches the *London Times*, we haven't much to go on, but if it's the *Bristol Mercury* or the *Edinburgh Gazette*, we've got at least some idea of the part of the country it was sent from."

But she wasn't looking at the letter. She was looking once more at him, remembering what he'd said about certain valuable skills he'd acquired in the military. Surely, the ability to identify obscure newsprint wasn't often required of ordinary soldiers.

If, on the other hand, one had spent the last seven years or more doing something extraordinary...

"What was it you said you did in the army? *Beachcombing*, wasn't it? I shouldn't think that would involve decoding many cryptic letters..."

The paper in his hand crinkled ominously, but he did not actually crumple it in his fist, as she'd feared he might. He was looking neither at the letter nor at her, but at the floor. "We'll both be better off if I don't answer that question. At least, not now. Every soldier's work is dangerous, but the more I reveal about mine, the less likely it is I'll ever be able to return to it. And surely"—he turned to her and smiled, though it did not reach his eyes—"you don't want me stuck at Dunnock forever?"

He didn't intend to stay in Balisaig? He wanted to return to the army?

She tried to tell herself this was good news. She would not be turned out of another home. But having lived here for years, she knew how desperately Dunnock and Balisaig needed better management. Leadership. And in truth—though it was not an entirely comfortable realization—she still cared enough for him that she would rather know he was here than putting himself in danger on the other side of the world.

"Of course not," she managed to agree, forcing lightness into her voice. "Even in a sprawling castle, Lord Magnus would surely run athwart Robin Ratliff now and again."

His answering laugh was derisive, humorless. He brushed his thumb across her knuckles, squeezed her fingertips, and then released her hand, which had only just begun to feel warm. "Don't. Please."

"Don't call you by your title? But you're the earl."

Those words sent him to his feet, his gaze focused on the door to the stairwell, which he had not closed. "I'm the son of a Glasgow schoolmaster and the simple Highlands lass he met on a walking tour. More important, I'm a lieutenant in His Majesty's army. I canna..."

The unfinished sentence hung on the air between them.

"You cannot?" she asked finally. "Or will not?"

His eyes shifted to take in the rest of the room, and all it represented. "This was not a decision I ever thought to be asked to make. What I have been, and what I am now expected to become, seem to me to be at odds."

"More like two sides of the same coin," she corrected gently. "Both cannot be uppermost at once, of course, unless you intend to stay balanced forever on the thinnest edge—a precarious position, to be sure. But a man with your history, your education, your experience seems to me to be precisely what Dunnock requires."

"My history," he scoffed. "Aye, the people hereabouts remember me as a mischievous lad. They willna—"

She, of all people, could speak with confidence on the character of Balisaig's citizens. "They will. In time."

His skeptical expression did not budge. "Well, in the meantime, I think I'd best stick to what I do best. Let's go over the letter. Together." He thrust it toward her. "Tell me what you notice."

After the slightest hesitation, she took the paper in a surprisingly steady hand. At first, the jumble of words swam before her eyes. Some sympathetic chord within her echoed his words: *I cannot.* But he obviously needed a distraction too. So she would do it. For him.

"Here," she said, jabbing at the paper with her forefinger and holding it out to him again. "This phrase is from the *Monthly Review.* 'Stupid and sickly prose'—I remember that. The nicest thing their reviewer said about *The Necromancer's Bride.*"

Thomas's brow darkened as he reread the phrase. "Tasteless hack," he muttered beneath his breath.

"Yes, I think he might have called me that too," she agreed with something like a laugh. "Oh, don't bother being offended on my behalf. The real victory was in infiltrating their hallowed pages at all. Don't you see? The popularity of *my* book forced the *Monthly Review* to acknowledge the existence of gothic novels. It is, perhaps, my favorite review of all."

With a mixture of amazement and amusement animating his features, Thomas shook his head. "Then we know the person who composed this note reads your reviews."

"So it would seem. And this bit here, 'shocking and scandalous, unfit for innocent eyes,' that's the *Critical Review.* Mr. Canfield had to print more copies, the book sold so well after that notice."

"And the newsprint here?" he asked eagerly, sitting down beside her. "Do you recognize it?"

"I can't be sure." Focusing on each individual scrap from which the letter had been constructed was far easier than taking in the whole. Still, Thomas's proximity—the heat of his body where it almost touched her side as together they held the letter and studied it, the mingled scents of his cologne and the damp wool of his greatcoat and the sweet spice of spilled tea—was itself a powerful lure. "What about these longer strips, the ones that call me a 'vile procurer doomed to hellfire' and the like? The paper's different."

"From a book, I'd say." He paused. "Odd. It's one thing to cut up a ha'penny broadsheet to make his point. But costly quarterlies? Books? Whoever wrote this must be a man of some means."

"Or a lunatic," she pointed out. "And why 'he'? Are you so sure this must have come from a man?"

"No, I can't be certain," he reluctantly admitted. "I suppose it's little consolation to you to know that if it was written by a woman, she's somewhat less likely to make good on this threat to 'carve your sinful words into your flesh with a quill.'"

Another laugh shuddered from Jane's chest. "Oh, a *very* little consolation, I should say. I myself can never seem to get a quill to stay sharp for more than a page or two. I hope he will at least share his secret."

At that bit of macabre humor, Thomas's eyes dropped shut, though a thin smile curved his lips. "I think it's time we called it a night." Even when he opened his eyes again, he did not look at her, but at the letter, which he folded carefully and tucked in the breast pocket of his greatcoat. "I'll make sure everything is locked up tight," he said, rising, "and that Dougan is on the alert. The dogs—"

"They might better stay with Mrs. Murdoch," she suggested. "She's all alone."

He froze. "And what about you?"

Tonight, she had pushed him to confront his fears. Perhaps it was time for her to confront her own. But what was it she feared?

Wanting him? Needing him?

Or losing him? Again.

She was used to being alone. But tired, so very tired, of being lonely.

She tipped her head slightly, in the way she did when she had a challenge to master. "I want you to stay with me tonight, Thomas." The invitation itself was only slightly more shocking to her than calling him by his given name. But it would be entirely incorrect for her to call him Mr. Sutherland now, and she had no desire to wound him with the title he so reluctantly bore. "That way, I'm sure to come to no harm."

Just last night, they had faced one another for the first time in seven years. How much had changed. And how little. The very air between them seemed to crackle.

"Jane." A whisper. A plea. His gaze darted past her, toward the door to her bedchamber. At last, he gave a curt nod. "All right. I'll stand watch here in the sitting room. But do me the kindness of leaving a blanket on that godawful sofa," he said, tugging up the collar of his greatcoat as he turned to leave. "And lock your chamber door."

The heat of anticipation melted into a cold ball of uncertainty in her stomach as she watched him duck beneath the lintel and disappear. Disappointed, she dropped her gaze to the floor.

In passing, her eyes caught the gleam of firelight over her silk banyan, saw the ink stains on her fingers. In spite of herself, a small smile rose to her lips. No, those had not been the parting words she'd longed to hear from him.

Fortunately, Robin Ratliff knew how to manage a reluctant hero.

Chapter 14

After discovering that the outer bailey was already well-secured, Thomas debated with himself before deciding to wake Dougan to tell him that someone might mean Mrs. Higginbotham ill. No point in bringing Ratliff's name into the discussion, and anyway, the old man seemed to have a soft spot for Jane. Despite his supposedly weak understanding, he latched quickly onto Thomas's words.

"Keep the gate locked? No one in or out? Aye, lad. Nowt'll harm Mrs. Higginbotham on my watch."

Thomas thanked the man and then returned to his own quarters, where he drew his knife from its hiding place in the bottom of his trunk and slipped it into the hidden sheath in the shaft of his boot. Arming himself against an unseen enemy was so familiar as to be almost soothing, but not at all what he had expected to find himself doing at Dunnock.

Then again, what *had* he expected?

He thought of what she had told him. For the first time, he considered the possibility that every moment in his life had been leading to this one. The threads of his life certainly had twisted themselves into a Gordian knot, impossible to unravel. Was he to take his blade and slice through the whole mess? But Jane—dear Jane, more sure of himself than he was, despite her own welter of worries—was part of the tangle, a tie that bound his past and present.

In the sitting room, he made a cursory attempt at straightening the mess he'd made earlier. On the floor lay volume three of *The Necromancer's Bride*.

I suppose you want to know what happens next?

God, yes. Why had she asked him to come back? Why had he agreed?

He could tell himself it was because she needed protection, and it was his duty to provide it. But that wasn't the whole truth. They wanted something dangerous from one another too.

The memory of a kiss had nearly driven him mad for seven years. What might happen if he were to be plagued by the memory of something more?

A shudder passed through him, longing and lust, and with them, something that might have been a flicker of hope. Or a foreshadowing of pain.

A smart man would plan some other entertainment for this interminable night. With a grimace, he picked up the book, slipped it into his pocket, and set about dousing the candles.

Once through the inner bailey, he made sure all was tightly latched and locked behind him, then set out to look for Mrs. Murdoch's room. He might have wandered for some time if not for Aphrodite and Athena, who began to howl as soon as his footsteps grew near. Perhaps they were better guard dogs than he'd given them credit for.

The door to Mrs. Murdoch's sitting room flew open. "Who's there?"

"'Tis I, ma'am. Forgive me. I only—"

"I might've guessed." With a shake of her head, she retreated into the room, and Thomas followed. It was a cozy space, almost filled by a pair of chairs with wine-colored upholstery sitting on either side of a high-polished walnut worktable. A pierced-tin lamp sent its speckled glow across embroidered cushions, pale green walls, and on the table, Mrs. Murdoch's work basket and a book lying facedown, as if he'd interrupted her reading. A novel, by its cover. One of Jane's?

The housekeeper reached into her pocket and tossed some small morsels to the dogs to quiet them. "Cheese parings," she explained as she wiped her hands on her apron. "Works a charm, but you wouldna want to sleep downwind of 'em after, if you catch my meanin'."

In spite of his grim mood, he found himself choking down a laugh. "Good to know." The dogs were watching him almost as warily as Mrs. Murdoch. True to her promise, however, they sat and were quiet. "I'm sorry to disturb you, but Mrs. Higginbotham asked me to tell you to keep the lassies with you tonight."

Mrs. Murdoch drew her chin to her chest, exuding skepticism. "How's that? Keep them here?" Her nose wrinkled, perhaps remembering her own recommendation of moments before.

"She's had some distressing news. That's why she sent for me tonight," he said, reluctantly reminding her of the note she'd delivered an hour before.

"Bad news? Should I go to her?" The dogs, hearing the anxiety in the woman's voice, strained forward, clearly wanting to hurry to her side.

"Please, ma'am. Let her rest. Keep the dogs here. She'll sleep better without interruption." Though the pronouncement had been meant mostly for himself, he looked sternly from one dog to the other and back again. Athena's hackles rose, but Aphrodite lay down almost submissively on the housekeeper's rose-patterned rug.

Mrs. Murdoch's gray eyes passed over him, taking in his state of undress. "You're on your way back down to the gatehouse, I ken?"

As he intended, she took his departing bow for assent. Or pretended to.

"G'night, Mr. Sutherland."

"Good night, Mrs. Murdoch."

Taking care to move quietly, he once more crossed the Great Room and ascended the spiral stairs. The door to Jane's study creaked when he opened it, but inside all was quiet and very nearly dark. Little more than glowing ash remained of the day's fire, and the single candle she'd left for him had almost guttered.

By that feeble flame, he found another candle and lit it, then scouted the room's shadowy corners. Empty. To his shock, she'd actually gone to bed, just as he'd ordered.

And for that, he tried to persuade himself to feel grateful.

She'd left both blanket and pillow for him, but they did little to disguise the miserable night that awaited him on that sofa. He could lie with either his head or his feet upon it, but not both at once. After depositing the book beside the candle on a small table, he shed his greatcoat, took up the blanket, and attempted to make himself comfortable in the leather chair instead.

But not too comfortable. Although he considered it unlikely that anything would happen, it would not do to be caught sleeping while on watch. He reached for the book and drew the candle closer. Based on his experience this afternoon, the conclusion to the story would keep him wakeful for some hours.

Recalling Jane's insistence that he could not guess what happened next, he was not surprised to discover that the first chapter of volume three opened not where volume two had left off, but in the cottage with Ophelia's foster family, wracked by guilt—as perhaps Jane had sometimes longed to imagine her own family after she'd gone. Though Lord Ruthveyn's money was desperately needed, they realized they'd wronged the girl by sending her into a monster's lair. Gathering together a small band of their fellows, armed with pitchforks, scythes, and torches, they prepared for a daring rescue.

Meanwhile, in the library, Ophelia knelt at Ruthveyn's feet, eyes downcast, waiting. Thomas sank a little lower in the chair, the relaxed posture entirely at odds with the anticipation thrumming through him.

The library carpet, though plush enough underfoot, prickled her knees through the thin muslin of her gown. In the heavy silence, she wondered whether he could hear her heart pounding. Still, she did not lift her head, keeping her gaze focused on his pale, long-fingered hand where it gripped the rolled arm of the chair with surprising ferocity. She had angered him. Disappointed him.

After what seemed an eternity, the hand moved, the lace trim of his sleeve slipping languidly over his wrist, his gold signet ring winking in the light. Slowly, he reached forward until his fingertips settled over her throat, his touch cool, light, and maddening.

He paused there for a moment as if taking the measure of her pulse, then ascended to trace her jaw, at last lifting her face to his. The pad of his thumb he dragged over her mouth, tracing the plump curves. With dark, heavy-lidded eyes, he eagerly watched the movement of his own hand. Willingly, she parted her lips for him.

"That's very pretty, my dear." His voice was hoarse, far rougher than his touch. "Very pretty indeed."

At the muffled grate of a key in a lock, Thomas jerked upright from his slouch and once more dropped the book.

Jane took three hesitant steps into the room. "Oh, it's you." Three steps farther, more sure-footed than the first, until she stopped before him. "I couldn't sleep."

Competing instincts warred within him. Stand up in the presence of a lady. Stay sitting so she might not see the telltale bulge in his breeches.

He wanted to blame the damned book for his condition. But equally responsible was the sight of Jane, her luscious curves painted by the candlelight, barely disguised beneath her nightgown. Wisps of hair had worked loose from the braid to caress her cheek, her jaw, her throat. For a moment, he wondered whether he had not, in fact, fallen asleep while reading and conjured this vision in his dreams.

Well, whether real or a product of his fevered imagination, if she took two more steps forward and dropped to her knees before him, he'd spill in his smallclothes, and that was that.

Jane, of course, did no such thing.

She crossed her arms over her chest, hiding her pert nipples from his view. "I wasn't sure you'd come."

He couldn't fault her skepticism; whether by leaving Tenchley so abruptly all those years ago, or seeking to hide his identity and the real reason he'd come to Dunnock, he'd given her ample cause to doubt him.

To calm his ill-timed ardor, he drew a deep breath and shifted his position in the chair, casting about for something to think of other than Jane's lightly clad figure. Something chilling. Sleet and snow and...*that horrible letter.*

For the merest moment, he'd forgotten the real reason she'd wanted him here. But, of course, *she* hadn't. The candlelight cast into sharp relief a furrow of worry etched across her brow.

In one fluid motion, he rose, snatched up the blanket, and draped it around her shoulders, then ushered her to the seat he'd vacated, closest to the fire.

"I told you I'd be back." He reached for the poker to stir the embers before adding more fuel.

"I meant earlier. When I sent the note." Out of the corner of his eye, he saw her watching him. Then she dropped her gaze to the floor, and her voice fell with it. "I wasn't certain you'd answer."

"You needn't have made it out to be Robin Ratliff's bidding." Dusting off his hands, he turned toward her again. "Surely ye ken I'd come at yours?"

She shook off the suggestion. "I don't know anything of the sort."

Boldly, he stepped into the path of her almost-vacant stare, forcing her to lift her eyes up, up to his face. "Well, now you do."

A flush—of pleasure, or so he thought—lit her cheeks. She fidgeted with the trim of the blanket where it lay against her breast, then seemed to recall he'd placed it there and tucked her fingers beneath her thighs to keep them more firmly under her control.

He held out one hand, palm up. "Up you get, lass. It's verra late, and you should be in bed."

"I'm not a child," she insisted, though the twist of her lips might fairly be described as a pout.

Eventually, however, she extracted one hand and laid it in his. With a playful tug, he brought her to her feet—and flush against his body.

He hadn't meant to do it, not really. A momentary shift in balance, a slight miscalculation of momentum. Nevertheless, there she was, delightfully warm and deliciously soft and in his arms again.

She gave a soft gasp, not quite an *oh!*, as if the collision might not have been entirely a surprise to her, but the resulting sensations were. Still, she did not pull away.

And he, God help him, did not immediately let her go. "Nay," he agreed on a whisper. "You're all woman. But if I'm to protect you, we canna—"

"Cannot? Or will not?" she said again. Once more the palm of her free hand settled possessively against his chest. Over his heart. "I think you're worried that if something happens between us tonight, you'd be taking advantage of me. Because I'm a lady, and you're a gentleman. Because you're the fierce Scottish warrior, and I'm the damsel in distress. Because you're the lord of the manor, and I'm your humble tenant."

Some ineffectual protest rose to his lips, but she cut him off before words could form.

"Have you forgotten, I write scandalous books?" The tip of her index finger was tracing a provocative pattern beneath his collarbone, and he had a sudden flash of the magic those fingers would work elsewhere... "They've made me obscenely wealthy." She tipped her head and looked up at him from beneath a fringe of dark lashes. "I've been self-sufficient for a very long time."

Self-sufficient. God forgive him, but he did not think she referred only to financial matters. It would be the end of his resolve to let himself imagine those wicked fingers of hers slipping between her own thighs...but he hadn't much resolve left anyway. He'd also been, ahem, *self-sufficient* for a very long time. Too damn long.

At his hesitation, she snagged her lower lip between her teeth and searched his face with wide eyes. It struck him as something a character in a novel would do, the sort of gesture Ophelia might have made to ensnare Ruthveyn. An innocent's notion of seduction.

But this wasn't one of Jane's books.

He ran the palm of one hand up her arm to cup the side of her head, then tugged her lip free with his thumb. "Tell me, in this plot you've concocted for us, what happens in the next chapter?"

"Well," she began in a more familiar voice, as if what she proposed was eminently practical, though her cheeks grew a brighter shade of pink, "if we give in to what's distracting us tonight, I should hope that we'll wake with clearer heads on the morrow. Once we can focus properly, we should be able to sort out who's been writing those ridiculous letters."

Should he tell her it wasn't likely to work that way, on either count? Unless he showed himself, the letter writer's identity would probably remain a mystery. And succumbing to the attraction between them wouldn't be like snuffing a candle, as she seemed to imagine. At least, not for him.

More like lighting a fuse.

Then again, perhaps she understood the dilemma perfectly. "In just a few days," she continued, "one or the other of us is going to leave Dunnock. Either I'll stay and go on being Robin Ratliff, or you'll stay and become Lord Magnus."

Surely there was another option? Another choice they could make?

The thought skittered away when her hand slipped downward, stopping once more over his pounding heart. "In all this time, neither of us has forgotten a simple kiss. Do you want to spend the next seven years, the next twenty-seven years, wondering what more than a kiss would've been like between us?"

God, no.

In some distant part of his brain, he knew he ought to answer her in words, and better ones than those. Preferably something romantic and flowery.

What he chose instead was a kiss. But this time, not a sweet, gentle kiss. A deep, demanding kiss.

The kind that could last a man twenty-seven years, if it had to.

One hand still cradling the side of her face, he brought his lips to hers, so eager he feared she might back away. Instead, she took another step closer, fitting her curves to his jutting angles. He moved his mouth over hers, hungrily at first, then slowly, reveling in her marvelous combination of suppleness and firmness, coaxing her to kiss him back. Finally, he dared to tease the seam of her lips with his tongue until she parted them and he could taste her sweetness once more.

If he broke the kiss, he knew he would regret it. Some of the blood that had departed his brain would return, and he would recall what a terrible idea this was. Years from now, he would think of this night and remember there was a moment when he could have been kissing her still and had stopped, and he would curse himself and the universe to boot.

So he went on kissing her, until he was breathless and she was too. Until her fingers curled in the fabric of his shirt and her other arm wrapped itself around his waist. Until he felt his feet move and realized he was guiding her—or she was leading him—toward her chamber, in the awkward first steps of a dance each was eager to learn.

Only when his foot struck something hard did he pause. She broke away enough to fix him with a wary glower and parted her lips to counter whatever feeble caution he might be planning to utter. Then she followed his gaze to the floor, where the third volume of *The Necromancer's Bride* lay, abused and abandoned.

One corner of her mouth kicked up. "Were you planning to bring it to bed? A bit of light reading to pass the time?"

He leaned toward her for a nip of a kiss, nudging her toward the bedchamber with his thigh. "I expect I'll have all the entertainment I need tonight."

It was her turn to stumble. Just a little. Before he could catch her, she'd already righted herself, taken another step. But a shadow of uncertainty had flickered into her eyes. "Thomas?"

He rocked back on his heels. "What, lass?"

Her gaze rose no higher than where his cravat should have been. "I should tell you that most of what I've written was merely a product of my imagination. I didn't have the benefit of, er, firsthand information."

"I can't say as I'm surprised," he said, not quite sure where the conversation was heading. "I didn't really expect you to have personal acquaintance with a dark magician who might have murdered his betrothed."

At that feeble witticism, a frown notched her brow. Suddenly, he understood. To the world, she was either scandalous Robin Ratliff or the widowed Mrs. Higginbotham, a woman perforce of some experience. She was trying to remind him that she was also still the innocent Miss Quayle he'd first met.

"Dinna ye ken, lass?" he whispered, dropping a soft kiss on her temple. "When it comes to lovemaking, imagination is the most important bit of all."

For a moment, she looked as if she weren't quite sure whether to believe him. Then her lips curved in an answering smile, just a trifle wicked. She picked up the candlestick and darted through the bedchamber door, dragging him behind her.

Chapter 15

He was still looking at her with that easy, mischievous grin when she released his hand and took a step away from him to set the candlestick on the nightstand. After turning the key in the lock, he crossed his arms before him to grab either side of his shirt and tugged it the rest of the way free from the band of his breeches. In one fluid motion, he slipped the tea-stained garment over his head and tossed it away.

From the waist up at least, every inch of him was as tanned as what she'd already glimpsed, and warmed now by the glow of candlelight. Either he'd had a habit of going about half naked, or the tropical sun had been strong enough to brown a man's skin right through the fabric of his shirt. The dark, curling hair on his chest grew in a diamond shape, thickest across his breastbone, then tapering to a thin line that disappeared into his breeches, like the tail of a kite.

She wouldn't let her gaze drop any lower. His lean, muscled arms and chest were quite enough to be going on with. She wanted to run her fingertips over every inch of skin he'd revealed, even the long, thin scar near his ribs, a reminder of the dangers he'd already survived. Wanted to rub her cheek against that silky hair and breathe in the manly scent of him. Wanted to...

"Turn about's fair play, lass," he murmured, and when she raised her eyes to his face, his eyebrows lifted suggestively. The knowing warmth behind his gaze made her press her thighs together, the movement thankfully hidden by the loose fit of her gown.

With a catch of breath, she let the blanket around her shoulders slip to the floor, then raised one hand to the ribbon that gathered the neck of her nightgown. She looked down at her fingers, tangled in the narrow silk. "I don't...Shouldn't we douse the candle?"

"Now, what would be the fun in that?"

He'd let her look. Now he wanted to see. Fair play, just as he'd said. Still she hesitated. Though he'd tried to hide it, she'd seen the state Thomas had been in while reading of fair, delicate Ophelia's willing submission to Lord Ruthveyn. "I—I'm afraid I don't look anything like the heroine of a Robin Ratliff novel."

Had more ridiculous words ever been uttered? Anyone could see she was...

Her mind cast around for a word, something other than *ample*, after their conversation earlier that day. *Sturdy* had been Mama's favored description of her daughter's frame, when she was feeling generous. A dressmaker had once called her *plump*, like a Christmas goose.

Thomas stepped toward her, reached for the ribbon—no, for her hand. His warm fingers encircled hers, not to urge her on, but to stay her fidgeting movement. "'Tis not looks that make a heroine, Jane. 'Tis spirit, and strength of mind, and bravery. All those you have." With one finger, he lifted her chin so she could not avoid his eyes. "And more."

Spirit. Bravery. Yes, she could do this. She wanted this. Beneath his light touch, she wound the ribbon around her index finger and slipped the knot free. With a bit of tugging and coaxing, the neckline of the garment loosened enough to slide over her shoulders, then lower. Over breasts entirely too full to suit the latest fashions. Over her soft, fleshy belly. Down dimpled thighs, and onto the floor.

When Thomas backed away from her, her eyes fell shut, and her heart hammered in her chest. No, she wasn't brave. She wasn't spirited. How could she have been so—?

"Turn around."

That growled command made her skin prickle, though not with fear. Slowly, carefully so as not to tangle her feet in her nightgown, she spun until she was facing away from him.

In the beat of silence that followed, she hugged her arms to her chest and tried not to imagine what he must he be thinking.

But it was impossible to forget what he'd told her before, about the day they'd first met. When she'd been so saucy as to favor him with her backside. And he'd...

"I'll not deny there's lads who like a slender lass." His whispered voice had not lost its rough edge. "But a writer such as yourself would do well to remember that not all heroes are alike." As he spoke, he moved closer, though still not touching her. "Not every man has an appetite that's satisfied by dainties." She shivered at the warmth radiating from his body. "I, for one, prefer a feast."

When he trailed a string of hot kisses along the curve of her shoulder, the prickle of his beard rough against her soft skin, her shiver turned into a shudder of longing. "What is it you want tonight, Jane?" His manhood nudged against her bottom, as if seeking an answer.

Strength of mind, he'd claimed she had. But in that moment, her thoughts were a jumble. The wildest flights of her imagination. Naughty pictures from a book she'd once stumbled upon—her first foray into "research" for one of her novels. Urges both new and familiar coursing through her blood and tingling in that hidden spot at the juncture of her thighs.

Then, in a flash, all of those trembling desires and heady fantasies coalesced into one. One urgent, primal need. "I—I want—" Her chest heaved with the effort of forming words. "I want you to hold me. Please—just hold me."

She would have spun to face him, but his arms came around her before she could move. She sagged against his strength, absorbed the sensation of his skin against hers. The hair on his chest tickled against her back as their ragged breaths rose and fell together. His lips settled on the crown of her head and did not move.

If she'd thought about it, she would have expected a man in this position to try to cup her breast, or even her mound. They were all but naked in her bedchamber, where she'd invited him, after all, and the evidence of his own desire was still pressed urgently against the small of her back.

But Thomas seemed to know that this was not yet the time for such intimacies. That, in this moment, what she needed was simply what she'd asked for: the feel of his arms around her. The human contact she'd so long denied herself. The care and understanding she'd always been denied.

How long they stood in that posture she could never afterward have said. Nor was she sure who moved first. But, eventually, she turned in the circle of his embrace, raised her arms to wrap them around his neck, brushed the aching tips of her breasts across the crisp hair of his chest. And he splayed one hand between her shoulder blades to draw her closer, rubbed lazy circles over her bottom with his other palm, and kissed her.

If their kiss before had been bruising, this was the balm, the gentle caress of lips willing to part for the pure pleasure of coming together again. When his tongue teased, she met it with the shy touch of her own, as they tasted one another's sighs and drank one another's breath. Need was coursing through her body, but she held it at bay, because she wanted these playful sensations too. Wanted everything this night could give her.

And more.

Oh, God.

Her heart leaped in her chest, like a startled doe desperate for freedom. More? Was she making a terrible mistake? What if she didn't wake up satisfied? What if she woke up aching? Every morning for the rest of her life...

She must have stiffened or pulled away or made some sound. Thomas stopped kissing her and looked down. One brow arched. "Jane?"

If she hesitated, she was lost. She tightened her fingers in the curls at his nape. "I need you, Thomas," she said, her voice remarkably cool and Mrs. Higginbotham-ish, betraying—she hoped—no trace of her desperation. "Take me to bed."

At those words, the old grin slid into place, and the dimple appeared on his cheek. She could almost forget what she'd glimpsed in his eyes. "I've never been one for following orders," he said. "But for you, I'll make an exception."

He released her long enough for her to clamber onto the high bed and settle between the luxurious linens, while he tugged off his boots and then went to work on the fall of his breeches.

His back was to her when he finally shed them entirely, and she was treated to a view of the paler globes of his bottom and the taut muscles of his thighs, dusted with dark hair. So the sun hadn't touched him everywhere?

Then he turned, and she saw all of him. As he walked toward her, his manhood bobbed, rigid and dark with need. The sight of it was both exciting and a little alarming. She was tempted to avert her gaze, but she couldn't bear the thought of wasting even a moment of this experience on shyness. He paused a few feet away to slick a hand over his length, somehow teasing her with it and offering it to her all at once. "Is there room in there for me, lass?"

She swallowed hard and nodded. Her head was full once more of decadent fantasies and illicit etchings, poses she'd doubted were humanly possible. One night to discover whether she'd been wrong.

But again what she wanted most was so utterly conventional, no doubt dull to a man who'd led a life like Thomas's. To lie on her back with her legs spread, to take him deep within her body, to bear his weight...

She shivered a little as he flipped back the covers and his knee pressed into the mattress as he prepared to climb into bed. When he was lying on his side beside her, and she could feel his heat from her shoulders to her knees, she began to shake in earnest.

"Cold?"

He reached for the blanket, but she shook her head. "I—I suppose I'm just a little nervous. I thought you would"—one hand flailed in a vague half circle—"you know, come on top and, um…"

He chuckled a little and shook his head. "It will be my very great pleasure, when the time comes. But ladies first."

With deft fingers, he undid the ribbon that finished her braid, then slipped each section free until her hair was loose and lay against her bare skin in cool, sensual waves. His fingertips stroked along her scalp, massaging away what felt like years' worth of tension. "Better? Now roll this way, just a bit."

She let him arrange her so that they were nestled together, her back leaning against his front. The position was reminiscent of the way he'd held her before, one arm cradling her head, the other encircling her waist. But this time his hands played over her skin, his touch at first light, then more determined. In her ear, his whispered voice poured a steady stream of praise as he dismantled every doubt she could have about her appeal.

"Like a work of art," he murmured, tracing a line from just above her knee, over the swell of her hip, to her round belly. "So soft. And when a man's hard, it's softness he craves, ye ken." His shaft, nestled in the cove beneath her bottom, nodded its agreement.

Then his questing hand rose to cup each breast in turn, and his groan of pleasure vibrated through her. "Ah, lass, shall I confess how I've dreamed of these, wondered over the shape and color of your nipples? But my imagination didna do you justice."

Until that moment, she'd been generally displeased by the rosy brown color of her areola, which were too large to easily be hidden by the shallow bodices currently in fashion. But as his thumb slipped back and forth over that petal-soft skin, until the edges crinkled and her nipples grew to stout peaks, she began to see the advantages of their size and shape. When he gently pinched her nipples between his second and third finger, she could not help but moan. When he pinched them harder, she found herself lifting her chest to his hand, seeking that glorious pleasure-pain. When he promised to suck them until she screamed, her whole body stiffened and shuddered.

"Perhaps not quite so self-sufficient after all, eh?" he teased.

Shock flared in her chest. Had he really thought that earlier she'd been referring to…*self-pleasuring*? Ordinarily she would have tried to claim she didn't know what he meant. Why, she would never!

Well, only rarely...

His hand slid down her body to toy with her nether curls. "If you're ready to come, then, open for me," he urged, and whatever denial she'd been poised to make evaporated in her throat. He eased her thighs apart, draping one of her legs over his so she lay spread to his touch. "Ah, that's it, lass. So wet. So eager."

As his fingers slicked through her folds, she squirmed against him, for at first he determinedly skirted her nub, then circled it with tormenting gentleness. "Please." She could manage no more than a hoarse whisper.

His lazy smile curved against her shoulder. "Since you ask so sweetly." Focusing his touch on the center of her pleasure, he quickly brought her to shattering release, still murmuring words of praise in her ear.

Boneless, she could do no more than make a soft mewl of protest as he extracted his arm and eased her back on the bed. Too soon for him to go, too soon to be left bereft of his touch, his heat. But to her relief, he levered himself over her, parting her thighs with his. His kiss was rougher, hungrier, and before she had stirred herself to respond to it, his lips and tongue were making their way down her throat to her breasts, sucking until she felt her need rising again.

Following a last lash of his tongue, he sat upright and watched himself run his work-roughened palms up the insides of her thighs where they lay open against his, his phallus rising between them. His thumbs skated back and forth along either side of her mound, where the skin was thin and delicate. She had never dreamed of anyone looking at her there, to say nothing of looking at her with such unvarnished lust in his face. Even she could not deny that he liked what he saw.

"If we had more time, I'd kiss you here. And here. 'Til you came for me again." The pad of his thumb slid once more over her nub, making her jerk. She couldn't pretend to be shocked at the notion, couldn't pretend she wasn't curious about the magic his mouth would perform.

Distraction, if she'd wanted such a thing, came in the form of one long finger slipping inside her, soon joined by a second. "But since it's just to be one night..." Her eyelids dropped almost closed when he took himself in hand and slicked his—*cock*, that shocking book had called it, though the word made her blush, then and now—through her wetness.

She'd expected some discomfort when he entered her, and it was a bit of a stretch at first. But she was still pliant and soft from her release, and her body welcomed his hardness, just as he'd said it would. Once they were joined, he came over her as she'd asked, caging her head and shoulders in his arms, tangling their fingers together, kissing her mouth, her jaw, her forehead. When he thrust, the hair on his chest teased her nipples and made them tingle again, and sooner than she would have thought possible, she was straining for another peak, lifting her hips to meet him, relishing his strength as he drove her down into the bed again.

Too soon, his rhythm grew ragged, and the breath began to saw from his lungs in uneven gasps. With a strangled cry, he jerked from her just as she began to clench around him. His seed spurted onto her belly, and he collapsed half on top of her. She squeezed her eyes shut and tried to imprint every last detail of the experience on her memory, the scent of sweat on his skin, the weight of his body pressing her into the mattress, the wet heat and pleasant ache that were the remnants of their passion.

Later she would tuck her newfound knowledge away in the dark drawer where such memories belonged. But for now she listened to the longcase clock in the study chime two and wondered whether it would be so very wrong to rouse him and do it again.

Chapter 16

At first, Thomas wasn't sure what had woken him. With some difficulty, he levered himself onto his side in the plush bed and scanned the room. Sunrise? No, well past. Though the windows were high and narrow here, as everywhere else in the castle, they faced east. Light flooded the room and made him blink drowsily and rub his eyes.

Beside him, Jane slept on, her back turned toward him, her hair strewn across the pillows. One pale, plump shoulder peeked from beneath the covers, tempting him to trace its curve with his fingertips. God, but she was so beautifully sensual. Three times he'd taken her last night—twice more than he'd intended and thrice more than he ought—and still his ungrateful cock had woken hard and eager. His hand moved, almost involuntarily, to touch her.

But no, he cautioned himself, forcing himself to lean back into his pillow and close his eyes. They'd spoken only of one night. And it was most definitely morning.

He didn't think he'd drifted off, but the sound of voices—a pair of them, at least, and one of them agitated—came from the sitting room and jerked him to wakefulness again. Was that what had disturbed him before? He glanced at the door; thankfully, the key was still in the lock. Probably just Esme, chattering to herself as she swept the hearth.

Before his body had begun to relax again, the door to the bedchamber shuddered in its frame as if struck. He sat bolt upright. From the sitting room came another muffled but urgent-sounding exchange.

"Jane!" he laid his hand on that tempting shoulder to jostle her as he spoke softly but sharply near her ear. "Wake up! I think someone's trying to break down the door."

Shoving hair from her face, she scrambled upright and clutched the sheets to her chest, evidently startled as much to find herself sharing her bed as by the news he'd imparted. "Wha—what did you say?"

But he had no need to repeat himself, for at that moment, something again rammed into the door, followed by a low moan and more scolding. And then a voice spoke near enough to the keyhole that the words could be clearly heard. "Och, Dougan, get up wit' ye, ye worthless lump. Mrs. Higginbotham, canna you hear me? Oh, what am I t' do?"

"Mrs. Murdoch." He and Jane spoke as one, and he felt sure it must be his imagination, but Jane looked...*amused.*

Whether or not she found the housekeeper's attempt to barge in upon them entertaining, she scrambled from the bed to put a stop to it. Thomas caught no more than a glimpse of her naked curves before she snatched up her dressing gown from a bench at the foot of the bed and slipped it on.

"You'll have to hide yourself," she urged, gathering up his clothes and boots and shoving them in his direction, "while I try to sort out what the devil has gotten into Agnes. In the wardrobe," she added impatiently, pointing toward that ancient piece of furniture while he was still searching for the doorway to a dressing room or the like. "There's nowhere else you'll fit."

Fit was overstating the case, for though the wardrobe was both tall and deep, it was also full of Jane's clothes, both mourning gowns and many others in brighter and paler shades, perhaps from before the time she had donned her Mrs. Higginbotham disguise. No chance of slipping into his breeches while hidden inside; try as he might, he couldn't even close both doors behind him.

The narrow gap between the doors did have an advantage, however. It allowed him to watch as Jane marched with surprising calm to the chamber door, twisted the key, and flung it open. Dougan, who had evidently been primed for another assault on the stout panel, came barging into the room instead, head lowered, and tumbled onto the floor.

Sweet Jane hurried to the man's side and bent to lay a hand on his shoulder. "Are you all right, Dougan? Have you hurt yourself?"

"An' if he has, 'tis no more than his duty," declared Mrs. Murdoch from the doorway. Aphrodite and Athena darted past her and began to sniff their mistress anxiously. "Gracious, Mrs. Higginbotham, what a fright you've given us."

"Fright? I don't—"

"It's not like you to lock the door, ma'am. Are ye feelin' poorly? I knocked and called for a quarter of an hour, and when you didn't answer,

I went to fetch Dougan. It's nearly ten, and I couldn't think what…" She shook her head in evident distress. "And then, o' course, there's the state of the rooms…"

"Rooms?" Jane echoed again, absently patting an agitated Aphrodite before she rose. "What rooms? Will one of you please tell me what is going on?"

"When Esme took Mr. Sutherland his breakfast," the housekeeper explained, a trifle impatiently, "she found the gatehouse empty and things in such upheaval—the tea tray overturned, and clothes thrown from his trunk—she feared something dreadful must have happened to 'im."

"I heard her scream." Dougan took up the story in his slow, methodical way. "Checked the bailey, just as he'd told me. No one in or out last night."

"Just as *who* had told you?"

"Mr. Sutherland," Mrs. Murdoch broke in. "Evidently he thought fit to warn Dougan that we might have an intruder at Dunnock. I wonder he didn't accord me the same courtesy."

"Well…" He heard the smile in Jane's voice, though he couldn't see her face. "Dougan *is* the guardsman."

Mrs. Murdoch's lips scrunched as if she'd bitten a lemon. "Be that as it may," she sniffed, "when I came up here to see that all was well, imagine my shock. Papers strewn about, a puddle of wax on the carpet, books on the floor…" She shuddered, a trifle theatrically to Thomas's way of thinking. So far as he recalled it was only one book. Surely, she'd seen worse messes than that? "I knew you'd never leave the study in such a state, ma'am. At least not willingly. An' then there's this." With a note of triumph in her voice, she produced her most damning piece of evidence: his battered greatcoat. "Mr. Sutherland's. Thrown behind a chair, it was. As if someone had aught to hide…"

"Mr. Ratliff received a threatening letter," Jane interjected smoothly, and he could not help but admire the calm in her voice as she plucked the garment from the housekeeper's bony fingers. "I was understandably alarmed. I worked late, but I asked Mr. Sutherland to keep watch last night, patrol the castle as it were. No doubt he came into the sitting room after I'd gone to bed, found things a mite, er, warm, and laid his coat aside."

Those words were rightly met with skepticism. No one had ever found any part of a castle in the Scottish Highlands in January "a mite warm."

Mrs. Murdoch's attention was quickly diverted by something else, however. "What's that you're fidgeting with, Dougan?" she demanded.

When Thomas realized what had caught her eye, he could no longer consider the distraction fortunate.

"Funny sort of a knife, innit?" Dougan held out the object. "Just lyin' there on the floor."

Instinctively, Thomas groped the boots he held. Empty. *Damn and blast.* The weapon must have fallen out when Jane had tossed his things to him, in the mad dash to hide all evidence of what had really transpired in that room.

"Mine." Jane reached out with her free hand and plucked the knife from Dougan's grasp. Thomas sucked in a breath, fearing one or both of them might slice off a few fingers in the exchange. But once more, Jane surprised him. Though he still could not see her face, he watched her handle the blade with surprising dexterity. "I thought it best to arm myself and lock my chamber door, under the circumstances."

Thomas relaxed, just a little. Dougan seemed entirely satisfied by Jane's explanations, and if the same could not be said for Mrs. Murdoch, she appeared ready to give up the interrogation for now, assured that Jane was at least temporarily safe. Gesturing impatiently at Dougan, she turned toward the door, intending to leave the room.

Two things happened, not unrelated, which evaporated that momentary illusion of triumph.

The wardrobe door creaked open, seemingly of its own volition. Startled, he looked down to see Athena nosing her way into the crack. When he flicked his fingertips to shoo her away, a low growl rumbled in the dog's throat.

Mrs. Murdoch, her attention evidently caught by either the movement or the sound, paused on the threshold and frowned. "'Tis all well and good to have another man on hand to keep watch o' things. But where is Mr. Sutherland now?"

Jane's head turned as she followed the housekeeper's gaze to the wardrobe, giving him a glimpse of her worried expression. If Mrs. Murdoch took it upon herself to investigate what the dog had found, that would be the end of it. Though his Jane was unquestionably a creative genius, if the housekeeper opened the wardrobe to find a naked man hiding there, a pair of boots clutched to his chest and the voluminous skirts of Jane's dresses covering what they could of the rest of him, even the famed Robin Ratliff could never concoct a story that would mollify her.

"Athena, come," Jane ordered, though the dog paid her no mind. "He wasn't in his rooms when Esme brought his breakfast, you said? Have you checked the kitchen, Mrs. Murdoch?" She glided between the housekeeper and the wardrobe, ushering both her and Dougan toward the door. "A man of his size, up all night...I'm sure he must've worked up quite an appetite."

His belly had the nerve to rumble loudly in confirmation, at which sound Athena gave a startled *yip* and flattened her ears.

Finally, he heard the door latch behind Dougan and Mrs. Murdoch. To his surprise, Jane did not turn the key in the lock but collapsed against the oak panel, barely containing her laughter. After studying her mistress for a moment, head cocked to the side in a quizzical pose, Aphrodite trotted over to aid Athena in the investigation of the wardrobe.

After counting to three, Thomas pushed open both doors of the wardrobe and stepped out into the room. The dogs skittered away at first, then snuffled past him into the wardrobe, and before he could stop them, they had found the breeches he'd dropped on the floor of the cabinet and begun a vigorous game of tug-of-war.

"Here, now. Here." Jane managed to choke out the admonition as she pushed away from the door and came to his rescue. With a sly glance at his person, she slipped past to snatch the dogs' prize from them. "Maybe you'd better put this on for now," she said, tossing his greatcoat in his direction.

He had to drop the boots in order to catch it. They landed on the floor, *thud-thud*, narrowly missing his toes. The noise earned him a reproving frown, though it quickly softened.

"A little worse for wear, I'm afraid." She poked her fingers through a row of holes in one thigh of the breeches, made by sharp canine teeth. "Esme's quite skilled at mending," she reassured him. "But they'll have to do for now." After depositing them on the rumpled bed, she began to walk toward the door, re-braiding her hair with brisk, methodical movements as she went. "While you put them on, I'll go down and try to keep Agnes busy long enough for you to sneak back to the gatehouse and get properly dressed. It wouldn't do to be late."

"Late?" *Properly dressed?* He'd been thinking rather fondly of the prospect of collapsing facedown on a bed for a few hours. Preferably not alone.

She glanced over her shoulder and this time did not look away. "For church. It's Sunday morning—or had you forgotten?" He must have grimaced, for a wry smile turned up one corner of her mouth. "I daresay it will do us both good."

Was she that eager to put the night's activities behind them? He gave a curt nod, not precisely intending to convey assent. "I'll have my knife back, before you go."

She stepped closer and laid the deadly instrument on his outstretched palm. "I hope you don't intend to do anything desperate."

Last night, yesterday, she'd opened herself to him, showed him parts of herself she'd never shown another soul—and for once, he wasn't just thinking of her body. He thought he'd been prepared for the trouble this morning would bring. The inevitable awkwardness. The realization, however painful, that things between them had changed.

But this playfulness was worse, far worse than he had let himself imagine. The Jane he remembered—silly and witty and clever—was still inside her, waiting to be set free. And he was more than halfway to falling head over heels in love with her.

Again.

"That depends," he said, twisting the blade to catch a beam of sunlight. "How dull are the parson's sermons?"

She laughed and shook her head, charmingly torn between honesty and irreverence. "Deathly."

Chapter 17

Standing in the otherwise empty Great Hall, Jane raised a gloved hand to the hair tightly coiled beneath her hood, then smoothed that same hand down the soft drape of her black woolen pelisse, taking stock after the night's adventures.

Her body was as sound and stout as it had ever been, perfectly unchanged... except for the mark left by one of Thomas's more fierce kisses, which was thankfully hidden beneath her bodice, and the not-unpleasant ache between her thighs. If her mind was not exactly sharper this morning, as she had hoped—she had not reckoned with the effect of very little sleep—neither had her wits flown entirely.

As for her heart? Her fingertips settled over her left breast. Perfectly steady, thank God. Last night's worries had been for naught. Last night need have nothing to do with today.

Or tomorrow.

She drew a deep breath and strode across the flagstone and through the inner bailey to the courtyard, where the castle staff had assembled beneath gray skies for their weekly march down to the village for Sunday services: Dougan in his much-patched kilt, and Mrs. Murdoch still reproving, Esme anxious to be reunited with her family, and Cook and the scullery maid shivering in the January air, missing the heat of the kitchen. Dougan had already raised the portcullis, so Jane gestured for the little band to start on its way.

Just then the door to the gatehouse grated open. Ducking his head beneath the lintel, Thomas stepped out to join them, the scarlet of his uniform stunningly bright against the gray stone and wintry landscape. Jane's fingers curled into the skirt of her pelisse, and her previously steady pulse kicked up a notch, just as it had when she'd been seventeen. He hadn't any right to look so handsome.

In two strides, he was beside her. "You did say 'properly dressed,'" he reminded her, as if he knew just what she'd been thinking.

He bowed a greeting to the others, who then continued their journey, all save Mrs. Murdoch, who paused to look him up and down before giving a satisfied tip of her chin and turning toward the path.

"You should consider yourself fortunate not to have fallen from Mrs. Murdoch's good graces," she said, trying to muster her usual cool voice.

"Indeed, I do," he replied in his customarily cheeky tone, "though I confess I'm more curious to know whether I've risen in your esteem."

"What nonsense. Do you dare to ask about—? On the way to—?" Her voice fell to a fierce whisper, and her eyes darted to the backs of the others, though they were already far in front and out of earshot.

He inclined his head and, under cover of the brim of his hat, gave her a naughty wink. "I'm pleased to hear I didna disappoint."

She parted her lips, but as happened far too frequently of late, no retort would come. Heat swept into her face, and with a huff, she looked away. After they'd taken a half-dozen silent steps, she said, "I'm not sure either of us is in the proper frame of mind for one of Mr. Donaldson's sermons." Then she pressed her lips primly together, at least in part to squelch a smile. "Or perhaps we're in precisely the proper frame of mind."

Thomas's eyes twinkled. "Will he rain fire and brimstone upon us? Is he the sort to make us tremble for our sins?"

As if she had not trembled enough already.

Mrs. Murdoch chose that moment to send a sharp glance over her shoulder. Jane could guess how they must look, walking side by side, heads together, laughing. Agnes obviously suspected something, but if she ever guessed the whole of it...

"Fine morning, is it not, ma'am?" Thomas called out, and to Jane's astonishment, the elderly housekeeper all but giggled her agreement before turning around again. Was there a woman alive he couldn't have his way with?

"How long has this Donaldson fellow been the parson?" he asked as they reached the edge of the village.

"Only a few weeks," she explained to his evident surprise. "In the autumn, old Mr. Parkham's health began to decline. I took the liberty of writing to Mr. Watson, Lord Magnus's—" Too late, she darted an apologetic glance toward him. "*Your* land agent, to inform him of the matter. I'm sorry if I overstepped, but I felt someone in a position of authority ought to know."

Thomas gave a brusque nod. "Shortly thereafter, Mr. Donaldson arrived, to function as a sort of curate, I suppose, if such a thing exists among Presbyterians. In spite of having help, though, Mr. Parkham still insisted on wearing himself to a shadow over Christmas. When his housekeeper went in to check on him on Boxing Day morning, she found he'd died in his sleep. Afterward, Mr. Donaldson simply...slipped into the clergyman's role, as no one was here to say anything to the contrary."

For a long moment, Thomas said nothing. Then, "Is he a young man?"

"In years, yes. But not in spirit." To Thomas's frown of incomprehension, she could only say, "You'll see."

The kirk stood on the far edge of Balisaig, hemmed in on two sides by the churchyard and on the third side by the manse. Once inside its stout stone walls, more than ample to enclose the small congregation, the castle servants filed into a pew near the back. Jane, without giving the matter much thought, walked up the nave to her usual seat in the Dunnock pew, to which she considered herself entitled, given the rent she paid.

After a hesitation so slight she could almost persuade herself she had imagined it, Thomas opened the pew door, which bore a faded coat of arms, and seated himself beside her, beneath a solemn plaque bearing the name of some previous Earl of Magnus.

He drew the congregation's notice—how could he not? If he'd intended to hide, a scarlet coat had been a poor choice indeed. Jane heard the buzz of whispered voices rise, then fall again when Mr. Donaldson came in.

Services began unenthusiastically, as they had since the advent of Mr. Donaldson's tenure, with some off-key warbling that passed for singing and a mumbled prayer. She tried to focus on the text, on the deliberate discomforts of the wooden seat, on the play of light across the chancel. Anything but the shape of Thomas's thigh, barely hidden beneath white pantaloons, or the breadth and strength of his shoulders when they nearly brushed hers. Perhaps she ought to have feigned a headache this morning.

Church was no place for a woman so entirely unrepentant for her sins.

Mr. Donaldson was a man of twenty-five or so, tall and rail thin, with dark hair and eyes. For all he'd lived his entire life in Scotland, his voice contained little of that pleasant Scottish burr. She suspected he had forced himself to abandon his natural accent for something he thought serious-sounding and respectable.

The people of Balisaig did not appear to appreciate his efforts. As he ascended to the pulpit, congregants' shoulders began to sag, as if the assembly had heaved a simultaneous sigh. She gripped the edge of the pew tight enough to make her fingers cramp, bracing herself for this week's onslaught on the simple pleasures enjoyed in the little community.

Of course, Mr. Donaldson did not have his predecessor's forty years' experience with Balisaig, did not have forty years' experience with anything. The sins of a city like Edinburgh, from whence he had come, were so far removed from life in a quiet Highlands village as to be laughable. Very little was to be accomplished by telling folks hereabouts that they ought to forgo the pleasures of the Thistle and Crown or that they must forswear gambling. After all, Mrs. Shaw's loss of an entire shilling at a game of whist in 1796 had still been a subject of some discussion in the community when Jane had arrived.

Which was not to say that the people of Balisaig were free from fault. Though she'd seen little evidence of gluttony or sloth, certainly wrath and envy were occasionally on display. And as they were only human, she had no doubt that they indulged from time to time in—

"*Lust.*"

When Mr. Donaldson shouted that single word into the silence of the congregation, like a lead weight launched from a catapult, it landed with a predictable *thud*. From somewhere behind her came a snort (almost certainly Edward Shaw, aged twelve, who had a twelve-year-old boy's interest in the sins of the flesh), followed by the slap of a hand (likely belonging to Mrs. Shaw or perhaps one of her daughters) against the side of the snorter's head. Jane gripped the edge of the pew more firmly yet, partly to stave off the laughter that was building in her chest, and partly to keep her mind from wandering in the direction of things best not dwelled upon in church.

The second motive was thwarted, however, when Thomas's hand slid from his knee and came to cover hers, his fingertip tracing a seductive pattern over the delicate skin on the back of her hand. The proper response would have been to pull away and fold her hands primly in her lap.

Somewhere in the last twenty-four hours, she had grown accustomed to his touch. She had lost the will to be proper.

"Again and again, Christ and his Apostles order us to avoid the temptations of the body," continued Mr. Donaldson, only slightly rattled by the Shaw family's performance. "And not simply to avoid them, but to cut off the hand that offends us, or to pluck out the eye. If sacrifice, if violence are necessary to control our sinful natures, to resist the lures of lust"—that fine bit of alliteration earned another snicker, from someone other than Edward this time—"then are we called to exercise righteous passion as the best means of defeating those passions which are anything but righteous.

"So too must we cull from our number those who would lead us into temptation." As he built to his conclusion, the young reverend paused to scan his audience, lingering on particular faces. "The immodestly dressed woman. The purveyor of liquors that inflame the baser appetites. The teller of lewd stories."

At that, Thomas playfully squeezed her hand. Jane jumped, drawing Mr. Donaldson's eye to her for a moment before he moved on. "There are those among us glad to do the Devil's work for him. Let us have no dealings with the Devil's middlemen." Out of the corner of her eye, she watched the dimple slide into place on Thomas's cheek, as if he saw himself in that description. "Following the exhortation of Saint Paul," Mr. Donaldson finished, "'abhor what is evil.'"

Under cover of the closing hymn, Thomas leaned down to her and whispered, "He left off the best part: 'hold fast to what is good.'" His eyebrows waggled suggestively.

Though it was surely sacrilege, it was impossible not to think then of the sensations she'd so recently experienced within the circle of his powerful arms. She narrowly managed to disguise a shivery gasp as a cough.

When the small crowd began to make its way out of the church, the buzz of conversation rose again. But when Mr. Shaw shouted out, "Tommy Sutherland, as I live and breathe," Jane realized she had misunderstood the nature of the village's curiosity.

With a slight touch to her elbow, Thomas left her side to go to the older man, who clearly had known him as a lad. From there, he was swept up in a whirl of greetings, even a kiss on one cheek from Elspeth, who would have been just out of girlhood when he last came to Balisaig. Mr. Campbell, the village blacksmith, who had been speaking quietly to Davina Ross, came forward with hand extended. Thomas brushed aside the gesture in favor of a back-slapping hug.

She smiled at the sight, despite the sensation of something in her chest tying itself in a knot. Would he be thinking of how—or even if—those same people would greet him if they knew he was Lord Magnus? Perhaps. But he must also see that he was beloved here, whatever mischief he might have caused in the past. They were glad to have him in their midst again.

Right where he belonged—if Robin Ratliff were not occupying his castle.

Quickly, Jane made her way to the back of the church, nodding politely here and there, and dipping a slight curtsy to Mr. Donaldson, who stood in the vestibule, the last obstacle between her and a sorely needed breath of fresh air.

But the clergyman was not to be put off with the mere forms of politeness. "And who is our visitor this morning, Mrs. Higginbotham?" he inquired, flashing his large yellowish teeth in something he probably intended as a smile. "I refer, of course, to the gentleman in regimentals."

Jane successfully fought down the impulse to glance over her shoulder, merely for another look at Thomas smiling among his friends. "Lieutenant Sutherland. Lately returned from the West Indies, where he was stationed for some time."

"A guest at Dunnock, I take it?" He seemed not at all bothered by the possibility that his questions might be considered prying.

Generally, she tried to avoid bald-faced lies to clergymen, particularly while standing under the roof of the church. But today she was grateful for her storytelling gift. All the truth was no longer hers to tell.

"Mr. Ratliff, my employer, has determined he will spend the rest of the winter in Edinburgh again. But he did not want to leave the castle residents entirely without a gentleman's protection. I'm sure you understand," she added, casting her eyes down to the flagstones. Though she would never claim to know Mr. Donaldson well, she felt certain he wasn't the sort to believe a woman could take care of herself.

"Indeed, I understand perfectly." When Jane lifted her gaze, his face was pinched. "Although I must say I am somewhat surprised to hear that Mr. Ratliff does. What I have been told did not suggest to me that he was a man of...finer feelings."

Jane stretched her own expression into something like a smile. "Perhaps, Mr. Donaldson, your next sermon should exhort the congregation about the evils of gossip?"

He gave an odd sort of twitch, ready to agree with the suggestion, yet somewhat suspicious of a trap. "You remind me, ma'am, that I intended to ask if you had time to step over to the manse after services? I would like to enlist Balisaig's leading ladies in an effort to raise the tone of our little village. Perhaps we might form a little committee to establish some regular entertainments, something more wholesome than one finds at the Thistle and Crown?"

When she returned a vague nod, he clapped his palms together, a more fervent expression of joy from him than she had ever seen. "Excellent. I'll just speak with Mrs. Abernathy and—Mrs. Shaw, do you think? I do worry about her son's immortal soul."

Jane was spared having to reply by his hurrying away to catch the apothecary's wife. When she let herself look back, she saw Thomas still enmeshed in conversation. She had little excuse to avoid the meeting at the manse entirely. Perhaps, however, she could get away more quickly by claiming they had agreed to walk back to Dunnock together. Though, of course, there had been no conversation of the sort. They had avoided all discussion of what would happen next.

Was there a way for the two of them to have a future together?

Rather than wait for the other ladies, Jane made her way to the manse, a picturesque stone building like the church, hardly more than a cottage, just two rooms up and two down. Mrs. MacIntosh would have been given the day off, of course, so she was not surprised to find the little house empty. The front door opened on a modest entryway, hardly wider than the stairs that dominated it. The walls had been painted a dun color, and the wooden floors were clean-swept but bare of any softening carpet or floorcloth. To the left and right, doorways led to the sitting room and the study.

Jane pushed back her hood, unbuttoned her pelisse, and prepared to wait in the former, where the furnishings were comfortable, though far from fashionable; the wallpaper was faded, and the carpet might fairly be described as threadbare. Mr. Parkham had wanted to change nothing that carried with it a memory of the late Mrs. Parkham, and doubtless Mr. Donaldson, a bachelor, had little interest in or concern for such matters.

After what seemed an eternity, and was doubtless less than a quarter of an hour, she pushed herself up from a chair covered in floral chintz and crossed the narrow entry hall to the study, from whose windows she expected to be able to see the front of the church. Probably Mr. Donaldson was having some difficulty extracting Mrs. Shaw from a chat with her friends, or he had thought of others to invite.

Though the sitting room was simply furnished, the study was crowded with bookcases, a large desk, a pair of leather chairs near the window, and a worktable between them. Given the clergyman's general air of fastidiousness, she was surprised to find every available surface covered by books, pamphlets, newsprint, and papers in haphazard-looking piles. As she made her careful way to the window, she brushed against the corner of an open book where it overhung the edge of the desk, sending it and several papers tucked beneath it and between its pages to the floor.

When she bent to retrieve it and return it to its place, she laughed aloud at the discovery Mr. Donaldson had been reading *The Necromancer's Bride*. Almost certainly for the pleasure of ripping it to shreds, she could guess, although she was curious whether he hadn't taken another sort of pleasure in it too.

As she began to gather up the other papers, a sardonic smile on her face, her eye was drawn to a number of furious underlinings. Not in the book itself, but on the other pages—clippings of assorted reviews of the book. The cruel phrases highlighted by the pencil markings were distressingly familiar after last night's letter. Hastily, she stuffed the loose papers inside the cover and laid the book in the place where it had been—or as close as she could come, hoping he would not notice the difference.

Moving more quickly now, she stepped toward the worktable, intending merely to peer through the curtains. But she could hardly avoid glancing down at the project on which Mr. Donaldson was currently at work. Like the desk, the table's polished surface was covered with stacks of books and various loose papers. Random newspapers, some sorely out of date. A jar of paste. And a tool, not unlike a penknife and wickedly sharp.

On the center of the table a book lay open to an essay entitled "On Female Virtue," in the main a critique of novel reading and the depraved young ladies who indulged in it.

What shall we say of certain books, which, we are assured (for we have not read them), are in their nature so shameful that she who can bear to peruse them must in her soul be a

The final word had been painstakingly excised by the nearby knife.

She knew exactly what the missing word was, but her mind skittered away from the truth. Was the room colder so close to the window? She was shivering. When Mr. Donaldson worked in his study, he must have a fire.

Prostitute.

That was the word that had been cut from the page. As in the threatening letter's shocking claim: *For the* prostitute *reader, you are the vile procurer.*

Without flipping to the title page, she also recognized the book from which it had been removed. Why hadn't she made the connection last night? Though forty years old, the ideas expressed in Reverend Fordyce's *Sermons to Young Women* still had their adherents—Mr. Donaldson evidently among them.

When she looked up, he was on the path from the church. No time to flee, no time even to slip back into the sitting room and pretend she had not seen what she had seen. So she turned to face the door, her hands gripping the table's edge behind her back as an hour ago they had gripped the pew, and waited. Waited while he stamped his muddy feed just inside the entryway and rubbed his bare palms together to warm them. Waited while he stepped into the sitting room and did not find her where she ought to have been. Waited as his footsteps sounded their way toward the study and he appeared in the doorway.

"Ah, Mrs. Higginbotham. There you are." He sounded remarkably pleased to see her.

"Where are the others?"

"The others?" He took three steps toward the desk, squared the book she had knocked to the floor, as if he could not bear the sight of such disorder. As she watched him tidy up, a hysterical laugh rose in her throat, but she swallowed it back. "Oh, you mean the ladies. I decided the meeting would be better put off to another time. When I'm sure their efforts would not go to waste."

"Wh-what do you mean?"

"With a wolf like Robin Ratliff at Dunnock, my flock is in constant danger, I'm afraid. Before the innocent lambs can be allowed to gambol, it is the shepherd's duty first to hunt down the predator." The man had never shied away from a strained metaphor.

"You wrote the letters."

"Letters?" His eyebrows lifted in mild surprise. For a moment, she thought he meant to claim ignorance. Then he gave a satisfied nod, and her heart sank in her chest. He would not confess so readily if he intended to let her tell anyone else.

"I am pleased to hear both of them reached their intended recipient," he went on. "I cherished little hope he would see the first. Having no other direction, I could only send it by way of his publisher in London. I had my doubts it would be passed along." As he spoke, he swept his bony fingers over the materials littering his desk, occasionally straightening or stacking. "I'm sorry you had to see them, Mrs. Higginbotham. I suppose I should have realized that Ratliff's post would be opened by his secretary."

"Amanuensis."

She almost smiled as she said it. Would she ever be able to speak the word without recalling how Thomas had jokingly blessed her as if she'd sneezed? Would everything she said or did from this point forward somehow carry with it the memory of him?

Donaldson's eyes flashed. Clearly he did not like to be corrected, especially not by a woman.

More's the pity. It was on the tip of her tongue to tell him the truth and hope it shocked him to death. "Yes, that's right," she said, matching his steely-eyed glare. "I have written out every one of Robin Ratliff's books."

"I would not have imagined a lady could be so intimately involved in the process of producing these execrable novels." As he spat out the words, he snatched the book from his desk and slapped it against the palm of his hand before tossing it toward the empty hearth.

"You—did you come to Balisaig on purpose, to find Robin Ratliff?"

"Heavens, no. In Edinburgh, I happened to make the acquaintance of a Mr. Matthew Watson, land agent to the Earl of Magnus. When Watson received your note about poor Mr. Parkham"—he clucked softly, though she struggled to believe that the sound reflected genuine sorrow—"he was kind enough to think of me. I found the situation here quite desperate. Obviously, Mr. Parkham had been unable to tend to his flock properly for some time. Sin was allowed to flourish right under his nose. That dreadful pub, for instance." He shuddered. "Though I did not know the worst of it then."

"The worst of it?"

"It was Mrs. Abernathy who happened to reveal that Ratliff was holed up at Dunnock Castle, like one of his own villains. Mentioned it just a few days ago, when she kindly brought me the post. I wonder no one had thought to warn me before."

Dear, sweet Mrs. Abernathy. She could never have suspected what Donaldson would do with a harmless bit of village gossip.

He sighed and shook his head. "And to think, you might have put a stop to it yourself."

"A stop to what?"

"Those vile books. You might simply have tossed the manuscripts into the fire."

An image flashed onto her brain, ink-covered paper curling in the flames. What had been fear became fury.

"Never."

At last, he looked up at her, his eyes cold and nearly black. "I wish I could say I was surprised. It sometimes happens that the she-wolf is just as dangerous to the flock as the male of the species. That being the case, I'm afraid you leave me little choice."

"Choice, sir?" She'd fought too hard for the freedom to make her own choices. No one was going to take that from her.

Nevertheless, Mr. Donaldson blocked the single path through the crowded room, between her and the door. Thomas had no idea where she was. She couldn't count on him to save her. But she saw no way to save herself. Unless...

Without any show of resistance, she let him approach, his hands raised as if he intended to wrap them around her throat.

Chapter 18

Outside the church, Thomas scanned the scattered churchgoers who remained, clustered in knots of conversation. Jane was nowhere to be seen. Disappointment stabbed through him, though he knew he had no right to expect to find her eagerly waiting for him. He saw no sign of Mrs. Murdoch, either. Doubtless they had decided to walk home together.

The same sharp gaze that had scoured the Caribbean Sea looking for danger passed once more over the people of Balisaig: a handful of sturdy farmers and their ruddy-cheeked families, a bespectacled man whom he took for the apothecary, the frail clergyman. Ridiculous, really, to imagine Jane had anything to fear here.

A hand settled on his shoulder. "You'll come and greet Mama," Theo Campbell said, and as it was not a question, Thomas made no answer except to turn in the direction of the blacksmith's forge, past the charming stone manse.

"How does she get on?" Thomas asked as they walked.

Mrs. Campbell had been a widow all the years he had known her, and he had wondered from time to time why she hadn't remarried, for he knew she had had offers. Still, he admired her loyalty to the husband with whom she had fled New York after the rebellion in the colonies. Like other free Blacks, most of whom had remained loyal to the Crown, they'd been uncertain about their future liberty when the colonists unexpectedly won the war. So they had accepted the British army's offer to escort them to a new settlement in Canada.

After the first winter, nearly overwhelmed by the desolation of Nova Scotia, they had heeded the advice of a passing Scottish fur trader to make their way to Britain when they could. The Scotsman had spoken so warmly of his childhood in the Highlands, the young couple had eventually made it their home too. Theo had been born here, and Mr. Campbell lay in its kirkyard, having taken his leave from this world too soon after his only child's entry into it.

"Well enough," said Theo, an echo of Ross's claim. But much like yesterday, Thomas heard worry in the other man's voice, as well as a measure of stubbornness. "Her rheumatism flares up in the winter, so she doesn't get out as much as she'd like. 'Twill be easier for her once Davina and I can wed."

He had seen Theo speaking to a young woman after services but had not recognized in her the girl he'd once known. Years ago, she had sported stiff braids and freckles and had taken her chief delight in tattling on her older brother. "Davina Ross?"

Theo regarded him seriously for a moment before a wide grin split his dark brown face. "Aye."

It was easy enough to guess what Davina saw in Theo, whose strength of body—his broad shoulders threatened every minute to overstrain the seams of his coat—now matched his strength of character. When they'd been mischief-making lads together, Theo had always managed to steer Thomas and Ross away from real trouble, though he was the youngest of the three and had not yet developed biceps that might have been hewn from stone.

"What's stopping you?" Thomas demanded. "Not Ross, I hope." He knew it must be a complicated matter for a man to see his sister marry his best friend. Hadn't Ross tried to tell him just yesterday that Theo enjoyed stringing the lassies along?

"Och, Ross'll be all right once he finally makes up his mind to marry Elspeth," he said. "Anyway, Davina says it's bad luck to marry before the heather's in bloom." But even as he offered those simple explanations, he glanced over his shoulder, toward the church.

Did the new clergyman have aught to do with the delay?

The question remained unasked, as at that same moment they arrived on the Campbell family's doorstep. In the main room, they found Mrs. Campbell dozing before a roaring fire, a colorful quilt draped over her legs.

"I've brought you a visitor, Mama," Theo said, bending to kiss her cheek.

"Not that Mr. Donaldson, I hope." She roused herself and looked sharply around the room.

When her eyes landed on Thomas, he bowed and came forward. "Thomas Sutherland, ma'am," he said, though he could tell even before the words were out that she needed no prompting to remember him. "How wonderful to see you again."

She favored him with a playful frown and tapped her other cheek. "If that's so, Tommy, then where's my kiss?" When he obliged her, she caught his hands in hers and held him at arm's length for an inspection. "I see from that uniform you've tried to make something of yourself."

"Aye, ma'am. With limited success."

"You needed my Theo and Eleazor Ross to watch out for you, as it used to be."

He shot his friend a look. "They have been sorely missed."

But how could he possibly tell any of them the truth? Once his real reason for returning to Balisaig was known, there would surely be an end of playful jabs and back-slapping hugs...although he would not put it past Mrs. Campbell to chide even an earl.

She urged him to take the seat opposite, close enough to the fire that it was almost too warm even for his thin blood. Theo dragged a wooden chair away from the table. Though the family did all its living in that small room, with its whitewashed walls and simple furnishings, all was neat as a pin.

A dozen years ago, the blacksmith's forge had been cold and the house adjacent to it little more than a shack. When or how Theo had stepped into the post and turned the tumbledown house into a home, Thomas did not know. That he had succeeded no one could have any doubt, though Thomas could easily believe Theo would not be satisfied with his achievements until Davina shared them.

"And have you seen the Shaws?" Mrs. Campbell asked, plucking at a knot on her quilt with knobby fingers.

"At church, yes."

"Young Edward is worse even than you were, Tommy," she pronounced with a shake of her head.

"Impossible." Thomas laughed. "It must only seem that way. He has all the year to make his mischief in Balisaig, while I had only a few weeks. I had to work harder at it."

"He feels the weight of his responsibilities," Theo said, more seriously. "Since his father's injury, he's been a good lad, but that farm, 'tis more work than one can do. Elspeth tells Ross they dinna ken how th' rent's t' be paid."

"I should like to see that Mr. Watson try to put the Shaws from their home," Mrs. Campbell declared firmly, and Thomas would not have put it past her to set herself in the land agent's way.

"Perhaps it will not come to that," Thomas said, almost under his breath.

He had it in his power to help them, and any of the others who suffered. He could even bring a doctor for Mrs. Campbell, to see what more could be done to ease her pain. But if he stayed...

His downcast eyes took in his scarlet coat. How was he to choose between British soldier and Highland laird? He could fulfill his oath to protect Great Britain, or he could protect the people of Balisaig. But not both.

"Put the kettle on the hob, Theo," Mrs. Campbell ordered.

But Thomas shook his head and rose. "I need to..." A dozen possible conclusions to that sentence suggested themselves, but at last, he said simply, "Go. I need to go. But rest assured, I'll call again another day, ma'am."

She accepted another kiss from him, and Theo walked with him to the door. "We're all glad to have you home."

There it was again. *Home.* Well, he might have come home, but he'd never felt so lost. He nodded his thanks to his friend and stepped into the cold.

Beneath lowering skies that threatened more snow, Thomas set out toward Dunnock on the wide lane that bisected Balisaig. Three or four hearty souls still stood near the church, but the others had dispersed to their homes—or perhaps the pub, despite Mr. Donaldson's jab at "purveyors of strong liquor." Ross's absence from the services had been conspicuous. Briefly, Thomas considered turning in at the Thistle and Crown when he reached it, but no. He needed to be alone. To think.

When he'd first settled into his post in the West Indies, the quiet had been its own threat. On occasion, a threat to his sanity. Though rationally he'd understood both the necessity for and desirability of silence—he'd rather be lonely than find himself on an island overrun by enemy soldiers—he had nonetheless craved the regular comradeship he'd left behind. His fellow intelligence officers. The friends of his youth.

Eventually, he'd grown accustomed to his isolation, but it had never ceased to be a weight. On his shoulders. On his soul. Though Dominica was an ocean away now, he found the weight had merely shifted, not lifted. If he stayed in Balisaig, would he not still be alone? Both Theo and Ross would soon be happily settled, while Lord Magnus sat high in his castle, all by himself, unapproachable, untouchable. Tommy Sutherland no more.

As he drew abreast of the church, he recalled the look in Theo's eye as he'd spoken of his wedding. Whatever Thomas decided about staying or going, he meant to see that Donaldson was removed. He would replace him with a man who understood the needs of this community. A man who—

The flutter in a window of the manse caught his eye, and instantly he was on alert. *Only a curtain,* he tried to tell himself, but after years of watching for sails, for flags, straining his vision against the darkness, against a blinding sea—well, old habits died hard. Automatically, he scanned the perimeter, lest the movement had been a distraction from some other threat, before focusing on the window.

Stone mullions framed a pair of figures: Donaldson and a woman, her back to the glass, the two of them locked in what appeared to be an embrace. Thomas fought a wry laugh. No surprise that the man who took such obvious pleasure in upbraiding others for their sins was a hypocrite. He might still have had the good sense to draw the drapes.

Thomas was on the point of continuing on his way, when his well-trained eyes noted the woman's fur-lined hood. Her rich brown hair slipping loose from its pins.

Jane's hood. Jane's hair.

And Donaldson's hands not on her back or her arms, but at her throat.

Before he was even aware of having begun to run, he was bursting through the front door of the manse, shouting for her, turning toward the room where he'd seen her standing. On the threshold of the study, he saw Donaldson jerk his head about to identify the intruder, a sneer of contempt twisting his features, even as his fingers continued to tighten around Jane's neck.

Then the man gasped, flinched. "Why you little whore—!" he gasped out as Jane pushed him away from her and he fell, striking his head on the corner of his desk before he hit the floor.

Jane looked down at her trembling hands, as if she too was bewildered by the dramatic turn of events. Thomas followed her gaze and saw blood coating her hands and spreading across her pelisse, a darker stain against the black, gleaming brightly against the blade of a small knife.

"Jane! Are you hurt?" He leaped across the room, shoving furniture from his path.

She tried to speak, couldn't, nodded her head, winced. Bruises were already forming on the pale skin of her throat.

Donaldson's blood, then. She'd taken advantage of the momentary distraction provided by his arrival to stab her attacker with the penknife that must have lain on the table behind her. But why had the clergyman—?

"He sent the letters," Jane croaked.

The letters? "Whist, lassie," he crooned, gathering her in his arms. "Don't try to talk." His frantic thoughts belied the stillness of his body, however. He'd failed to protect her. Surely, he'd missed some important clue connecting Donaldson to the threats. Why, just now, he'd almost passed by. If the curtain hadn't fluttered as Jane struggled, then—

He was spared further self-recrimination by the arrival of two others: the apothecary and his wife, who must have seen him run into the manse.

"Is something amiss here?"

"Mrs. Abernathy," Jane whispered, and before Thomas quite knew what had happened, the apothecary's wife, a fair-haired fashion plate of a sort rarely seen in the Highlands, had pushed him out of the way to gather a sobbing Jane in her arms, oblivious to the blood.

Abernathy knelt beside Donaldson. "He's been stabbed!" He fixed Thomas with a look that demanded explanation.

"He tried to choke the life out of Ja—Mrs. Higginbotham. He must be mad."

Abernathy's eyebrows shot above the rims of his spectacles. Shaking off his disbelief, he returned to the examination of Donaldson, who groaned as the apothecary examined both the injury near his belly and the lump rapidly forming on his skull. "He'll feel that knock on his head for a good while. But so long as no infection sets in," he concluded, "the stab wound is too shallow to do much real harm."

Thomas's fingers twitched as he contemplated reaching into his boot for a blade that would finish the job.

"Mrs. Higginbotham?" Another voice came from the doorway, this one belonging to Elspeth Shaw, who was backed by her slower-moving father. She took a step toward the desk and looked around in horror, taking in what no one else had yet had time to observe: the piles and stacks of books and papers, a mess at odds with anything one might have guessed about the clergyman.

"The letter you brought, Elspeth," Jane began, over Mrs. Abernathy's attempts to keep her quiet, her voice still hoarse from the press of Donaldson's fingers on her throat

"The one for Mr. Ratliff?"

"It was a death threat." Jane's eyes were dull, as weary as her voice. "Mr. Donaldson wrote it."

Hectic color flooded the young woman's cheeks. "Oh, God. Mrs. MacIntosh swore when she gave it tae me that it had only been mixed up with his post. Said Mr. Donaldson had told her to give me half a crown to take it right tae Dunnock and explain as how it'd been mislaid. And we did so need—" Her father's hand settled on her shoulder, silencing her.

Donaldson had preyed on the girl's desperation, her honest desire to help her family. Despite the vitriol he had spewed from the pulpit, how could she, or anyone, have imagined him capable of this?

Still, Thomas could not shake the conviction that *he*, both laird of Dunnock and trained intelligence officer, should have known.

"Abernathy, tie his wrists behind his back before he wakes," he said, drawing every eye to him. The apothecary nodded, patting his pockets with one hand. Wordlessly, his wife tugged loose one of her elegant silk ribbons and handed it to him. While that was being done, Thomas gave the next order: "Someone else fetch the constable."

Blank eyes met that request. Mr. Shaw shook his head. It seemed Mr. Watson had not seen fit to charge a local man with such responsibility.

"Then I'll take him before the magistrate myself." The threat rumbled from Thomas's chest like distant thunder. If Donaldson didn't survive the journey, so much the better.

Jane, who had once more leaned her head against Mrs. Abernathy's breast, turned to look at him. *That's you*, she mouthed.

He would almost rather she had stabbed him with the bloody knife she still held. Of course, Lord Magnus, the gentleman of highest rank for miles around, would be the magistrate.

How, under the present circumstances, could Thomas continue to hide from his responsibilities?

Gruffly, he cleared his throat and addressed Mr. Shaw. "There's something I must say. You know me of old, sir. I have the very great honor of being a son of Balisaig by virtue of my late mother, Anne Maguire. All who knew her thought themselves blessed by the acquaintance of a kind and generous lady—"

"Aye, lad," Mr. Shaw interrupted, understandably a little baffled by the recital of genealogy at a time like this. "And the same goes for your gran, God rest 'er."

Thomas acknowledged the kindness with a bow. "Unbeknownst to me, and I do heartily believe to my father, both those good women could trace their lineage to a noble clan, though their branch of it was quite far removed from the main trunk of the tree, as it were. Still, no matter how distant the relation, 'tis a true one, and so it is that I come to be the last in a long line of Maguires."

Mr. Shaw, who had been leaning against the doorjamb for support, straightened his posture, as if he suspected what was coming.

"Any one of you," Thomas continued, letting his gaze take in the whole room, passing the lightest over Jane, "may recall that the late Lord Magnus also had Maguire blood."

Mrs. Abernathy gasped. "Och, this is better than the theater. Are you going to tell us next that you're the new earl?" The question held a teasing note, but a hint of wariness too, as if she could not make up her mind what to think.

Thomas drew a deep breath, but Jane spoke first.

"He is."

After a beat of shock, Mrs. Abernathy fluttered into a deep curtsy, and her husband rose to his feet merely to bow. Elspeth seemed not to know what was expected of her and looked to her father for guidance. Mr. Shaw alone continued to regard him with a firm eye.

"That's all well and good, lad. Now what do you mean to do about it?"

Thomas's eyes darted from the Shaws, to the apothecary and his wife, even to the clergyman lying supine on the floor, though he still had not begun to stir. In his head he could hear General Scott's voice, ticking off his responsibilities in Scotland. *Conduct an assessment of the property and its tenants' needs...Make your determinations about the estate's management before the spring planting season...*

He had sought and lived a life of adventure. Nevertheless, this duty had become his, just as Scott had said. Would he let the people of Balisaig go on murmuring about the earl's failings?

Last of all, he settled on Jane, who looked as pale as he had ever seen her, her own gaze blank and distant. God, how he wanted to gather her into his arms again and assure her all would be well. To vow to heal not just this hurt, but all the others that had befallen her. To guard her from future harm.

Why, maybe you'll even meet some likely lass and decide to settle down...

And just like that, he realized exactly what he had overlooked. He understood, at last, how wise Scott had been.

Th' canny auld bastart.

Yesterday, last night, he'd thought in terms of either-or. Either he left Dunnock, or Jane did. But, of course, there was another way. It had just taken him a little while to see it.

"I mean to do my duty by the people of Balisaig, Mr. Shaw," he said, though he was still focused on Jane. "I intend to make Dunnock my home."

It would be work, of course. But, God willing, he wouldn't have to do it alone.

Chapter 19

Late that night, snow began to fall. Jane stood at the window of her study, her forehead pressed to the cold, diamond-paned glass, and watched. Imagined it coating the roof of the manse, where Thomas, Mr. Campbell, and Mr. Abernathy were keeping watch over Mr. Donaldson. When the clergyman awoke, if he awoke, he would be imprisoned and tried. The story of what had happened must even now be flying through Balisaig like the snowflakes.

It was still falling in the morning when Mrs. Murdoch brought up the breakfast tray. Jane was sitting at her desk, the pages of *The Brigand's Captive* spread before her. The almost preternatural hush that had fallen over the castle ought to have made it easy to work, but she found it quite impossible to pick up her penknife, sharpen a quill, and begin.

I intend to make Dunnock my home.

"Word came in the wee hours o' the morning that Mr. Donaldson was awake," the housekeeper said as soon as she crossed the threshold. "Mr. Sutherl—'is Lordship—has taken him on to the jail in Inverness."

"This weather will delay his return." What might have been the journey of a morning would take all day at least.

Agatha nodded. "He swore he'd be back tomorrow, no matter the snow."

Tomorrow was February the second. Candlemas. The day the earl was to meet with his tenants and servants, pay salaries, collect rents, sign new leases.

"Where shall I leave this, ma'am?" The housekeeper's gaze flitted over the desktop, looking for a place to put down her tray.

Jane waved the food away. "Thank you, but I'm not hungry."

I intend to make Dunnock my home.

"A cup o' tea, then? You must take something, Mrs. Higginbotham. After what happened yesterday—"

"Very well," Jane agreed, though she had no intention of drinking it. Anything to send Mrs. Murdoch on her way. "And please ask Dougan to bring up my trunks."

"Your trunks, ma'am?"

She had been so worried about being forced to leave, she had forgotten she still had the power to choose. This time, it would be her choice to go. "I've delayed far too long already."

Worry creased the elder woman's lined face. "You're leaving? But I had such hope that you and—"

"The tea, please, Mrs. Murdoch." Jane's voice was still hoarse. "And the trunks. That will be all."

Quiet was said to be conducive to thought. She refused to let herself think, afraid she would second-guess herself.

She packed her clothes, leaving behind all her widow's weeds and the bloodstained pelisse. When she started over—and she would start over—she would no longer be Mrs. Higginbotham. The dogs, who had no memory of any place that was not Dunnock, curled up on their cushions in front of the fireplace and sulked.

She packed her books without flipping through the pages, packed her papers without a second glance. When she reached her destination, she would write to Mr. Canfield and explain the delay in the delivery of the promised manuscript. She did not expect any complaint. Mr. Canfield could not afford to reprimand Robin Ratliff for tardiness.

By morning, everything was neatly ordered. Nothing remained but one leather-bound book, lying in the center of the desk. She gave a decisive nod, satisfied with her labors, and reached for the bell.

Even before she had rung it, Mrs. Murdoch appeared in the doorway. She took in the trunks and bandboxes with a disapproving glance, then thrust out a folded piece of parchment. "Lord Magnus asked me tae give you this."

"He's here?"

"Aye, ma'am. In the Great Hall."

Jane looked about at her luggage, the otherwise empty room. "Did you tell him?"

Mrs. Murdoch's lips were set in a thin line. "No, ma'am."

Relief flooded through her. "Thank you. I would rather explain myself. Please have Dougan fetch my things and put them in the cart. And have Esme run down to the Thistle and Crown to buy me a seat on the stage."

"But Mrs. Higginbotham—"

Jane held up her palm, still not perfectly steady, but improving. Who would ever imagine she had stabbed a man with that hand?

"I will go down and speak with him. When a quarter of an hour has passed, please bring the dogs to me."

After a bewildered Agnes nodded confirmation, Jane gathered up her skirts in one hand, still clutching the parchment in the other. For the last time, she descended the spiral staircase, pushing aside the remembrance of Thomas's hand brushing—possessively, she now knew—across the stone.

I intend to make Dunnock my home.

Though when she thought of what he'd told her the next night in her study, she was forced to admit to herself that she wasn't being fair. She knew he'd assumed the mantle of earl most reluctantly. Only the fiasco at the manse had forced him to tell everyone the truth—and very nearly revealed hers, in the bargain.

At the bottom of the stairs, she paused to gather her courage. A dozen strides along the corridor took her to the arched entryway into the Great Hall. Unlike a few days before, it now blazed with light, a fire roaring in the enormous fireplace, conversations ringing off the stone. And in the center, beside a large trestle table, sat Thomas—*Lord Magnus*—rocked back in a wooden chair, laughing at some story the man standing across the table from him had told.

He might have passed for a farmer himself, clad in the buckskin breeches the dogs had torn and Esme had mended, paired with his old scuffed boots and a drab green wool coat. As usual, the knot of his cravat had worked scandalously loose.

In other words, just as handsome and charming as ever.

Her ordinarily steady heart began to thump at the sight of him. *Strong,* Thomas had called her. But she wasn't sure she had strength for this.

When she'd invited him into her bed, she'd told herself she wanted nothing more than a distraction. She'd asked for just one night, and he'd given it to her, generously, passionately. Fortunately, she had the better part of a lifetime's experience with keeping her memories, even the pleasant ones—with keeping her very self—firmly under lock and key. How very close she'd come to thinking she needed him, to giving something of herself in return.

One night must never again be allowed to change everything.

She clung to the shadows, listening to his exchanges with the tenants who came before him. Carefully he went over the terms of each lease with them, now and then striking an unfavorable clause or adjusting the rent. When Mr. Shaw stumped across the floor and was invited to sit, a concession to his injured leg, she watched the farmer stay standing as he carefully counted out his coins.

Then she watched Thomas scoot fully half of them back across the table. "A loan," he insisted over Mr. Shaw's incipient protest. "And Jamie MacIntyre has volunteered his boys to help your Edward this spring."

Mr. Shaw looked on the verge of sobbing in relief at this unlooked-for kindness, though he hid it with a brusque handshake before he scrawled his name on the lease. Jane felt the sting of tears in her own throat. Thomas's generous, easygoing nature was clearly welcome here. But was it wise? If there was a poorhouse for earls, he'd soon find himself in it.

Strange to think she would never know what became of these people, whether Mr. Shaw's leg healed properly or how Edward would behave when he got past the difficult adolescent stage, what the weather would be like when Davina Ross married Mr. Campbell, or when Mr. Ross would finally realize he and Elspeth made a fine pair. She would never see the sort of place Dunnock Castle became under Thomas's management.

Would never see Thomas...

When the last tenants left the hall and he bowed his head over the desk to make a final notation in some record book, she fortified herself with a determined nod, strode briskly across the flagstone, and stopped before the table.

The scrape of his chair legs echoed loudly as he pushed back and stood. "Jane—at last." He reached out for her hands, but she kept them folded in front of her, wrinkling the paper she'd almost forgotten she held. "Are you well?" he asked, letting his hands fall and looking her carefully up and down, pausing longest over the muffler she'd wound around her neck to hide the ring of fingertip-shaped bruises there. "No, of course you're not. How could you be, after what happened? But rest assured, he's locked away now. I made sure of that myself. He'll never hurt anyone again."

To that, she had no reply. He would doubtless be shocked to discover how little was the part Bartholomew Donaldson had played in her thoughts over the last two days.

After an awkward pause, he nodded toward her clasped hands. "You got my note."

With trembling fingers, she unfolded the paper. Her disbelieving eyes had to scan the page three times before she could take in what was written there.

"A lease to Dunnock Castle?" She looked up at him, astonished.

"Aye."

Carefully, she refolded the parchment and held it out to him. "That's very generous of you. But it won't be necessary." When he would not take it from her, she tossed the lease onto the table, desperate to be rid of it. "I believe I'll buy a little cottage somewhere—I really haven't any need for a castle, or a red racing curricle, or an enormous bed." At the mention of the bed, Thomas's pupils flared. She pretended not to notice. "When one rents, one is always at the mercy of the landlord, and as you know, I prefer to be self-sufficient."

"Jane." His voice was nothing more than a whisper as he came around the corner of the table to stand beside her. For just a moment, she thought he meant to take her in his arms, and her heart began to hammer—part fear, part longing. The rare shadow of doubt flitted across his expression, as if he could see her pulse race. He kept his arms at his sides. "I only meant to tease you a bit," he said, glancing down at the paper.

She managed a ragged-sounding laugh. "Oh, I know. Very clever. However, I've already made arrangements to go."

"Nay, lass," he replied dismissively, but not unkindly. "You're in shock. 'Tis no time to be making decisions. Stay. Stay as my guest, if you must—I'll gladly go on sleeping in the gatehouse. Better yet, stay as my—"

"My trunks are already packed," she spoke across him, averting the temptation to hear what his next word would have been. *Stay. Stay as my guest. Stay as my*—His *what*? Though curiosity ate at her, it was better not to know. She had long been, and would remain, independent. How could she be Thomas's anything? "My ticket is purchased. I'm leaving as soon as our business here is done."

Before he could reply, or even react, Athena and Aphrodite burst in, their shrill yaps echoing in the vaulted hall. They raced toward her, skittering and skidding a bit on the stone floor, jumping up against her skirts when they reached her to demand pats and praise.

As she knelt to run shaking hands over their wriggling bodies, she came face-to-face with Thomas's legs, encased in scarred brown leather and patched buckskin. She let her gaze rise no higher than his knees. The dogs had brushed right past him—in fact, Aphrodite had likely slipped between his feet. Even now they were scrabbling over the toes of his boots, paying him absolutely no mind.

Her first thought was that they understood, somehow, that Thomas was in charge at Dunnock now and must not be barked at or growled at any longer. Her second thought, more ridiculous still, was that they could sense, in their doggy way, a change in their mistress's feelings for the new master.

Good heavens. If she were going to accord some meaning to the dogs' behavior, she ought to have done it when Thomas first arrived. Oh, how they'd tried to protect her that night, the sweet, silly things. But in the end all the snapping and growling had done little good. She had still ended up in danger. In danger of believing she needed Thomas Sutherland, Lord Magnus. In danger of giving up part of herself. In danger of falling in love.

Abruptly, she rose, dusting off her hands. Over Thomas's shoulder, she caught a glimpse of Mrs. Murdoch under the arch of the doorway, looking on the verge of tears. "Dougan says the cart is ready when you are, ma'am. Esme's gone on ahead t' hold your seat."

"Thank you, Mrs. Murdoch." Her arms and legs ached with the effort of not running to the woman, yearning to be enfolded in a motherly embrace. "Thank you for the kind attention you have shown me at Dunnock."

"You'll meet Mr. Ratliff in Edinburgh, I ken?"

Jane darted a glance at Thomas. "That is the plan, yes."

"Verra good, ma'am." Her head hanging uncharacteristically low, Agnes turned to go, then paused. "May I take the liberty of saying you'll be missed?"

"Of course, Mrs. Murdoch. And I shall miss you."

Nothing more was said until the *clip-clip* of Agnes's brisk footsteps disappeared down the corridor. Jane snapped her fingers to bring the dogs to her side. She would say her goodbyes to Dougan and Esme and to the Abernathys when she reached the village. Which left only one other goodbye to say.

But when she turned toward Thomas, he spoke first.

"What would have been your answer if I'd proposed to you, all those years ago?"

The reply came to her lips without hesitation. "I would have said yes." Surprise and pain mingled in his expression, driving her to explain. "The girl I was then dreamed all the ordinary dreams—love, marriage, children. It just so happens that I dreamed an extraordinary one, too, one that surely would have languished if I hadn't been pushed from the nest—"

"Ripped from your home and rejected by your family, you mean." The heat in his voice was unmistakable.

"I'll not deny that the experience taught me some hard lessons," she conceded. "But knowledge is often acquired with difficulty. Because of what happened that night, I learned things I would not otherwise have known. I discovered I had the strength to stand on my own. And I realized the importance of leaving on my own terms."

Finally, his strong, broad shoulders curved, as if bending reluctantly to her will. "I've never been one for taking orders, lass, so I've no intention to begin giving them. If you wish to go, I'll not stop you. You'll make your own choices, like any Robin Ratliff heroine. But," he added, "let me take you to Edinburgh. I canna abide the notion of you traveling alone."

"I thought you understood," she replied crisply. "I *want* to be alone."

He flinched, then tried to disguise the movement with a shake of his head. "Alone is dangerous."

"No," she countered. "Alone is safe."

But *alone* was not the same as *loneliness*, as she well knew. Loneliness was a piece of paper held above a flame, just out of reach of that tongue of fire. For the longest time, the heat touched nothing, caused no damage. Then, in the blink of an eye, a black spot appeared in the paper, then a hole, and finally, all was ash.

He laid his hand lightly over hers. "Please remember, if there's trouble or—or anything else, you've only to bid me come to you, and I will."

I shan't call for you.

The words were right there, waiting to be said. She should say them, if only to make them real to herself. Instead, she stretched onto her toes and kissed him, the merest brush of her lips across his. Ending just as they had begun.

Then she withdrew her hand from his and whispered, "Goodbye, Thomas."

Chapter 20

From the earl's chambers on the northeast corner of Dunnock Castle, Thomas watched the breeze ripple the dark surface of the loch, much as he'd once watched a warmer wind curl the blue Caribbean into foamy waves. Spring was still little more than a promise on the distant horizon of time, but he'd spent the day planning for it nonetheless, making sure his tenants had what they needed until the frozen ground thawed and the sky, at last, began to show more blue than gray.

Much remained to be done. He'd not yet sold his commission, though he'd borrowed against its value to pay for some much-needed repairs. He'd not found a replacement for Watson, whom he had unceremoniously dismissed in a letter for poor management of the estate's income. He'd not appointed a new clergyman, either, though he'd written to an old school friend in Glasgow about the post.

With a grimace, he stretched, trying to ease the tightness in muscles unaccustomed to the work of bending over a desk all day. He needed action. *Perhaps not the sort that involves invaders crossing the water,* he acknowledged to himself, turning away from the window. But, surely, he could be allowed to lend a hand when a roof was being thatched or a fence rebuilt? Not waved off or reminded in doubtful, deferential tones that Lord Magnus's work lay elsewhere. Couldn't they understand the muddle he was in? This earl business was worse than he'd feared.

Ledgers and letters and the like would never be enough to drive Jane from his mind.

On occasion, he considered giving it up and begging General Scott to take him back, to give him some assignment he wouldn't survive. Then again, the general demanded bravery of his men, and what sort of soldier wasn't brave enough to tell a woman he loved her?

Though there was never a moment he found himself in danger of forgiving himself for letting her leave Dunnock without a fight, Mrs. Murdoch was nonetheless ready and waiting to remind him of his mistake. Just yesterday she had looked him up and down, wearing a stern expression that put him in mind of his gran.

"Beggin' your pardon, my lord, but you look as if you haven't slept this week. Surely you'd fare better in the south chamber. Mrs. Higginbotham left that fine big bed—she had it from a cabinetmaker in Perth, an' she did. 'Tis more suited to a man o' your stature, I'd say. Won't you at least look at it?"

He'd only narrowly avoided retorting that he'd already seen the bed, thank you very much. In fact, he'd even managed to snatch a few moments' sleep in it—when he hadn't been pounding into Jane with the wild abandon of a fool who'd imagined he would never know misery again.

No, he meant never to set foot in that room, to say nothing of rest his head on those pillows, again.

Bad enough that the earl's chambers were a mirror of hers, divided by nothing more than a wall. One night, he had even taken up his candle to search for a passage between them. Surely there'd been one once, probably bricked up in centuries past because some long-ago countess had had enough of her husband. But he had found no sign of it. No way in, except by the south tower stairs, which he'd avoided for almost a month and could surely go on avoiding. Ten years in the army had surely given him discipline enough for that.

Is she safe? Is she happy?

Tonight, those two questions dogged—*dogged*? Damn and blast, couldn't he at least be free of the memory of those ill-mannered spaniels?—his footsteps as he strode from the bedchamber into the study. From the study down the narrow spiral staircase of the north tower, where he always managed to recall the sway of Jane's hips when she'd first led him up. To the dining room, where he took a lonely meal—or rather, drained three goblets of something purporting to be wine and pushed food around a plate. From thence to the Great Hall, where he pretended to admire the tattered tapestry he'd been studying when he'd first heard her voice again after all those years. And from there, of course, it was but a few steps to the south corridor, the south tower, and the suite of rooms at the top...

In most respects, Jane's study—and it would always be *Jane's study*— was unchanged. The same murky prints hung on the wall, the terrible sofa still sat near the hearth. But the life had gone out of the room. The hearth was cold, swept bare, cushions removed. The bookshelves were empty. And the desk...

He took three cautious steps closer, candle in hand, though he knew without inspecting the volume lying there just what she had left behind: the final installment of *The Necromancer's Bride*. He hadn't forgotten about the tale—she was too good a storyteller for that—but neither did he have any desire to pick it up, to read the final chapters. No doubt the villagers stormed the castle and freed the girl, while the dissolute lord died alone in his castle.

But so long as those pages remained unread, the ending—Jane's and his ending—remained unwritten.

"Lord Magnus?"

At the sound of that soft, feminine voice, he jumped, nearly dropping the candlestick. Slowly, he turned. "Yes, Esme?"

"I've looked ev'rywhere for you, sir, I have. Never once woulda thought tae look here. Good that I saw your light. Dougan's fetched up the post for you."

"At this hour?" Beyond the window, the skies were nearly dark.

"Och, he went down at midday, he did. I s'pect he tucked it in his pocket and forgot tae give it tae Mrs. Murdoch until just now. It happens that way, from time tae time." The girl had a salver tucked under one arm, a stack of letters clutched in one hand—not quite the fashion in which the housekeeper had ordered her to deliver the post to the master, he suspected, though he himself saw little reason to stand on ceremony. "Here you be, sir," she said, coming forward and holding it out to him, belatedly remembering to curtsy. "Mrs. Murdoch says tae tell you there's a letter there for Mrs. Higginbotham. She said you'd know what was t' be done with it."

"Thank you, Esme." With apparent calm, he took the letters from her hand and watched her leave before turning toward the desk, thumping down the candlestick, and shoving the book out of his way. His hands shook as he riffled through the stack. Bills, mostly, and a reply from his friend in Glasgow.

At last, he found what he sought.

He'd been half expecting to see the childish scrawl with which Donaldson had disguised his hand, or the too-neat copperplate belonging to some clerk at Persephone Press. But it was neither, merely unremarkable penmanship, probably a gentleman's, which spelled out *Mrs. J. Higginbotham* and the direction. *Dunnock* was missing an *n*.

He turned it over in his hands, contemplating. His dilemma wasn't precisely a moral one; he knew how to open and reseal a letter such that the intended recipient would never suspect. It wasn't the logistical challenge posed by the letter that made him hesitate either, though he certainly could not forward it to someone who had told him quite frankly that she did not want to be found. No, it was the realization, cutting through him with the searing pain of a dull-edged blade, that if he opened it, it would be as good as saying he expected never to see her again. That she was so entirely lost to him, he'd as well toss the letter in the fire.

With pointless care, he lifted the seal, preserving the fragile wax medallion and making sure the paper did not tear. Slowly, he unfolded the letter—a single sheet, with just a few hastily written lines slanted across it—and laid it open on the desktop, pinning it down with his splayed hand while with the other he drew the candle closer.

> *My dear Jane—*
> *I pray God may direct this note to your hand, though I*
> *cannot. I write to confess something most dreadful. Papa*
> *discovered your last, with the new direction in Edinburgh,*
> *which I had not yet committed to memory. We had words,*
> *as you may imagine—as a last jab, I told him you'd made a*
> *dashing success of your writing. That you'd grown quite rich*
> *& were ever so much more generous with me than he. My dear*
> *sister, can you ever forgive my foolish temper? He stormed out,*
> *calling for his horse, saying he would 'have his fair share.' I*
> *fear if he finds you, he means to deliver the punishment he often*
> *says you evaded all those years ago.*
> *With all my love, & a most sincere plea for your*
> *forgiveness—*
> *Jonathan*

Thomas's hand curled convulsively, crumpling the note before he caught himself and then smoothing it out again. He recalled her telling him that her brother had been the only one with whom she'd kept in contact. And evidently, in seven years, her father had not forgiven her for the pages her mother had found.

He pushed to his feet, pinching the flame of the candle between his fingers to extinguish it as he snatched the letter from the desktop. He would find her, somehow, though she'd sworn to make it difficult. After all, his training as an intelligence officer must still be good for something. He would not let her father harm her again.

By the time he reached the bottom of the stairs, he was shouting orders to whomever might be in earshot, more soldier than earl and eager to charge into battle, with or without a plan of attack. Esme brought his greatcoat and gloves at a run, while Mrs. Murdoch searched her memory for any detail that could help him to discover where Jane might have taken lodging in Edinburgh, even which name she was likely to use.

A fool's mission, if ever he'd undertaken one—next to nothing to guide him to a woman who didn't want to be found. He would never succeed without help—but where in Balisaig was help to be given? Though he'd been thinking recently of his isolation in Dominca, at least there had been other soldiers only a distress signal away. And long before that, when he'd found himself in trouble, he'd turned to—

"Of course," he fairly shouted, cutting through Mrs. Murdoch's agitated babble. "I'm going down to the Thistle and Crown."

"The pub? At a time like this?" squeaked Esme.

The astonished housekeeper drew herself up straight. "My lord! Have you forgotten you're the Earl of Magnus now?"

"Not at all, ma'am." He shrugged into his greatcoat, then laid a hand on her shoulder and beamed down at her. "But just in the nick of time, I've remembered I'm Tommy Sutherland too."

As he expected, awkwardness descended when he swung open the door to the Thistle and Crown and stepped into its warmth. Conversation had steamed the window and seemed to hang heavy in the air. A moment passed, in which one man laughed heartily at the joke he'd just told, before another nearby jostled him into silence with an elbow. Elspeth Shaw paused in the act of thumping two pewter mugs of ale onto a table, causing foam to slosh down a fellow's shirtfront. The man yelped in protest, then swallowed whatever oath he'd been about to speak and tugged off his wool cap instead. Others hastily followed, until Thomas raised a hand to halt their unwelcome obeisance.

"Nay, lads. Go on about your business. I've only come to speak with Ross."

All eyes traveled to the bar, where Ross stood polishing a glass with a linen rag. Ross merely looked at him, not a bit deferential, eventually jerking his chin in a sort of greeting. "Aye, then. Go on."

Still, Thomas did not approach. He knew he'd left this conversation too long, seeing the wariness in the face of one of his oldest friends, a man who must now wonder how he was to act before the new earl.

It was pointless to deny that Thomas's change in status made a difference between them. But because for more than a month now he'd been too embarrassed to seek out Ross and Theo, to shake their hands and beg their pardon for his deception, he'd let the title become a far greater barrier than it might have been.

"I need your help, Ross," he said simply. "Yours and Theo's. If you're willing."

Ross gave the glass a final swipe and set it aside. "Might do."

It wasn't *yes*. Nor, thank God, was it *no*. As Thomas stepped closer, noise rushed in to fill the space between them, as if the small crowd had previously agreed that carrying on their own conversations was by far the best cover for listening in on the one about to take place between the earl and the publican.

When he reached the polished oak slab on which generations of Ross men had served countless pints, Thomas laid an elbow on the bar and leaned close enough that he could not be easily overheard. "It concerns Mrs. Higginbotham."

Ross's eyes scanned the pub, refusing to meet Thomas's. "Th' way I heard tell it, th' lass wants nowt tae do with you."

"Aye," Thomas readily conceded. "And I may never change her mind. But she may be in danger again. I have to do something. And I canna save her on my own." Ross said nothing, though his gaze ceased to flit about and focused on some distant point. "You'll not believe me if I say I'd rather this thing had never come between us." The other man made a scoffing noise in his throat. Who, given the choice, would rather be a poor man than an earl? "I've not forgotten that you saved my worthless hide more than once, Eleazor Ross," Thomas continued, drawing the man's narrowed blue eyes to him. "Now I'm asking you to help me save her. Please."

"That'll do," he said, shaking his head and reaching out a hand to slap Thomas on the shoulder. "But call me Eleazor again, and I'll break your jaw...Magnus."

"Fair enough." Relief rushed from his chest in a huff of laughter. "Now, where will we find Theo?"

Ross's only answer was to reach behind the bar for a broom, lifting its handle to knock three times on the ceiling. In a few moments, a breathless Davina threw open the door behind him, revealing the steep wooden staircase that led to the family's rooms above.

"Whisht, Ross," she scolded. "Didn't I just get Da settled in for the night? And now he's wonderin' what's the trouble."

Ross waved off her complaint. "Fetch your mantle, lass. Go and tell your fella that 'is lordship's darkened the door o' the Crown at last, an' is askin' after 'im."

Davina, who had paid Thomas no mind until that moment, jerked in surprise, favored him with a wide-eyed stare, and scampered back up the stairs.

Theo's broad shoulders filled the Crown's doorway before Thomas had downed half a mug of ale. "Ye sent for me?" His dark brown gaze flitted between Thomas and Ross.

With his rag, Ross shooed two men from the table in the secluded chimney nook, declaring their chess match a draw, and motioned Theo and Ross to the empty chairs. "Now, then," he said, pulling over a third chair and straddling it, "tell Theo what you told me."

Though he knew Ross referred to what he'd revealed about Jane, Thomas first laid a hand on Theo's iron-thewed forearm. "Years ago, you first honored me with your friendship. I hope you'll think of me as your friend still."

For a moment, Theo said nothing. Ross broke the silence. "Och, go on, then. Yer ma'll be thrilled to know her wee lad's friends with an earl." When Theo at last cracked a smile, Ross continued, "You'll always be one of us, Magnus." He spoke the title with a teasing edge. "Didna ye ken? Now, what's this about Mrs. Higginbotham bein' in danger?"

"Mrs. Higginbotham?" Theo echoed, and the concern in his voice warmed Thomas's heart.

"When she was little more than a girl, her father cut her off, told her to leave," he explained, speaking low. "Tonight I had a letter, addressed to her from her brother, saying that their father was coming to Edinburgh to find her."

Ross scowled. "I dinna suppose he means to make amends."

"Nay," Thomas agreed. "He's got the start of me for sure, though I haven't as far to go. Still, I must get there quick as I can to warn her."

"The mail coach is your fastest bet, but it won't come through again for two days."

"I cannot wait." For a moment, they all looked thoughtful. Then Thomas said, "This is mad, I know, but there's a racing curricle at Dunnock. She'd go like the wind, if a man had horses."

Ross sighed at the impossibility, but Theo only lifted his shoulders. "If that's all, I reckon I can borrow a pair."

"How?" the others demanded. "From whom?"

"Best no' tae ask questions when ye dinna want the answer."

Alarm surged in Thomas's veins; he'd asked for help, for friendship, not for this. But Ross spoke first. "Theo Campbell, if ye get yerself hanged for horse thievin' afore ye can make an honest woman o' my sister, I'll kill ye again myself."

Theo's answering laugh was somehow somber. "Then I'd best not get caught. Look for me at Dunnock's north gate, just before dawn."

Thomas gave a curt nod of understanding. "The curricle holds two," he said, hardly daring to make another request.

"Theo wouldna want tae leave 'is ma alone," Ross pointed out. "An' the less tae connect him tae those 'borrowed' horses, the better."

"Then you, Ross," Thomas said, turning toward him. "Will you come with me? Help me find her?"

Disbelief sketched across his friend's face. "Of course, ye great numpty." Then he paused, a frown wrinkling his brow, as if contemplating a problem of some complexity. "If there's room for but two in the carriage, how do you mean tae fetch her back?"

At that moment, Elspeth slipped by on her way to a table and brushed Ross lightly on the shoulder with her hand—not precisely to get his attention, Thomas realized, but simply to reassure him she was near, that she was his. And perhaps to remind him he was hers. Ross reached up and covered her work-reddened fingers with his, squeezed and released them, and Elspeth went on her way. Not a word nor a glance passed between the two of them. Just a momentary contact, almost unnoticeable, and yet the intimacy of it pierced Thomas.

If Jane was lost to him, he would never know its like again.

"I fear she'll not be coming back to Dunnock."

Theo and Ross exchanged a look. "Whatever you say, your lordship," Ross said with a skeptical laugh, sketching a showy half bow with a flick of his wrist and a theatrical dip of his head. "But when she does, you'd best not ask me tae walk home."

Chapter 21

*Incredulous, Allora raised her chin and met her captor's hazel eyes.
"You mean you don't know the source of the glowing light either?" she
demanded. When he shook his head, the moonlight glossed his hair, and
she found herself fighting the unanticipated temptation to curl her fingers
in its dark waves.*

Jane brushed the feathered tip of her quill across her lips. How *was* she
going to explain the glowing light? Shouldn't a writer of her experience
have had that business sorted long before now?

And just when had the brigand begun to resemble Thomas?

Swallowing a groan, she crumpled the sheet into a ball and sent it
to join a growing pile of similarly rejected pages on the floor near the
hearth. Aphrodite's ears perked up. An hour past, she had been ready to
give chase, but this time she didn't lift her head from her paws. Athena
pretended not to notice at all.

Mr. Canfield had been most understanding about the delay, assuring
her that he believed the book would be all the better for it. Jane, however,
had her doubts.

Rather than waste more paper, she laid aside her pen and rose. Four
swishing strides took her to the rear window, which overlooked what she'd
been assured would be a lovely garden, come spring. Though the days
were getting longer, it was still early enough in the year that the light was
beginning to fade, though it was only just past four o'clock.

While deciding where to settle, she'd taken half of a little house on
the edge of New Town, one room up and two down. A girl came in every
morning to keep things tidy, and her landlady's servant brought in two

meals a day. The widowed landlady, Mrs. Rutherford, lived next door, in the other half of the house. She'd asked remarkably few questions of Jane and seemed inclined to let her go about her business, so long as she entertained no gentlemen and the rent was paid on time.

Four swishing strides took Jane back to the desk. It really was an ideal arrangement as far as her work was concerned. Though she'd originally intended to find somewhere remote, like the cottage she'd described to Thomas, Edinburgh allowed her to be perfectly anonymous. A few rooms in town were more than sufficient for her needs.

Only occasionally did she wish for a bit more compass for her imagination. It was difficult to work out a particularly thorny problem of plot in a room only half a thought wide. At times like these, a writer needed space to stretch both her legs and her mind. Such as...a cavernous hall so long it was difficult to see from one end to the other, or perhaps in finer weather, a grass-carpeted courtyard between the tall stone walls of an ancient castle.

With a sigh, she threw herself into her chair. She who prided herself on her self-sufficiency, in every sense of the word, missed Dunnock and Balisaig with an ache unlike any she had ever known. She missed Agnes and Esme and Mrs. Abernathy, the warm greetings at the pub, and the distant blare of Dougan's pipes. Without intending to, without even trying, she'd built up a little community—a little family—around herself.

Years ago, she'd been forced to leave her home and family. She had vowed never to need such trappings of sentiment again. This time, however, she'd had a choice about leaving. Had she made the right one?

Most of all, she missed Thomas. Seven years ago, scrabbling for survival, she'd hardly had the luxury of pining for what they might have had. Doubtless he, sailing into dangers unknown, had felt the same. But now, she had entirely too much time to think.

As if she were a character in a Robin Ratliff novel, she raised a hand to lay her palm against her chest. From time to time, she fancied she felt a sort of twinge there. The pain of a heart that would never be solely hers again, for despite her best efforts, a piece of it had broken free and flown to him.

Still, beneath her hand, that organ beat with such steadiness and strength, one could almost imagine it was whole. Evidently, it was possible to go on living with such a wound.

Oh, if only there was some way of knowing how he fared. Whether he missed her. Whether he wanted her. Was he broken-hearted too? If she could see him, just once more, then she could look into his eyes and see the truth...

You've only to bid me come to you, and I will.

With a shake of her head, she picked up her pen, dipped it into the ink, and held it above the page, waiting for words to come. Eventually, a drop of ink splashed onto the page, very like a tear. This would never do. Methodically, she blotted up what she could of the droplet so as not to waste yet another piece paper or the sheets beneath it. Afterward, she cleaned the tip of her quill, corked the ink bottle, and put everything away.

This time when she rose, Athena lifted her head hopefully. So far, Edinburgh had been a grave disappointment to the lassies, as all the attention they received from their new circle of acquaintance involved an occasional pat on the head and a few words of praise. No one carried bits of cheese in her pocket just for them. The girl who came to clean didn't even seem to like dogs. Still, the pair was resiliently hopeful.

Jane smiled down on them. "Come, Athena, Aphrodite," she said, with a snap of her fingers before going to fetch her new pelisse of slate-blue wool. The dogs scrambled to their feet. Before a small oval looking glass, she paused to don her fur-trimmed hood, which she had kept for its practical warmth, of course, and not at all because she associated it with that walk with Thomas or his almost-kiss. "Let's go for a walk."

When their leashes were fastened, the trio descended the steps and walked in the direction of her favorite bookshop. The cobbled street was narrow, a little crooked, and lined with a mixture of houses and shops. Pungent coal smoke threaded through the brisk air. At the end of an uphill climb that pinked her cheeks and left them all a little breathless, she entrusted the dogs to Davy, a local lad who was as glad to earn his coin by watching them as by sweeping the crossing.

A bell tinkled above the door when she entered, and the clerk, who was wrapping books in brown parchment for another customer, nodded in her direction. She drew in a deep breath of the soothing bookshop smells of leather and paper. A tall gentleman was leafing through the latest titles, spread out on a table near the front; upstairs, two young ladies were whispering and giggling over what might well have been a Robin Ratliff novel. Jane smiled privately to herself and moved on. She wasn't looking for anything in particular—nothing, that was, but an excuse to get out of the house. And perhaps, while she was at it, something that would stimulate her imagination and give it something to think about other than a certain Scottish earl.

History, Biography, Geography...She strolled aimlessly past shelves, eyeing the spines of slender volumes and thick ones, plain ones and those that had been embellished and embossed. Geology, Chemistry, Natural Philosophy...Here, the range of possibilities sparked something unexpected.

The glowing light—could it be an alchemical experiment gone awry? She began to browse more intently, now and then pulling a book from the tightly packed shelves, until her arm was full of a weighty stack of ideas. Now to find a place to peruse at length.

Mr. Murray, the bookstore's owner, had long since discovered that customers who stayed longer bought more and so had arranged the shop to encourage dawdling. A table with two wooden chairs had been claimed by a university student poring over the volumes spread open before him, running his eyes over each in turn as if comparing information. In a more secluded corner, a gentleman and a lady were thumbing through a single book together, paying far more attention to one another than to its pages. Jane found a chair with well-worn upholstery and made herself comfortable, one book on her lap and the remainder tucked on either side between her hips and the chair's arms. She opened the first, a cheap and battered edition of Sir Robert Boyle's *The Sceptical Chymist*, and began to read.

Halfway through, a possibility took root and began to blossom. Surreptitiously, she reached one hand up to ease the knot forming in the side of her neck, a sure sign she'd been at it too long. Davy would wonder what had become of her. Just a moment or two more. She'd purchase this book, certainly, and maybe another of Boyle's to study at more length, but she believed she'd at last solved the problem of the glowing light, and possibly figured out how to make the brigand respectable. Not *too* respectable—the shadow of mystery always hung around her heroes, even at the end—but respectable enough that readers would not have cause to doubt Allora's happiness.

A shadow fell across the page she was reading. She blinked, trying to bring the words back into focus. But before she had looked up to see what had made the light fail, a voice spoke. A masculine voice, low and familiar.

"Well, well, well. Robin Ratliff. I've found you, at last."

* * * *

The racing curricle did indeed go like the wind. Frozen ground aided their progress, so that they arrived in Edinburgh late on the second day, more wearied by the journey than the spry horses Theo had brought to them under cover of predawn darkness—"a loan, merely, an' the less said about it, the better."

Still, not quite two days and a hundred fifty miles provided more than enough opportunity for Thomas's anxiety to grow. His traveling companion had been relentlessly sharp-tongued and seemingly unsympathetic—had

Thomas actually imagined that his own change of status would alter Ross's salty nature?

"Here now." Ross, who had been driving since the last stop, slowed the horses as they approached the city, with its narrow, bustling streets. "We've made it."

"Aye. But I've as yet no earthly idea where to find her in all this, to warn her." And even if he managed, she'd likely not thank him for the interference.

I thought you understood. I want *to be alone.*

"Well, ye'll see nothin' of her if ye sit gazin' at yer own navel." Ross jostled his arm with a nudge from his bony elbow. "Look about yerself."

Thomas did as he'd been bid—observation was too ingrained a habit for him to shed it entirely, even when it seemed unlikely he'd see anything at all.

"What happens if we find her and she wants nothing to do with me?"

The question had been running through his mind for days, though he'd feared to give it voice. Even now, the words might easily have gone unheard over the rattle of wheels over stone. A few moments passed before Ross made any reply.

"Mrs. Higginbotham always struck me as a woman of sense. She'll be glad enough o' the warning about her da, and ye've only done what her brother set out to do. She canna fault ye for that."

Thomas managed to nod as if in agreement, blaming the tautness of the movement on the bulk of his garments and the tightness of his shoulders, strained after two days of cold, hard travel.

"Can it be you were hopin' I'd tell you she's *no'* a woman of sense?" Ross prodded.

Yes. Because love wasn't sensible. But she had built up so many walls and barriers around her life, around her heart. If she was determined to guard them strenuously, even a trained intelligence officer had very little chance of sneaking past them...to say nothing of breaking them down.

Then again, she had opened the door to him on occasion. Taken him into her confidence. Into her bed. And the glimpse he'd had of the woman inside those stone walls—a thrilling, heartache-inducing combination of Robin Ratliff's creativity and sensuality and Jane's quiet vulnerability— meant he had privileged information. Something no one else had seen.

Besides, would a truly sensible woman have such a soft spot for her—

"Dogs!" Thomas grabbed for the reins. Had the thought of them called the image into his mind, or had he really just spotted Athena and Aphrodite tied to a lamppost?

The horses lurched, and Ross muttered an oath under his breath. "What're ye on about now, Magnus?"

"Ja—Mrs. Higginbotham's dogs. Right there." He pointed toward the pair of little brown and white spaniels and waited for Ross to tell him he'd lost his damned mind.

"Well, I'll be—" Ross whistled between his teeth. "It could be them, I s'pose. Worth a look."

Thomas was out of the carriage before its wheels had stopped rolling. He approached the dogs with an abundance of caution, as if he expected any moment to discover his mistake. When he got close enough to reach out and let the first sniff his fingers, he knew he had to have been wrong. No growling, no shrill yapping. Just a nudge of his hand from Aphrodite, asking to be petted, followed by a great deal of wriggling from both them.

"Hey, now." A dirty boy emerged from the shadows, brandishing a broom. Thomas stood upright and looked down at him with a frown, but still the lad did not quail. "You leave Mrs. Thomas's dogs alone," he demanded.

"Mrs.—Thomas, did you say?" The most wretched coincidence imaginable. Unless...

"Aye. She's just gone into the shop." He jerked his chin toward the door behind him. *R. Murray, bookseller* read the gilded lettering on the glass.

"Wait here, Ross," Thomas called to his friend. "I won't be a moment."

Above his head, a bell tinkled as the door closed behind him, forcing him to step farther into the warm, dusty room. A clerk was lighting a lamp against the oncoming gloom of evening. "Can I help you, sir?"

"I'm looking for Mrs. Thomas."

The young man looked thoughtful. "Och, she popped in an hour or so ago. Upstairs, most likely—if she's still here."

Hope dared to rise in his chest, despite the fact that it might easily be another woman, so absorbed in a book that she'd lost track of time. *A young woman? With brown hair and eyes that will linger in your memory for years?* He couldn't bring himself to ask.

"If you find her," the clerk added as he blew out the curl of paper with which he'd lit the lamps, "you might tell her it's nigh on six."

"If I find her, I'll do that."

On one side of the shop, a steep wooden staircase rose into shadow. Thomas took the steps two at a time. At first, he saw nothing but shelves of books, old and new, thick and thin, too closely packed for him even to be able to determine the color of the paint on the walls. A few volumes lay scattered across a nearby table, left behind by some would-be customer. He crossed the floor, conscious of every creak, glancing around the edges of tall shelves, seeing no one. Then, in one dim corner, he spied a chair, and in it a woman, surrounded by books, bent over one lying open in her lap.

The curve of Jane's neck, surely. The rich color of her hair, so neatly pinned. Still, the shadows made it difficult to be certain. The woman had shed her pelisse and laid it over the back of a second chair. Not the one he'd last seen her wear, but surely the fur-trimmed hood was hers...?

He approached, expecting her to look up at any moment. But the book still absorbed her entire attention. At the side of her chair, he paused, trying to determine what she was reading. Some treatise on chemistry—no. Alchemy? He smiled to himself. But of course...

"Well, well, well. Robin Ratliff. I've found you, at last."

Her head jerked up, and it seemed to require an extraordinary effort for her to bring him into focus, as if she did not trust her eyes. "Thomas?"

He held out a hand to help her rise, and after a moment's hesitation, she laid her fingers in his. Books slid from the chair onto the floor.

"Why—? How—?"

Fragments of questions seemed to be all she could manage, but still he strove to give her answers. "Your brother sent a letter to Dunnock, hoping it would reach you. Your father found your direction—he's on his way to Edinburgh. I feared he might—" His voice broke as she searched his face, his eyes. He did not let go of her hand. "I needed to know that you were safe."

"This—this cannot be real. How did you find me *here*?"

"I saw the lassies outside."

Despite her obvious confusion and uncertainty, a smile twitched across her lips. "My watchdogs let you in?"

"Aye. You might almost say they welcomed me." He squeezed her fingers as amusement mingled with surprise spread across her face. "I guess the only question left to answer, is...whether you'll welcome me too."

"Actually," she said, pressing her lips together, though she could not seem to iron the smile from them entirely, "*I* have a number of additional questions. But I'll answer yours first."

To his utter shock, she launched herself into his arms, wrapping her own around his waist and laying her cheek against his chest. "I missed you. More than I had thought possible."

His better angels urged caution. Missing him was a good sign, but it made no promises for the future. The devil on his shoulder whispered, *Kiss her. Find out how much.*

Whether wise or not, he listened to the devil.

He swept her quite literally off her feet, lifting her with one arm and turning her until her back was against one of the tall shelves. When a gasp of surprise left her lips, he covered them with his own, firm but not demanding, letting her set the tenor of the kiss.

Eagerly, she peppered him with a half dozen little kisses, pulling back each time as if to make sure he was still there, still real. Then she settled her lips against his more possessively, her arms tight around his waist, banding them together. Bracing himself with one hand against the shelf above her head, the other on her hip, he surrounded her, caged her. Let the world try to touch her. She was his to protect. Forever.

"As soon as the carriage wheels began to roll, I wished I'd never left Balisaig," she murmured between kisses. "I'd been so happy there. But I thought—that is, I couldn't seem to think—"

"You were in shock," he reminded her, brushing a loose strand of hair from her cheek.

"I couldn't see a way to stay that wouldn't mean giving up the independence I'd fought for. I feared I'd be giving up a part of myself." She paused to swallow something suspiciously like a sob before she could continue. "But it was the going that seemed to break me in two."

"It's all still there waiting for you, if you're willing to come back. To come home."

"Home?" Her answering kiss—alternately soft and demanding, the brush of lips giving way to a tangle of tongues and then gentling again—was broken by a creak on the stairs, the sound penetrating the fortress they had made.

"Mrs. Thomas?" The clerk called tentatively from stairwell. "Is everything all right?"

"Oh. Oh, yes, thank you."

Thomas could not help but chuckle at her breathlessness. "May I say, I approve of your latest secret identity, Mrs. Thomas?" he whispered against her ear.

She laid a hand against his chest and shook her head, the gentlest possible scold. "Mr. Thomas will be right down with two books for you to wrap, please, Mr. Smith." Slipping beneath his arm, she moved to gather her things. "I haven't brought my reticule, so please send the bill."

"*Mr.* Thomas?" If the clerk had made any effort to hide his astonishment at her revelation of the gentleman's identity, he had failed. "Yes, ma'am."

She winked and whispered. "I suppose that's a demotion, isn't it, my lord?"

He settled his hungry gaze on her face. "Indeed not, ma'am," he said, and he could not remember a time when he had been more serious. "I can think of no higher rank."

Jane sobered too. "My father will be more than happy to try to disabuse you of such notions, I'm sure."

"I don't intend to stay and hear him. Come down, and we'll be off yet tonight."

"No." She deposited two heavy old volumes in his outstretched hand. "I'm not afraid of him. Seven years ago, I felt I had no choice. But I won't run from him now." Her voice was firm. However soft her exterior, she had steel in her spine.

"At least let Ross and me deal with him."

She paused in the act of slipping on her pelisse. "Mr. Ross is here?"

"Aye. We came in your curricle," he confessed, slightly abashed. "Theo found us horses."

The details of his journey seemed to astonish her even more than his presence. "Well," she said, tying her hood beneath her chin, "I hope you didn't scratch the paint. Now, go down," she ordered, waving him toward the stairs. "Have Mr. Smith wrap those. I'll be right behind you."

As soon as they had left the shop, the clerk locked the door behind them. The lad on the street was equally eager to return Aphrodite and Athena and be off. Thomas reached into his pocket for a coin, but Jane was quicker, withdrawing a shilling from the finger of one glove. "Here you go, Davy. Were they good girls?"

"Thank you, ma'am. Aye, ma'am." He nodded toward Thomas and tipped his cap. "They seem tae like the gentleman." And indeed, the lassies were jumping against his shins and sniffing him eagerly, a transformation for which he could offer no explanation.

Jane smiled. "He's a likable-enough fellow, I suppose. Particularly when he has his pockets stuffed with cheese."

The bewildered lad nodded and scampered away, while Thomas scanned the darkening street. Ross was nowhere to be seen.

"My curricle?" Jane asked, one eyebrow cocked dubiously.

"I suppose he didn't want the horses to stand in the cold." Thomas prayed the explanation was not something more serious.

She took the dogs' leashes but let him carry the books. "No matter. My rooms are just down the hill."

Before they had gone very many steps, he heard the jingle of a harness. Ross drew abreast of them. "Evening, ma'am. I'm relieved tae find you well."

"What a pleasant surprise, Mr. Ross. I thank you for coming all this way. I feel quite like a princess in a fairy tale, to inspire such a thrilling rescue. You've left the Thistle and Crown in your future bride's capable hands, I suppose."

"Aye, ma'am." Even in the fading light, Thomas saw the color rise in Ross's face. "Now, if his lordship will hand you up…"

"Oh, thank you, but no. Lord Magnus will walk me home. There's a posting inn two streets over. Stable the horses and take a room for the night—at my expense, of course." Athena tugged impatiently at her leash. "We shall discuss our plans for defeating the dragon in the morning."

"*Our* plans? Dragon?" Ross echoed before shaking off his incredulity and tipping his hat. "Aye, ma'am. As you wish it." He sent a glance toward Thomas and winked. "I won't wait up for you," he added in a voice that was not as low as Thomas would have liked. Then, with a chirrup to the horses, he was off.

It was Thomas's turn to feel heat spread over his face. "I would not have you think, Jane, that I told Ross—"

Her lips quirked. "People don't always need to be told." The mischievous twinkle in her eyes was matched by a saucy tilt to her chin. "For instance, I don't believe Mr. Ross has actually proposed marriage to Elspeth Shaw. And yet…Ah, here we are." The dogs raced up the steps of Number 17, nearly jerking the leashes from Jane's hands.

"I do not like the thought of leaving you here alone, lass." He glanced uneasily up and down the street. "We've no idea what your father intends nor when he might arrive."

"I'm afraid tomorrow will have to be time enough for talking," she said, fishing for a key. "My landlady lives beside me, and she does not allow me to entertain gentleman callers." Once unlocked, the door swung open, and the dogs surged through, their leashes dragging behind them. Jane climbed two steps before turning back to him, now meeting him eye to eye. One finger came out to touch his lips. "So if I let you in tonight, you'll have to promise to be very, very quiet."

Desire bolted through him. A gentleman would surely refuse to come in, to say nothing of stay. Then again, she might be in danger. How could he bear to leave?

When she turned to ascend the remaining stairs and enter the house, he followed on the silent feet of a well-trained spy.

Chapter 22

Inside the door, Thomas paused to take in his surroundings: a small sitting room, simply furnished, and beyond that a dining room whose good-sized table was presently covered by stacks of paper. Stairs, presumably to the bedchamber, rose before him. All seemed pleasant enough, but he could not help but wonder why a woman who could afford to rent a castle would have chosen to stay in a cramped Edinburgh flat. Had at least some small part of her hoped he would come looking for her, despite her avowal to the contrary?

Jane was busying herself with untying the dogs' leashes and giving them fresh water and food in the other room. As at Dunnock, their plush cushions lay before the hearth. While they ate and drank, Thomas laid aside the books, then toed off his boots, the better to maintain the directive of silence, and stood them near the door. His greatcoat he hung on one of a row of pegs above them, and in another moment, Jane had come to hang her pelisse and hood beside it. At last, she locked the door, then turned to him, an uncertain smile barely curving her lips.

He took her head between his hands, searching her face by the fading evening light. She had not lit so much as a candle. Still, he could see traces of sorrow, of worry, in her bright eyes. If he could have spoken, he would have told her what was in his heart, would have begged her to lay every burden she bore on his broad shoulders.

Then again, there was an unexpected appeal to the unbroken silence, to the necessity of *showing* her all he felt. Perhaps sometimes, even for a famous novelist, words were not enough.

Slowly, he lowered his lips to hers for a single kiss, soft, though not without heat. Then he dropped to one knee before her, cushioned only by the thin wool rug that lay before the door. Before they took another step, she must understand the place she already held in his heart. Surprise flared in her eyes as he took her hand, circled the finger that would soon bear his ring, kissed the path his fingertip had traced. Finally, he laid her palm against his chest, pushing aside both coat and waistcoat so that nothing but the thin fabric of his shirt separated them. Scottish law required very little more than the joining of hands to declare a man and woman husband and wife.

If she'd have him, then tonight would be the first night of the life they would build together, their true wedding night.

Her lips parted, as if she would speak. The sound of a woman's voice would not alarm the landlady, of course; Jane must on occasion at least talk to the dogs. But she too seemed to sense the power of the silence that surrounded them. For once, even Athena and Aphrodite were quiet, worn out by their walk and curled together on a single cushion, already near sleep.

Instead, with her free hand, Jane gathered her skirts and knelt, never lifting her other hand from his chest. Taking up his right hand, she kissed his palm and laid it on the stretch of bare skin over her left breast, linking them heart to heart. Then she looked into his eyes and nodded solemnly. *Yes.* A vow seven years in the making.

From this moment forward, they belonged only to one another. Forever.

When their lips met again, he could feel her pulse rise beneath his hand and knew she must feel his heart too, hammering in his chest as if he'd just raced a mile. Or perhaps a hundred fifty miles, not knowing whether agony awaited him at the finish line. Now, though, he tasted nothing but sweet, sweet victory, her mouth moving against his with tenderness and gentleness and, yes, love.

When his hand began to move over her skin, his fingertips skating over her collarbone and tracing the little hollow at the base of her throat, his thumb slipping beneath the gathered neckline of her dress, she responded by curling her fingers into his shirt, tugging at the hair on his chest. His thumb dove lower, teasing the puckered edge of her areola, then finding her pebbled nipple. Their kisses grew more frantic, little nips of pleasure, the clash of teeth as she opened beneath him, surrendering to his plundering tongue.

With very little urging, he could have taken her there on the floor, his pleasure only heightened by the cool, hard wood and the rough burn of the carpet. But wedding nights were for proper beds and a least a modicum of gentleness, weren't they? Awkwardly, he hoisted himself, hoisted them both, to standing, unwilling to break their kiss, though he was forced to concede the necessity of removing his hand from her strained bodice, despite her quiet whimper of disappointment.

Finally, he lifted his head and turned her toward the stairs, prompting her ascent with a playful tap on her bottom with his palm. Through her skirts and petticoats, she could have felt almost nothing of his touch, but nonetheless, wild desire flared in her eyes, and she scrambled up the steps with such eagerness she nearly stumbled.

He followed without hesitation, catching up with her on the landing when she paused to fumble with the latch, and pinning her against the door for another searching kiss. Behind her back, she managed to get the door open, and they nearly fell into the room. A quick glance took in a washstand, a plain-front armoire far smaller than the wardrobe at Dunnock, and a narrow rope bed—made for one. Or two, lying one atop the other.

He dragged his lips along her jaw, down her throat, to the swell of her bosom, relishing every sweet inch of her soft skin, then turning her to kiss the back of her neck, the top of her shoulder, the tender places he'd watched her rubbing anxiously as she read. His fingers went to the fastenings of her dress. Pleasant and easy as the banyan had been, tonight, he'd have the pleasure of unwrapping her: first the light wool gown, and then her corset, and finally her silky shift, at each step letting his hands sweep over the plump curves he revealed.

She was panting with need by the time he finished and came around to face her, her eyes dark with desire. Just her stockings remained, and she gave a startled gasp as he knelt to untie her garters. Only the discovery that she was wearing the charming pair he had rescued from the snow stopped him. The clocked design marched temptingly up her calves toward her knees. His little bluestocking. He ran a hand up each leg, one at a time, suddenly glad he had spent the last few weeks laboring with no implement heavier than a quill, for work-roughened palms would have snagged the delicate silk.

He liked the sight of her this way, naked but for the lace-edged garters encircling her dimpled thighs. Laying a string of kisses across her soft belly, he breathed in the musky, womanly scent of her. Once more he swept his hands up her legs, over her hips, across her bottom, at last dipping his fingertips into the hollow at the apex of her thighs, brushing the damp, crisp curls that guarded her entrance.

She shifted, ready to part her legs for him, pressing against the band of his arms encircling her. Slowly, he rose, following the soft lines of her hips, her back, her waist to her breasts. Cupping their weight, he took each lovely, large nipple into his mouth, one at a time, laving, then suckling until he heard a strangled cry gurgle in her throat. So marvelously sensual and responsive—one day soon, he would bring her to release that way, then start over again with his face between her thighs. But right now, he needed...

Lightening his touch, he caught her hands, which she'd kept clenched at her sides since her shift had fallen to the floor, almost as if she were fighting some foolish impulse to cover herself, to try to hide her beauty from his eyes. With his thumbs, he pried her fingers loose, uncurling her fists, massaging her palms, and finally kissing the sharp, half-moon indentations carved into her soft flesh by her fingernails.

When her hands were pliant, he laid them against his chest, beneath his coat, silently pleading with her. *Claim me. Make me yours, as I need to make you mine.* For the space of a breath, she hesitated, watching her hands, not meeting his eyes. Then, in a rush, she pushed his coat over his shoulders and down his arms, sending it to the floor to join her clothes. Next, her fingers flew to the buttons of his waistcoat, the knot of his cravat, the fall of his breeches, each yielding readily to her. With a very little assistance, he was soon as bare as she—barer, for his stockings did not seem to exert an equal fascination to hers.

First her eyes, then her hands explored his body, muscled and tanned and dusted with coarse hair, so unlike her own. On each pass, however, her questing fingertips skirted his cock, and he was not certain how long he could last before he broke down and begged for her touch, for never in his life had he been so hard and hot with need.

At long last, her cool fingers encircled him. Too much. Not enough. He kissed her to forestall the string of epithets that rose to his lips. Placing his own hands on her shoulders, he steered her toward the bed. When they reached its edge, he intended first to lay her down. At the last moment, though, he switched their places, tossing back the coverlet and reluctantly freeing himself from her hands to lie on his back against the cool linen. Crooking one finger, he invited her to come on top of him this time.

Despite the room's deepening shadows, he saw surprise, perhaps even a little uncertainty, flit across her face. At Dunnock, she'd wanted him above her, surrounding her. She had seemed to crave those reminders of his strength, the proof of his ability to protect. Tonight, however, he wanted to remind her of her own strength, her own power. Though she'd been hiding behind false names and widow's weeds, he'd seen her, how strong she was. Now she needed to see that he found *her* strength equally alluring. Arousing.

Just when he was resigned to breaking the silence, to attempting to put into words what his heart felt, she set one knee on the edge of the bed, leaned forward, and kissed him. Slowly, tentatively, she aligned their bodies, straddling his hips with her thighs, surrounding him. Reaching between her legs, she guided his cock into her womanly heat.

God, what a glorious thing to carry her, to be ridden by her, to watch her seek pleasure even as she gave it. Lightly, he encircled her with his arms, careful not to restrict her freedom, letting her set the pace. Slow at first, then fast, then slow again, pressing her breasts into his chest, then rising almost onto her haunches so that they swung temptingly before him. Lifting his chest, he caught one pert nipple between his lips, drawing sharply in time with the shallow thrust of her hips, until he felt her clench around him, a silent cry parting her lips, calling his seed from him in a rush of heat.

Afterward, she collapsed against him and lay still, the drowsy weight of her more soothing than he could have imagined. He listened to her quiet breathing and recalled the soft sigh of the ocean. In Dominica, he had dreamed of peace. He had dared, sometimes, to dream of Jane. At last, those dreams had come true.

At Dunnock, in the afterglow of their lovemaking, he had pushed away any thought of what the future might bring, for him or for them. But now he welcomed it, the knowledge that *this* was their future: days of drowsy lovemaking; swift, silent coupling in the dark; and all the moments in between, standing beside one another, supporting one another, together through whatever they must face. Including tomorrow...

A wry smile curled the corner of his mouth, and a huff of breath lifted his chest as he drew his arms more firmly around his bride, his countess.

Her enemies didn't stand a chance.

Chapter 23

Jane jerked awake to the sound of someone pounding on the front door. For just a moment, she was back at Dunnock again, the pleasant ache between her thighs, Thomas's scent on her pillow, Agnes demanding to be let in to assure herself of Jane's safety. But as the fog of sleep lifted, driven off by the incessant hammering of a fist against oak, she realized she was in Edinburgh. In the narrow rope bed. Alone.

She glanced hurriedly around the small chamber. Her dress and shift hung crookedly from the towel bar of the washstand. No sign of Thomas's clothes anywhere, no proof of that strange, silent interlude except that which she carried on and in her body. Not a dream, then. But when had he left? And where on earth had he gone?

"All right, all right. I'm coming." She slipped her arms into the sleeves of her banyan as the dogs howled and the visitor knocked relentlessly. "Hush," she ordered as she reached the bottom of the stairs. Athena at least did her the favor of pausing to consider the command before rejecting it.

"Who's there?" she called, remembering that the person on the other side of the door might be her father. How could Thomas have left her at a time like this?

"Mrs. Rutherford. I demand you let me in this instant."

Her landlady? It couldn't be more than an hour past sunrise. Cautiously, Jane opened the door enough to peer out. "Ma'am?" A pair of brown and white noses thrust themselves past her ankles and into the gap to carry on with their protest, at least as energetic in their animosity toward Mrs. Rutherford as they ever had been with Thomas.

Perhaps the dogs had better judgment than she'd given them credit for having.

"Open that door, Mrs. Thomas." Her chin jerked to underscore the demand, though her iron-gray hair did not move with it. On the whole, Jane would much rather have had to face Agnes's discovery of Thomas hiding in the wardrobe. "And silence those dogs," Mrs. Rutherford snapped.

Snatching up a dog under either arm, Jane let the door swing wide, sparing a quick glance into the street. Across the way, a tall gentleman leaned against a lamppost, wearing a familiar greatcoat and slouching slightly as if to disguise his height. Before she could decide whether her imagination was playing a trick on her, the man lifted the brim of his hat with one finger, just enough to reveal his eyes, and favored her with a wink. *Thomas.* But how—? And why—?

A nod from him sent her looking farther up the street, and sure enough, there was Mr. Ross, or so she gathered, his hat also pulled low and one booted foot propped on a neighbor's area railing. They had formed their own guard, it would seem, and the realization gave her a moment's relief, all the more needed when she closed the door and turned to face Mrs. Rutherford.

She was standing in the middle of the sitting room, but craning her neck to see past Jane and into every corner. "I don't know why you're smiling, Mrs. Thomas. A blush of shame would be more fitting." Jane bristled, thinking of Mr. Donaldson's last sermon. "You entertained a gentleman here last night," the woman went on. "Expressly against the rules."

"I beg your pardon?"

"Betsy saw his boots and coat by the door when she came in this morning to light the fire."

And indeed, for the first time, Jane noted that the hearth was blazing and a tray sat in the center of her desk. Someone had already helped himself to the toast and jam.

A man of his size, up all night...I'm sure he must've worked up quite an appetite.

She pressed her lips together to keep from laughing outright. "I haven't the faintest notion what you're talking about, Mrs. Rutherford," she said when she could trust herself to speak. "I have long suspected, however, that Betsy has an aversion to dogs. Perhaps she's just trying to stir up trouble."

Mrs. Rutherford looked askance at Athena and Aphrodite, then back at Jane. "Then you won't object if I look upstairs?"

Something rose in her—the memory of her mother's prying, her father's heartlessness, along with a surge of rebellion against a world that considered itself entitled to sit in judgment on her choices. "Certainly not, Mrs. Rutherford," she replied, her voice sweet enough to set her own teeth on edge. "And in turn, you will, of course, understand that I shall be leaving by the end of the week."

"Well, now, Mrs. Thomas, I shouldna think that would be necessary," Mrs. Rutherford began, in no doubt the most mollifying tone she possessed, though that wasn't saying much. The landlady was evidently partial to keeping a tenant who paid her rent—at a slightly higher rate than advertised, of course, to ensure that Mrs. Thomas was a lady of quality.

"Oh, but it is." Jane stretched her thinned lips into a smile. "If you'd be so kind as to have your manservant bring down my trunks from the attic? Today?"

"Well," Mrs. Rutherford huffed as she brushed past on the way back to the door. "I'm only trying to keep a respectable house, ma'am."

"Of course. But I'm afraid I'm done with houses, Mrs. Rutherford." Her false smile softened into something genuine. "I've decided I'm quite ready for a home."

Thoroughly baffled, Mrs. Rutherford huffed again and left, slamming the door behind her. Jane wandered into the next room to pour a lukewarm cup of tea as the dogs began to settle themselves.

What exactly was she supposed to do now?

Restless feet carried her back to the window, but a quick glance showed no sign of her watchmen. Reluctantly, she returned to the desk. While sipping her tea, she unwrapped the two books she'd bought yesterday. Uppermost sat Boyle's *Experiments and Considerations Touching Colours, with Observations on a Diamond that Shines in the Dark.* Somewhere in its pages lay the solution to her glowing light problem in *The Brigand's Captive.* Returning her cup to its saucer, she tucked the book under her arm and went upstairs to dress.

When she descended the stairs, the sitting room was no longer empty. "G'morning, ma'am," Mr. Ross greeted her around the last morsels on the breakfast tray, hurrying to his feet.

Thomas, who'd been reclining easily on the little sofa near the window, rose too. "Well, now, lass, I hope you had a good night's rest," he said, and winked. "Ross here says he never heard me come in last night, but how he expects to hear anything over that snoring, I'd like to know."

"Yes, well." Jane willed herself not to blush, though heat was rushing through her veins. "It was, on the whole, a remarkably quiet night."

Thomas laughed, glanced at his friend, who had bent one fair brow into a skeptical arch, and quickly turned that laugh into a cough. "Now, then. I figured we'd be lucky to beat your father to Edinburgh, and it turns out, we've only just done it. Ross charmed the innkeeper's wife into letting him see the register this morning, and a Mr. J. Quayle arrived late last night. He stole your last letter to your brother, so he knows right where you are to be found. I'd expect to see him at any time."

A shudder passed through her, as if she'd been doused with cold water. Thomas stepped closer to her, took her hand in his, and led her down the remaining three steps. When she reached the bottom, he did not let her go. "What do we do now?" she asked.

"You go back upstairs and wait. When he comes, Ross and I will deal with him."

For a moment, Jane said nothing. "Deal with him?"

"Persuade him tae go back where he came from and leave ye in peace," explained Mr. Ross.

Her gaze shifted between the two of them. She could guess exactly what sort of persuasion they had in mind. "He expects to find me alone. He'll never even come through the door if he sees two strapping men prepared to set upon him."

"Well, we have a plan."

"Och, now, Magnus, ye canna be serious with all that?" Mr. Ross chimed in, sounding anguished.

"If you'd be so kind, lass," Thomas said with a mischievous smile, "bring down that fancy dressing gown of yours, and any sort of a mobcap, if you have one."

Jane blinked.

"Ross, as the shorter of the two of us, will sit just here at the table, wearing your banyan and cap, with his back to the sitting room. When your father knocks, I'll open the door. He'll see someone he assumes to be you at work and step in, and we'll have him, you see?"

Jane's lips twitched. "Mr. Ross is going to dress as me?"

"You said naught about a dress, Magnus," he sputtered in protest.

"Not a bit of it. Just lay the thing over your shoulders and shake it off the moment I've locked the door."

It sounded a rather elaborate plan, merely for the pleasure of telling her father off—a pleasure, if she understood things correctly, she would not even be allowed to witness. But she trusted Thomas, whose words and gestures seemed to regard the whole event as a lark, though now and again she caught a shadow of something else in his eyes. "I'll run up and fetch what you need."

An hour and a quarter later found her sitting on the edge of her bed pretending to read Boyle's century-and-a-half-old treatise on light and color, but mostly tracing the stitching on the faded coverlet and watching the light travel across the pale green walls. When she at last heard a rap on the door, she nearly dropped the book. As she had hoped, the dogs were too busy worrying the bones she had given them, snapping at one another now and again for sport, to pay any mind to another visitor.

Hurrying to the door of her chamber, she opened it just enough to hear voices rising from the rooms below: Mr. Ross's high-pitched attempt at an English accent inviting her father in, Thomas's deeper tone as he ordered her father to drop his walking stick.

Latching the door behind her, she hurried down the steps, reaching the sitting room just in time to see Thomas pin her father to the floor with a knee to his chest and the walking stick across his throat.

Her father looked older, of course, though not frail, his brown hair liberally sprinkled with gray. Right now, his face was a familiar shade of puce, and that equally familiar glob of spittle had begun to form in the corner of his mouth as he hurled epithets at his captor. Whatever she felt in that moment, it was not pity. Mr. Ross, who loomed over the pair with the poker from the fireplace upraised in his hands, would have looked more threatening if he had shed the mobcap along with the banyan.

She took a step closer. "Wait."

"Jane." Thomas and her father spoke as one. Mr. Ross tried to prevent her approach, but she slipped easily past.

"I need to speak to him," she said softly to Thomas, whose expression was contorted into a mask the likes of which she had never seen before. His was not the face of a man who'd spent his time in the West Indies relaxing on a sandy beach. "Let him go."

The words took several long minutes to reach him, but at last, he rose, keeping a firm grip on the walking stick, and allowed her father to scramble to his feet.

"Jane." His blue eyes were hard as he glanced at the two men before focusing on her. "You were expecting me."

She took an involuntary step backward. "I had a note from Jonathan."

"Ah, yes. That worthless young man."

"Enough. I was subjected to your ranting and raving for years. I will not hear you abuse my brother. In fact, I'd say it's your turn to listen."

His gaze narrowed, but he let her speak.

"Seven years ago, you declared me dead to you. You ordered me—a seventeen-year-old girl—from your house. All over a story I had written, of which you did not approve. Now, as I understand it, you consider yourself entitled to some share of what I earned from those words, *my* words."

"I hired your governess, didn't I?" he broke in. "I bought books and paper and—"

"Do not pretend you educated me for my benefit. You did it to ensure you had a marriageable daughter. It was always your goal to be rid of me. You cared nothing for me at all."

Foolishly, she had thought he might deny the claim. He set his jaw and said nothing.

"You intimidated me then. You will never do so again. So here is the return on your investment." She tossed him a black woolen stocking—the last of her widow's weeds—into the toe of which she had tied a few coins. They jingled when they landed on the floor at his feet. "Three shillings, eleven pence. A generous accounting of the value of the paper and ink I used to compose my first novel, one copy of which you tossed into the fire. I hope you consider it ample recompense for your journey. You'll receive not a penny more."

Mr. Ross gave a humorless laugh as he stepped toward her father. "Now, didna ye hear the lass? I'd say it's past time for ye tae go."

Glowering, her father held out a hand for his walking stick. Thomas, whose stern expression appeared to have been carved from granite, held the other man's gaze as he snapped the stick as if it were no thicker than a twig.

"You Scottish ruffian! How dare you abuse me or my possessions! I suppose you've had your hands on my daughter, too? I'll—"

"That Scottish ruffian is the Earl of Magnus," Mr. Ross explained coolly. "And if ye were half as smart as yer daughter, ye'd be out the door afore he uses what's left o' that stick on yer heid."

This final threat, though spoken in Mr. Ross's thick brogue, seemed to penetrate the haze of her father's anger. With a final curse, he kicked the knotted stocking aside and strode out the door.

Shaking, she sank to the sofa. Mr. Ross picked up the banyan and laid it gently around her shoulders. Thomas studied the jagged ends of the walking stick. "You should have stayed upstairs, Jane, and let me deal with him."

"Let you bloody his nose, you mean," she said, amazed to hear a hint of laughter in her voice. She felt freed, as if she'd cast off an enormous weight she had not known she was carrying.

"At the very least," he agreed, softening at last. Some of the usual twinkle returned to his eyes. "If I'm ever to protect you, lass, you've actually got to let me do it."

"You did something far more important, Thomas. You saved me from myself, from what I might've become. I was so busy proving I could survive on my own, I almost forgot what it was to laugh. What it was to love. Now, take me home," she commanded, launching herself into his arms. "Home to Balisaig."

A moment later, Mr. Ross gave a discreet cough. Jane would have taken a step back for propriety's sake, but Thomas held her tightly. "I suppose you'll be takin' her in the curricle," Mr. Ross asked irritably.

"Still worried you'll have to walk?" Thomas teased. "No, I'll hire a coach for the lady."

"And leave Mr. Ross to drive my curricle? I don't think so."

Thomas chuckled low. "Very well, then. Ross can ride comfortably in the coach. With Athena and Aphrodite."

"Nay, Magnus. Not the dogs. We had an agreement," he protested.

But she was too busy kissing Thomas to hear the rest.

Chapter 24

The closer they drew to Balisaig, the quieter Jane grew. Thomas at first suspected discomfort; the journey was wearing, and though they'd enjoyed a surprisingly mild stretch of weather, it was still chilly for travel in an open carriage, no matter how well bundled up they were. He ought to have insisted she ride in the closed carriage with her trunks and her dogs and kept Ross in the curricle with him.

Or perhaps she was thinking through the plot problem she'd been trying to solve. She'd explained last night, over dinner at a posting inn, that the old books she'd been studying at the shop when he'd found her had presented a possible solution to her dilemma, but that she was still working through her idea.

Mostly, though, he feared she was dwelling on something that might not be so easily resolved.

Out of the corner of his eye, he watched her gaze focus alternately on the jagged, rocky horizon; on the soft green carpet that edged the roadway and crept across the field, blanketing the ground in a promise of spring; on the steady gray rumps of the horses trotting ever onward. The sun was low in the sky, and the gold and blue of afternoon was slowly bleeding into the orange and purple of twilight—they would only just reach Dunnock by nightfall—when she gave a firm jerk of her chin, as if she'd reached some silent conclusion.

Expecting her to announce that she'd finally devised a way for her characters to live in perfect felicity, he was more than taken aback when she declared, "I refuse to give up my work once we're wed."

Surprise jerked through him, causing the reins in his hands to twitch and the horses to slow. With a soft chirrup, he urged them back to their steady pace before turning to Jane. "Who asked you to?"

Still stiff, she turned warily toward him. "I realize we had not discussed..." Beneath the lap blanket, one hand made a restless circle, a gesture that might have been intended to take in any number of things. "But I feared you might not think it proper for your countess to..."

"As it seems you may not be well acquainted with the lass, I'll just tell you that my countess has a mind of her own. Nor am I overmuch concerned with propriety, if it comes to that."

She weighed his response for a moment. The clip-clop of the horses' hooves was loud in the stillness. "You'll also be marrying a woman with a substantial fortune to her name. Though according to the law, everything I have will be yours."

"Aye," he agreed. "A scandal, if you ask me, but I canna change the law on my own, lass. I can only tell you I intend to order the solicitor to draw up papers to settle what's yours however you see fit." He shifted the reins to one hand so that he might slip the other beneath the heavy wool lap blanket in search of hers. "On our children, if you wish it," he said, curling his fingers around one tightly balled fist.

Leaning forward just enough to peep around the fur edge of her hood, he watched her cheeks pink, and the slightest curve of a smile rise to her lips. "Do you suppose one day they'll learn the truth and wish their inheritance had come from some more respectable source?"

"An' who, may I ask, is raisin' these bairns, that they haven't the sense God gave a goose?" That earned him one of those tinkling laughs he loved so much. He squeezed her fingers again. "What's more respectable than a book that makes folks happy?"

"Did you—?" She sounded hopeful, though she tried to hide it when she spoke again. "Of course, you must have found the volume of *The Necromancer's Bride* I left for you."

"I did, though not at first. It was some weeks before I could bring myself to go into your study."

That too seemed to surprise her. "Oh. Well, when you did find it, did you finish the story?"

"Not yet. You may recall, I had to see to my own happy ending first."

Her head tipped to the side. "If you haven't read it, how can you be so sure Ophelia and Ruthveyn's story ends well for them?"

"Well, now, I *had* considered that her family might drag her away from Ruthveyn, and then the miserable sot would cast some spell or the like to turn everyone to stone, including himself..." He leaned forward a bit farther, trying to see her expression. "But I realized if they'd been punished for wanting each other, if you'd made their story into a tragedy, your readers wouldn't be so wild for it. And those high and lofty critics wouldn't have been half so unhappy with you."

Freeing one hand, she pushed her hood back slightly and turned to face him with wide, bright eyes, as if she couldn't otherwise take in what he'd said. As if she'd never considered it in quite that light before.

"I'm proud of you, lass," he insisted. "An' if we're blessed with children, they'll be proud too. My only regret is that so much of Robin Ratliff's reputation rests on that aura of mystery he cultivates. I'd dearly love to shout the truth from the north tower of Dunnock Castle, so the whole world knows what you've done."

Her chest rose and fell in a little huff of laughter. "The north tower? Unless there's a creature dwelling in the depths of the loch, who would hear you if you did?"

"There could be," he insisted with a wink. "But one fantastic story at a time. First, you've got to get the brigand and his lass—what's her name?"

"Allora."

"—out of that glowing cave in one piece. An' what it is they've found again?"

"A rare, luminescent gem."

"Worth its weight in gold, I suppose."

"More," she agreed with another ringing laugh. "And you're right. Mr. Canfield is most anxious to receive the completed manuscript. When we reach Balisaig, I must write out the ending and send it off, first thing."

He released his grip on her fingers to shake free of his driving glove and slide his hand onto her knee. "First thing? I confess I had something else in mind for our first night at Dunnock as husband and wife."

"Husband and wife?" Sounding skeptical, she shifted slightly beneath the heat of his palm. "I know what was in my heart when we knelt together and clasped hands in Edinburgh. But I don't think even Scottish marriage laws are quite that lax. I cannot possibly stay with you at Dunnock until we're actually married. And unless something has changed, Balisaig is short a clergyman."

"Dinna fash yourself, lass." Beneath the lap blanket, he tugged at her skirts, inching them slowly higher. "I've a surprise for you."

Her breath quickened as his fingertips brushed over the soft skin of her thighs. "Thomas," she scolded. "Hand me the reins."

"Aye?" he teased with both his whispered words and his touch. "Did you want my undivided attention?"

"Most certainly. Otherwise, you're going to land us in a ditch." With an exaggerated sigh of annoyance, she reached across both their bodies with her right hand and grasped the reins, even as beneath the blanket, she eased her legs apart, inviting him into her softness. "This is still my curricle. And I won't have you wrecking it."

* * * *

When Thomas turned and planted a kiss on her head where it leaned against his shoulder, Jane clung stubbornly to sleep. With a nudge of his chin, he brushed back her hood, and she felt the cool night air caress her face. "I can see Balisaig just ahead, lass."

"Mmm?" Drowsily, she burrowed deeper into the pillow she'd made in the slight hollow where his chest met his shoulder.

"Best wake up, or you'll sleep through your own wedding."

Those words succeeded in rousing her. "Wedding?"

"Aye. And here's your surprise."

At last, she lifted her head and blinked sleepily at the little specks of light that pierced the darkness. Too small to be the windows of the village, they flickered and twinkled like stars. Unlike the driver of the Royal Mail, Thomas slowed the horses as they rounded the bend and entered Balisaig, just east of the apothecary's shop.

Candles twinkled along the edges of the street, warming the hands and lighting the faces of every villager. Mr. and Mrs. Abernathy waved merrily before she bent to say something to little Mary MacIntyre, who nodded and scampered down the road ahead of the horses. Across the way, Elspeth Shaw stood before the Thistle and Crown with her family about her, each one with a candle upraised in welcome. Farther along came other familiar faces. Mrs. Murdoch and Dougan. Dunnock tenants. Anyone and seemingly everyone who called this piece of the Highlands home.

As she and Thomas passed, they all saluted and cheered and fell in behind the curricle, ushering them finally to the Campbells' little house, where Ross greeted them. He'd reached Balisaig ahead of them? She rather thought she might still be dreaming.

"And here we are," Thomas announced, stopping the horses and hopping from the seat, then turning to lift her down.

"I don't—" Between smiles and answering curtsies, she rubbed the sleep from her eyes and tried to tuck a few loose strands of hair beneath her hood. "What's going on?"

"Your wedding, Mrs. Higginbotham." Mrs. Abernathy and Mrs. Murdoch stepped up on either side of her, and each taking an elbow, they swept her toward the house. Ross clapped an iron grip on Thomas's shoulder and dragged him in the opposite direction.

The Campbells' little sitting room was empty. "My wedding?" Jane repeated, bewildered.

"Och, aye. You'll see." With a twinkle in her eye, Mrs. Abernathy reached up to untie Jane's hood.

"Oh, no," Jane protested, shaking her head when Mrs. Abernathy tried to lay the hood aside. "My hair must look a fright." She could feel the normally tight chignon hanging low on her neck, and wisps of hair tickled her face.

"I can't think when I've ever seen it—or you—look lovelier," insisted Mrs. Murdoch. "That softer style suits you. Och, I'm that glad you've come back to us, I am," she said, taking Jane's hands in her own gnarled ones.

"And I'm ever so glad to be here," Jane agreed, drawing the elderly housekeeper into an embrace. No more keeping the world at arm's length.

A knock at the door prompted Mrs. Abernathy's final preparation: the removal of Jane's kid gloves. "You'll see," she promised as she tugged them free before gesturing her outside once more.

The people of Balisaig, all smiles, formed a candlelit path leading toward the forge. Though open to the night air, the fires made it a cozy shelter. The sharp scents of peat smoke and damp wool clothes and rusty iron mingled in the night air. A smaller gathering awaited them there— Mrs. Campbell in a warmly situated chair, freshly-washed Athena and Aphrodite content on her lap, the fur that normally hung in their eyes tied back with pink ribbons. Davina standing devotedly beside her future mother-in-law. Ross and Theo Campbell sporting wide, devilish-looking grins. And Thomas, clad in a kilt.

She lifted a hand to cover her own smile. So that was why they'd hurried him away!

Oh, but it suited him, his strong, shapely legs just visible between its hem and the tops of his boots. The Earl of Magnus. The Laird of Dunnock Castle. The Highland warrior of her dreams.

Mrs. Abernathy nudged her toward him, and she reached out a hand to take the one he held outstretched. The little crowd surged into the blacksmith's forge behind her.

"We had the right idea that night in Edinburgh," Thomas said to her, his voice low. "It just needed witnesses." Then he darted a glance at the assembled company and laughed.

She laughed too, love and joy bubbling up from a deep well inside her that had been capped for far too long. Mrs. Murdoch produced a length of white linen and handed it to Mr. Campbell, who took Jane and Thomas's clasped hands and began to bind them together with it.

A handfasting ceremony? Performed by the village blacksmith? She'd heard of the like before, of course. But this was not exactly what she'd been expecting when Thomas had mentioned a wedding.

"Is this...legitimate?" she whispered to him.

"Quite," Thomas assured her. "But I've a friend from Glasgow who's agreed to come to Balisaig and be our parson. He can do the deed, if you'd rather wait a fortnight or so."

Wait? His eyes twinkled mischievously, as if daring her to recall what they'd done a few nights ago. Or in the curricle an hour past.

But she let her gaze drift around the little—well, not so very little—gathering. Candles still flickered in the darkness, setting aglow the cheerful faces of the people who had welcomed her. Befriended her. Who had made Balisaig home to her, when she'd believed she would never have a home again. Who were eager now to see her become their countess.

Her eyes returned to Thomas, who'd been watching her, his own expression that maddening mixture of amusement and affection. His eyebrows rose and fell, prodding her for an answer.

"Wait?" she echoed aloud. "And for what? There will never be such a storybook perfect moment as this, Lord Magnus." A cheer went up from the assembled company, muffling her next words so that only those closest to her could hear. "And I could not love you more than I do right now."

"That's decided then," Mr. Campbell said, laying their joined hands on the anvil and covering them with his own.

"Aye," agreed Thomas, leaning toward her, brushing her lips with a perfectly scandalous kiss. "An' after seven years of waiting, 'tis sure I'll never love you less."

Epilogue

Staring down a blank page—pen at the ready, though no words would come—Thomas wondered how Jane managed to do it again and again. *The Brigand's Captive* was still flying off the bookshop shelves, and she was already at work on *The Pirate's Prisoner.*

Pretending a pose of thoughtfulness, he glanced around the room. Very little had changed in its transformation from Jane's study to Lady Magnus's, though he had enlisted Dougan's help in silently swapping the miserable sofa for its more comfortable twin from the gatehouse. Jane's brother, Jonathan, who had gladly accepted the offer of the post as Dunnock's steward and would soon take up residence in the gatehouse, need be none the wiser.

Near the empty hearth lay Athena and Aphrodite's cushions and toys, though at the moment, the dogs were distracted by Jane herself, kneeling on the rug to brush their slick, spotted coats. They continued to tolerate Thomas's presence in their house, though he always carried a few cheese parings in his pocket, just in case.

"How's the letter coming, my dear?" Jane asked without turning her eyes away from her task.

Thomas once more focused on the blank page before him and heaved a quiet sigh. "I canna do it, lass. What is it you would have me say?"

"Do you not wish your general to know you're enjoying civilian life? How well things get on at Dunnock and in Balisaig?" She twisted to study him over her shoulder. "His last order to you was to send you here, Thomas. I know you've resigned your commission, but surely he deserves the courtesy of a letter about all that's happened since."

"But I've told you, he'll ken all that without my telling him."

"Oh, Thomas." Shaking her head, she rose from the floor and brushed the loose fur from her skirts. Since their wedding, she'd continued to wear her rich brown hair in a comfortable knot at the nape of her neck, with a few wisps playing about her throat and ears. The tighter style had always tempted him to pluck the pins and set her free, but this one was even more distracting, putting him in mind of how she looked when she'd been well-tumbled.

"I know you told me he's a *spymaster*." As usual, she spoke the last word on a whisper, though none but the dogs were in earshot. He had weighed carefully whether or how much to tell her about his time in the army, the years in Dominica. But in the end, he'd decided he was done with secrets, though he could not shake the habits of watchfulness and wakefulness upon which his survival—and so many others'—had once depended.

With a saucy sway to her hips, Jane approached the desk, coming around the corner to lay a hand on his shoulder and *tsking* over the blank sheet before him. "But really, Thomas, how could he possibly know what goes on all the way up here?"

"I canna say *how*. I'm only certain he *does*."

Increasingly convinced that General Scott had known exactly who and what Thomas would find when he arrived at Dunnock, he could not persuade himself to believe the man needed a letter to convey the details of both momentous events and more mundane ones. If he wrote at length about Davina and Theo's quaint little wedding at the kirk, or the improvements in Mr. Shaw's leg, about the larger than usual number of wobbly lambs and curly-haired calves with which the Dunnock farms had been blessed that spring, or Elspeth and Mrs. Abernathy's joint venture of a tea shop next door to the pub where the ladies of the village could gather—absolutely none of it would be news to the general. Of that he was certain.

"Well," she said, tracing one finger up his cheek and around his ear, "I can think of one thing he can't possibly know."

"Oh, aye? And what's that, lass?" he asked, favoring her with a skeptical lift to his brow.

For answer, she plucked the quill from his fingers and laid it aside, then took his hand in hers, laying the flat of his palm over the curve of her belly.

A long minute passed before the full meaning of the gesture managed to make its way to his brain. Then he was on his feet with his arms around her, the letter forgotten. "A baby? Jane, my love, my lass, are you sure?" After all, they'd only been wed a few weeks.

She laid her cheek against his chest and nodded. "Much like your general, I can't say how I know," she said, and he could hear the smile in her voice. "I just do."

He dropped a kiss on the top of her head, drawing in the sweet fragrance of her hair—not night-blooming jasmine now, but the fresh, wild scent of a Scottish spring. She was going to bear his child, their child.

A family. A home. All the things they both had imagined could never be theirs. And now they would have them. Together.

* * * *

General Zebadiah Scott tossed the letter onto his disconcertingly empty desktop—Captain Collins had been straightening up again—and tilted back in his chair. Once more, he'd failed in his chief duty to the Crown: to train and retain the best intelligence officers in the world.

But did he not have a parallel duty to his men? A duty to ensure their health and welfare and even happiness?

These brash young men all seemed to consider themselves indispensable. Scott, however, had been at this long enough to know that enemies came and went. If one war ended, another soon began. Anyone, even he, could be replaced.

So on occasion, when an opportunity presented itself—an unexpected inheritance, for instance—he seized the chance to remind one of those obstinate fellows that there was more to life than spying. Or at least, more to life than the sort of spying he'd been doing.

With a smile that even a stranger would recognize as self-satisfied, Scott picked up the letter again and tucked it into a file in a drawer no one but he ever opened. A good agent, even when he resigned his commission, was never really lost to His Majesty's service. Thanks to a little strategic maneuvering—what civilians called matchmaking—he had spies in places no one would suspect.

Now including Balisaig.

Before he could push the drawer shut again, a rap sounded on the door between his office and his aide's.

"Enter."

Captain Collins stuck his head into the room, looking unusually agitated. "We've just got word about the delivery, sir."

Scott motioned him in with a wave of one hand. Collins crossed the threshold, dragging his steps in a show of obvious reluctance, and shut the door behind himself. With deliberate motions, Scott paused to light his pipe, drawing in little puffs until the flame caught. Smoke curled from around the pipe stem as he parted his lips to say, "Something's gone awry, I take it."

"Yes, sir." Collins's confession was choked, though he could have had nothing to do with the mistake. "Lieutenant Hopkins had to hand off the package unexpectedly."

More smoke. "I see. Who has it now?"

"A—a woman, sir." He ran a finger beneath the collar of his coat. "Another customer just leaving the bookshop. As best we've been able to determine, her name is Lady Kingston."

Scott turned in his chair, studying the startlingly blue spring sky through the window behind him. Soon, the familiar madness of the Season would descend upon London, the whirl of parties, musicales, balls. Secrets—not all of them state secrets—would fly from lips to ears in passionate whispers.

He'd met the Earl of Kingston years ago, at a charity ball organized by his lovely, lively young wife—now widow. Why, she must be out of mourning by now. Without much difficulty, he could picture her delicate brow wrinkled in a frown as she puzzled over the contents of the book she'd just unwrapped.

Useless to her. Priceless to many others—not all of them on the right side. And if any of those on the wrong side suspected it was in her possession, she would be in grave danger.

"Retrieval could be a delicate operation. We mustn't alarm her. Send Major Stanhope right away," he ordered without turning around.

"The Magpie, sir?"

At Collins's incredulity, Scott curved a wry smile around his pipe stem. The man despised that moniker, though he'd earned it in part by his cleverness. But like his namesake, he could be sociable when he chose. The perfect agent to charm that book out of the countess's hands.

Could Stanhope be charmed by her in return?

Every mission carried with it a risk. Now it was time for Scott to decide whether he could afford to risk losing his best agent. After a moment's thought, he nodded decisively and spun the chair to face Collins again. "Indeed. The Magpie and Lady Kingston." Silently, he toed shut the drawer filled with his personal files related to his retired agents, all now happily married. "Oh, and Captain," he called after his aide, who had already moved to put the order into action, "do keep me apprised of any... interesting developments in the case."

Keep an eye out for

more adventures in the

Love and Let Spy series

Coming soon

from

Susanna Craig

and

Lyrical Press

Dear Reader,

Thanks so much for picking up *Who's That Earl*! I hope you enjoyed traveling with Jane and Thomas on their journey to happily ever after. If you have a minute to share your thoughts with others by leaving a review, I'd really appreciate it. Reviews, even short and simple ones, help match books to the readers who will love them.

Don't miss future installments in my Love and Let Spy series: sign up for my author newsletter by visiting www.susannacraig.com/newsletter. I'll use it to keep you in the know about new releases, sales, and other book news (and I promise I'll never spam you or share your email address).

If you're new to my books, please check out the Rogues & Rebels series, in which the rebellious Irish Burke siblings match wits with an assortment of English rogues, and the Runaway Desires series, stories that sweep you from the West Indies to the West Country. Find more information at www.susannacraig.com/books. Each story stands alone, with the series connected by themes and characters. All my series exist in the same historical world, so you'll find a few familiar faces popping in from time to time. And of course, every book delivers romance, history, adventure, and a happy ending...guaranteed!

Until we meet again, happy reading!

Susanna

SEP 2020